# SHERLOCK HOLMES

## AND THE **TELEGRAM** FROM **HELL**

## ALSO BY
# NICHOLAS MEYER

### FICTION

*From the memoirs of John H. Watson*

*The Seven-Per-Cent Solution*

*The West End Horror*

*The Canary Trainer*

*The Adventure of the Peculiar Protocols*

*The Return of the Pharaoh*

*Target Practice*

*Black Orchid* (with Barry Jay Kaplan)

*Confessions of a Homing Pigeon*

### NONFICTION

*The Love Story Story*

*The View From the Bridge — Memories of Star Trek and a Life in Hollywood*

# SHERLOCK HOLMES

AND THE **TELEGRAM** FROM **HELL**

EXTRACTS FROM THE DIARIES OF JOHN H. WATSON, M.D.
JUNE 1916–NOVEMBER 1918

EDITED BY

# NICHOLAS MEYER

THE MYSTERIOUS PRESS
NEW YORK

*For Michael Phillips, Frank Spotnitz, and Steven-Charles Jaffe*

ϑ

SHERLOCK HOLMES AND THE TELEGRAM FROM HELL

Mysterious Press
An Imprint of Penzler Publishers
58 Warren Street
New York, N.Y. 10007

Copyright © 2024 by Nicholas Meyer

First Mysterious Press edition

Interior design by Maria Fernandez

Library of Congress Control Number: 2023922349

ISBN: 978-1-61316-533-1
eBook ISBN: 978-1-61316-534-8

10 9 8 7 6 5 4 3 2 1

Printed in the United States of America
Distributed by W. W. Norton & Company

# INTRODUCTION

Toshiro Watanabe
Kurosawa Heavy Industries, Ltd.

*March 26, 2022*

*Dear Nicholas Meyer,*

*I was until recently the personal secretary to the late Hikaru Mishima, president & CEO of the above.*

*As you know, Mr. Mishima died last year, a victim of the worldwide Covid pandemic, which has taken so many lives.*

*I am writing to inform you that Mr. Mishima's estate has gone through probate and his bequests are now being disbursed. Mr. Mishima had many relatives, foundations, and charities, and a wide range of interests, most of which need not concern you. (One of his passions was research into mental telepathy; another was the SETI project.)*

*However, among his bequests is the last tranche of entries from Dr. Watson's diary, which Mr. Mishima purchased at auction from Sotheby's in 2019. Two sets of these pages Mr. Mishima previously entrusted to you for editorial purposes, believing your prior work in this area made you ideally suited to evaluate and edit his purchase.*

*Mr. Mishima approved of your work on the pages you titled* The Adventure of the Peculiar Protocols. *Though he did not live to read your subsequent work on the section you titled* The Return of the Pharaoh, *I make bold to say he would have approved that as well.*

*In the hospital in Kyoto, consulting with me while on a ventilator, Mr. Mishima expressed his wish that you edit the last section of Dr. Watson's diary; entries commence in June 1916 and cover approximately one year.*

*Therefore a courier for Kurosawa Heavy Industries, Ltd., will contact you shortly regarding delivery of said item.*

*Below you will find several documents, which I suggest you have your lawyer review before you sign and take possession of the pages.*

*Please let me know how you would like to proceed.*

*Kind regards,*

*Toshiro Watanabe*

Personal Secretary, Hikaru Mishima, CEO

Kurosawa Heavy Industries, Ltd.

Tokyo, Panama, Amsterdam, Buenos Aires

Even with the mixed blessing of the internet, the to-and-fros of lawyers, the damn boilerplate took almost five months. But I am now finally in possession of what I am told is the last chunk of Watsoniana purchased at Sotheby's in 2019 by Mr. Mishima and doled out to me piecemeal ever since.

Mr. Watanabe was right to be cautious: these pages are unlike anything of Watson's that I've ever read. It is not, let me be clear, that the style renders the diary entries suspect. On the contrary, while I can only claim limited smarts in this department, it isn't the handwriting that gives me pause; *it's the content*. While Holmes and Watson during a collaboration of almost thirty years had occasion to deal with many unusual mysteries and problems, I'm betting even by Holmes's standards (his preference for the "outré"), this section takes the cake. It may be the fitting conclusion to a career unique in the annals of crime, a crime that (had it been successful) would have affected all our lives.

Referring to it as a crime may be legally incorrect, but, well . . . you decide. Watson certainly labeled it one.

Readers will also form their own opinions as to the authenticity of what they read.

With this ms. I have somewhat altered my editorial approach. Where I was formerly inclined to smooth out the bumps and errata in Watson's narrative, here it seems appropriate to interfere less. I hope you'll see why.

Dates, as Holmes always maintained, are crucial and nowhere more so than here.

It is interesting to note that what starts as a straightforward narration succumbs, as events unfold in rapid succession, to more disjointed entries, with tenses confused. Sometimes Watson's verb tenses are so mixed it's hard to know whether he was writing before, during, or after the fact, but in order to preserve the flavor and urgency of the narrative, I have chosen on this go-round to simply leave them as diary entries. For the most part, entries appear to be made more or less on the days when events transpired, but there is also evidence some entries were revised. By whom must remain an open question, though the cramped penmanship certainly resembles the doctor's hand. There are ink stains, arrows, and insertions enough to confuse the most scrupulous reader, but the pages themselves all appear to come from the same series of WHSmith notebooks in which Watson seems to have written most of his Holmes chronicles. There were entries that had nothing to do with the major narrative, and these I've struck out. (There's a lot of culinary detail, but I judged menus and recipes were not the point).

One important caveat: in the following, Watson admits to signing an early version (1911) of the UK Official Secrets Act—and to subsequently defying its prohibition against recording or disseminating what was covered under its provisions. It is beyond my pay grade to ask why Holmes's biographer was prepared to risk so much, but evidently in his mind the benefits outweighed the illegality and its possible personal consequences.

I have supplied footnotes where I think they may be helpful (but you can always ignore them), and also photographs of the participants where I could locate them.

Finally: in all my previous editing chores on his manuscripts, I have followed Watson's example by never including the name Sherlock Holmes in the titles I gave the finished books. Now, for the first time, I am breaking with that tradition and precedent for reasons I hope the reader will find self-evident.

I now turn the story over to John H. Watson, M.D.

—Nicholas Meyer
Los Angeles, 2023

# EXTRACTS FROM WATSON'S DIARY

**2 June 1916**. Another blood-soaked day. I am spent after ten hours in surgery. It was nightfall before I could eat the cold supper Maria had set out for me and bring myself to read the *Times*, there to learn of more millions dying on the Western Front where the slaughter continues unabated.

As both patient and surgeon I have known the terrible price of battle, but this surpasses anything in my experience. It is hard to believe the extinction of an entire generation is the price England must pay to prevent the German double-headed eagle waving over Buckingham Palace and the imbecilic Kaiser sitting on his grandmother's throne.* I had thought to retire after Juliet's death but instead of finding time for grief, I am obliged to exhaust myself amid the stench of ether and carbolic, treating maimed and disfigured young men—many little more than boys—who return from France amid a never-ending flood of

---

\* The Kaiser's grandmother was Queen Victoria.

viscera and missing parts, some arriving still in the remnants of the uniforms in which they were wounded. All bear the same faraway look, as though they were seeing not what was before their eyes but something unimaginable behind them. Fulham Road is choking on a river of ambulances streaming from the train stations. I am literally trembling with fatigue and know my days as a surgeon are numbered.

But the day's travails turn out to have scarcely begun. Sitting alone at my dining table, I became aware of a moaning that I originally imagined to be a summer breeze soughing in the chimney, but the sounds soon resolved themselves into what was unmistakably human. Maria was weeping in the pantry. Maria, who has been with us for more years than I care to remember, first engaged by Juliet at the start of our marriage, has served us since with never a murmur of complaint, helping nurse Juliet during the last terrible months of her illness and then staying on to see to my widower's needs ever since. She had a gentleman friend some time ago, but lately I've not seen or heard of him. I dare not ask why.

The sobs persisted so I set down my napkin and wandered into the larder where I found the poor woman in her chair, trying to muffle her cries in a tea towel.

"Maria, what is it?" She started and looked at me as guiltily as if I'd caught her stealing the spoons.

"I'm so sorry, doctor." She dabbed furiously at her eyes with the towel. "Forgive me!"

"I'm sure there's nothing to forgive, Maria. What's wrong?"

She shook her head, unwilling or unable to reply. I put a hand on her quaking shoulder. "Come, tell me."

She allowed my hand to steady her. Taking several deep breaths, she removed the towel and spoke into it. "It's Harry, my nephew . . . Mont Sorrel—wheresoever that is!"

"Oh, Maria."

"My sister's youngest. Only seventeen!" she wailed. I knew for a fact scenes like ours were played out daily. There was not a home untouched by the war. It was as if the Old Testament angel of death had flown over Britain instead of the Egypt of Moses.

"Are they certain?"

She nodded vigorously. "They got the telegram this morning. Poor Nellie's youngest," she repeated. "And that after Garth and all the rest!" And then, unable to contain herself, she threw herself into my arms, bursting into hot, bitter tears once more. "Why? Why doesn't it end? Will it never end?"

I held her awkwardly. "You might better ask why it even began," I murmured.

She lifted her red, tear-streaked face to peer up into mine. "Why did it? Why must they all die? Everyone said it would be short. They promised!"

"'Home before the leaves fall,'" I remembered. "Come, let me pour you some brandy."

"I never touch it, doctor."

"Just tonight." I lowered her into the chair, fetched a plain glass, and poured a draught into it. "Come, only a swallow."

She obeyed, coughing on the drink, wiping fresh tears away with the back of her hand. "No one understands! We hate the Germans. The Germans hate us. But the royal family, ain't they German too? Only seventeen!" she repeated, swallowing the rest of the brandy at a gulp and huddling, bent over, gasping for breath as the liquor did its temporary work.

Poor girl. What could I tell her? How to explain the quicksand of entangling alliances that dragged all Europe into this cesspool of blood? Alliances I can scarcely understand myself, no matter how many times speeches and posters have attempted to pound the facts into my head. That an Austrian archduke's assassination in faraway Serbia (wheresoever that is, as Maria might say) had somehow brought in Austrians, then the Germans and their strutting, war-hungry kaiser to back them on the one side, forcing Russia, France, England, and Australia (Australia!) to honor *their* alliances with little Serbia on the other? None of that would account for her nephew's death, or her father's or two brothers', all of which she had stoically endured to this point with British resolve and a stiff upper lip. But young Harry torn to pieces at Mont Sorrel was the straw that broke the camel's back.

Amid these saturnine reflections we were startled by the bell. Instantly Maria was on her feet, straightening her apron. "I'll see to it, doctor."

"Nonsense, Maria. Go up to bed. I'll deal with whoever it is. Go on now."

"Thankee, doctor." Scouring her eyes yet again with the heels of her hands, she fled upstairs. The bell rang again. Would this day never end? Wondering who on earth might be calling so late, I slipped on my jacket and unbolted the door, astonished to behold a figure emerging like a wraith from a thick, sulfurous fog.

"Holmes!"

"May I come in?" His voice was ragged, not the familiar, crisp tones to which I was long accustomed.

"Certainly."

I had not seen my singular friend in over a year. Always favoring a touch of the dramatic, the detective could not have devised a better entrance. I stood aside to let him pass, wondering not only at his unexpected presence, but also his appearance, for despite the indifferent lighting I could see that he sported a black eye and a chipped bicuspid.

"And a cracked rib, I fear," he confided, noting my confusion.

"Come into the surgery. Let me see."

"First let me sit." Knowing better than to insist, I gestured to a chair by the hearth, though at this time of year there was no need of a fire. Holmes lowered himself carefully into the chair and sat still for several moments, his eyes closed.

"You are not at the front?" He spoke at last without opening them. "How fortunate—for me. Didn't you say you intended going?"

He had raised a sore subject. "After Juliet's death, I volunteered at once. The training and skill of a battlefield surgeon I knew would be of inestimable value, but I was rejected on account of my age and my leg. It is hard for me to stand for long periods. Thus I was posted to the Royal Marsden, treating secondary wounds, though these are bad enough, including sepsis and gangrene, many ultimately involving amputations." It still rankled that I had not been accepted for active service. London was crawling with older men—and women—in one form of uniform or another and I felt it a blemish, even if no one else was of that opinion, but the detective's appearance drove these considerations from my mind.

"Holmes, what has happened to you? Who has done this? Could you see the blackguards? And why are you not in Sussex, attending to your bees?"

"I did it to myself, Watson. Or rather, it was done at my direction. I'm too old for this," he added in a murmur, echoing, as it happened, my own ruminations. But whatever "this" was, his battered appearance confirmed his statement. I was relieved to see his imperious, beaky nose had not been broken, though in addition to the other changes in his physiognomy, I now noticed a scraggly goatee I had seen once before. The memory of that disguise did not bode well.

"Holmes, let me have a look at you," I repeated. "It shouldn't take long."

"There's no need," he replied, closing his eyes. "The shiner will heal, as will the rib, and I daresay the tooth can be replaced somehow or other."

"At least let me draw you a bath and let you have a hot soak." It was obvious he hadn't had a wash in days.

"Later."

I took a chair opposite and repeated my question.

"What *hasn't* happened?" he answered. "I must admit my rosy prognostications of two years ago were at best . . ." here he hesitated before concluding ruefully, "premature. You might well be entitled to whisper *Norbury*, Watson."*

With slower movements than usual (I now perceived the knuckles of his right hand were bruised and swollen as well), he took out his silver case and with some difficulty extracted a cigarette and tapped it clumsily on the cover before lighting it, at which point his grateful inhalation was usurped by a cough.

"Holmes, you must let me bind your ribs."

"In due course," he replied, shutting his eyes briefly once more. "Might I trouble you for a glass of water?"

I had learned from a lifetime in his company there was no point arguing with him. Rather than presenting himself at a hospital, he

---

\*       Norbury was the site of one of Holmes's failures (*The Yellow Face*) and a codeword he encouraged Watson to use whenever the doctor felt the Great Detective was getting too big for his britches.

had come here with some definite end in view, which he would communicate in his own good time.

"Of course. And something to eat? Let me make you a sandwich.
You look starved."

"Thank you, just water for the moment."

"Wait here." Allowing him to sit there, his eyes still shut, I
stared at that unpleasant goatee and rose to fetch his drink. As I
ran the tap, it was easy to remember, to drift back two years (only
two, and yet a lifetime) and recall those optimistic prognostications, following our capture of the German spymaster, Von Bork,
near the cliffs of Dover in that scorching August of 1914. Holmes
had said to me then:

> *There's an east wind coming . . . , such a wind as never blew*
> *on England yet. It will be cold and bitter, Watson, and a*
> *good many of us may wither before its blast. But it's God's*
> *own wind none the less, and a cleaner, better, stronger land*
> *will lie in the sunshine when the storm has cleared.*

"Premature," the detective repeated, reading my mind as though
he were inside it, "but not inaccurate." Opening his eyes, he took
the glass I handed him. "Though I maintain my prophecy. The sun
will shine again on England."

"You will forgive me saying so, but it is hard to imagine the sun
shining upon England when her best blood is presently irrigating
Flanders's fields." I could not forbear thinking about Maria's poor
nephew.

"I've been wrong before," the detective allowed. He sipped the
water, wincing as he swallowed. "Still each of us must do what we
can to see that civilization survives."

"And what have you been doing to save civilization?" I rather dreaded to learn. With his snaggle tooth, his smile more nearly resembled a snarl. Though I knew him to be sixty-six and he was clearly the worse for wear, yet those gray eyes—the left admittedly bloodshot—shone brightly as ever. "Holmes, come into the surgery. I insist."

"Very well." He allowed me to lead him there, where I clicked on the lights and gingerly helped him out of a tattered mackintosh and dirty singlet. In the light, his slender torso was black and blue, his rib cage clearly visible, so emaciated was he now.

Seeing my look, he smiled grimly. "Where I've been they don't give you much to eat and what they serve up is scarcely digestible."

"And you've been kicked."

"Set upon with hobnailed boots, aye."

I located the damaged rib and palpated gently. "Cracked but not broken. I don't think an X-ray will be necessary. If you don't stress it overmuch it will knit on its own."

He accepted this news without comment. I sponged his chest, applied salve to the bruises, and began wrapping his rib cage. What was one patient more? I had been all day piecing together broken men.

He suffered my ministrations in silence save for an occasional intake of breath. When at last he spoke again, his words were a bolt from the blue.

"As we sit here, the jury is debating the guilt of Roger Casement."

I could not tell from his tone whether this non sequitur was a statement or a question. "Holmes, I've learned over the years that in some quarters I am accounted a dullard, but I daresay I am no more so than my neighbors, whom, I venture to suggest, would be just as confused by your change of topic as I am. I simply cannot follow your train of thought."

"I will slow the train for your benefit, my dear fellow. Casement is the topic, I assure you. You have been following the case?"

"All England is following it. The swine should hang, in my opinion. Too tight?"

He shook his head but drew less emphatically on his cigarette. "The 'swine,' I remind you, was knighted only five years since by His Majesty for 'services to humanity' for exposing the crime of human trafficking and the horrors of King Leopold's Belgian Congo."

I applied more salve around the black eye and sticking plaster to a fingernail. "Holmes, what has Roger Casement to do with these injuries? Nowadays Sir Roger's 'services to humanity' consist of fomenting Easter Sunday's uprising in Ireland while England fights for her very life, stabbing those who honored him in the back. Let him hang, I repeat. Hold still."

*Sir Roger Casement*

Holmes sighed and obeyed. "I repeat: Casement is why I am here. He will hang, doubtless. The jury is bound to convict—if only on the basis of the diaries. May I put on my shirt? I'm cold."

I helped him slip into the ragged garment and did up the buttons that remained for him. His cryptic remarks further bewildered me. "Casement's diaries? You don't believe they were forged to help convict the man? His defenders are convinced they were."

The detective appeared to consider this possibility. "A spurious record of the man's sexual dissipations disseminated by Whitehall to discredit his heroism and character?* To send him the way of Oscar Wilde, only more permanently?"† He scowled, dismissing the idea. "I doubt that would serve. Sir Roger has ardent and prominent admirers, our old friend Bernard Shaw among them."

"Shaw is another Irishman, come, you know this perfectly well. Though he has for the moment forsworn his pacifism and now professes to support the war, who's to say where his true allegiances lie?" Holmes said nothing to this but allowed me to clean and bandage his other fingers. A right thumbnail was almost torn off.

"But how do you explain Sir Arthur Conan Doyle's defense? He maintains the sexual contents of the diaries merely prove Casement insane."

I tied off my bandage. "According to what I've read, Casement refused to plead insanity. Besides, isn't Doyle yet another Irishman? They all stick together."

"The United States Senate has begged for clemency."

---

\*    There has to be something bleakly hilarious in the idea of some nameless Secret Service flunky inventing (or remembering!) homosexual exploits to insert (somehow?) into Casement's diaries.

†    Wilde's homosexuality earned him two years' hard labor in Reading Gaol (prison).

I refused to be drawn into the labyrinth of American politics. "Holmes, what has Roger Casement to do with your wounds?"

He sniffed, wincing at the pungent odor of antiseptic. "As I said, he is bound to hang." He sighed. "Might I now trouble you for some tea?"

He followed me docilely into the kitchen and settled himself into a pantry chair while I lit the kettle. I was in the act of adjusting the gas when he said quietly behind me—

"Do you miss it?"

I turned to face him. "Miss what?"

"Come, confess. I see it in your face. The old days in our shared rooms before the cozy fire in Baker Street of a winter's night. Victoria is on her throne and all's right with our world—an empire upon which the sun never sets. There's a knock on the door—a stranger in desperate straits! A speckled band—!"

"An emerald carbuncle!"

"Carbuncles are blue. Reread your own account, Watson."

"A solitary cyclist!" I recalled, undeterred, falling into the spirit of the thing. "The dog that did nothing in the nighttime!"

"The league of red-headed men!"

"The hound!"

He sat back with a sigh. "Ah, yes, the hound. The world was simpler then. Or so it seemed. A purloined goose . . ." Then, leaning forward, his bloodshot gray eyes peered intently into mine. "Watson, those palmy days are gone forever."

"I hardly manage to write anything these days," I admitted.

"Nowadays, who has leisure to read?" the detective said by way of consolation.

"In any event, now you are keeping bees, you've no cases."

"True. No cases—only Casement. I knew him, you know."

Holmes never failed to astonish.

"You knew Roger Casement? How on earth?"

"In America, during the two years I toiled undercover as the Irish-born sympathizer, 'Gideon Altamont,' Casement was there as well, agitating on behalf of Irish independence, soliciting money, aid, and arms in her cause. As Altamont, I did much the same. There's an enormous Irish population in the States, as you know. Our paths crossed more than once. In Chicago, Buffalo, and later, New York City."

I tried not to picture Holmes with that hideous beard and doubtless perfected Yankee-Gaelic lilt, charming money and arms for sedition, even with the long-term rationale of penetrating Von Bork's gang of saboteurs. I shuddered involuntarily at the disagreeable thought.

"I remind you that in 1912 when Mycroft dispatched 'Altamont' to America, England was not at war." The detective had again made himself at home in my mind. "My assignment was to keep watch on Von Bork, whose job—anticipating the conflict—was to lobby resistance to the idea of America's entering a war on the Allied side. According to the Foreign Office there are almost two million German Americans in the United States, which does not include another ten million of Teutonic descent, all vehemently opposed to any anti-German activity. When war finally came, President Wilson found himself confronted by such strong isolationist headwinds, he could only sit on the fence, choosing like Nero to fiddle while Rome burns."

"While all Europe burns," I amended.

He did not contradict me. "Poor Mycroft. What cold comfort to know my brother did not live to witness this." A wave of his uninjured hand took in the cataclysm as the kettle whistled. "Though it would not be inaccurate to say he anticipated it."

"You were lucky in 1912," I reminded him, spooning oolong into the pot. "As you crossed the Atlantic on the *Lusitania*, you might have predeceased your brother."

"It could have been worse. That year I might have sailed on the *Titanic*." He yawned and ran a hand through his matted silver hair, which wanted trimming. "What is luck, really, save a name we give to something that cannot be defined?" He shrugged philosophically. "Call it fate, fortune, kismet, or destiny, by any designation it remains mysterious." The detective managed a lopsided smile. "We don't know what luck is, yet we cannot help acknowledging it. I have been lucky."

So far, I thought, though at present he did not *look* lucky. How many of his nine lives had Holmes used up by now? I wondered also at his frame of mind, but he abruptly threw off his brown study no sooner than he'd entered it. "In point of fact, poor Mycroft brings me to the reason for my visit."

"I was wondering when you would get round to it." I could not help noting how easily we fell into our familiar pattern of relations. No matter how long it had been, the detective and I seemed always to pick up exactly where we left off. Perhaps that is one definition of friendship.

He blew on his tea and sipped it. "Watson, would it interest you know why I am in this condition, dressed as I am and where I have spent the last week and half?"

"Holmes!" My patience was at an end.

"In prison with Roger Casement." Before I could expostulate, he leaned forward again, tapping me on the knee with a bony forefinger. "Every time I attempt to step away, they pull me back! As you know, since our return from Egypt, I have been comfortably rusticating with my bees on the South Downs, trying not to read the news."

"Yet you persist in keeping our old Baker Street digs, which suggests you are not completely satisfied with your bucolic life."

"Watson, how very observant you have become!" His eyes twinkled as of old. "My pied-à-terre, yes. I cling to my old address as tenaciously as President Wilson does his neutrality. I run up to Town now and then to attend concerts and the opera. My gramophone is no substitute for a live performance and I must have my musical injection now and then. It is one habit I cannot break. Mrs. Turner sees to it our old rooms are kept tidy."

"But it wasn't a concert that brought you to Town this time."

"Right again! Really, my boy, you surpass yourself. I was approached by Sir William Melville, intent on luring me out of retirement. He is director of the newly created British Secret Service, more properly SIS, the Secret Intelligence Service."

"Never heard of either."

"That's as it should be. He goes by the code name 'M.'"

"Not very subtle—choosing a code name with one's own initial," I felt bound to point out. The whole business was making me distinctly queasy. I felt as if I were literally at sea—and I am a poor sailor.

"He chose his code name to honor the memory of his mentor," the detective said quietly.

"Ah." I felt dry land beneath my feet once more. "Mycroft. Of course."

Neither confirming nor denying this, Holmes resumed. "Neither side may admit it, but this much is clear to both: like two bull moose with their antlers hopelessly entangled, England

and Germany are locked in a struggle to the death where only one side can be victorious. The loser will lose all."

I thought of Maria's nephew, who had already lost all. "Go on."

"SIS could get nothing out of Casement, but knowing of my American association with the man, Sir William asked if I would be willing to be tossed into the traitor's cell to see if he might share secrets with a fellow Irish terrorist. Before he most assuredly is hanged," he repeated.

"What a singular proposition."

"And you know my taste for the outré. The more I thought about it, the more . . ." He stopped in search of the right word.

"Appealing?"

"Plausible. The more plausible it became. I was desperate to be of war use, though at my age I couldn't imagine what that might be. Sir William's proposition seemed simple enough." He slurped more tea through his broken tooth.

"Sir William thought Casement might know something of Germany's intentions?"

Holmes studied his bandaged fingers as he attempted to flex them. "He thought it not unlikely. The moment war was declared, Casement rushed from America to Germany. By November of 1914 he was attempting to convince Irish prisoners of war in Hamburg to reenter combat. On the German side."

"What nonsense."

Holmes lit another cigarette. "It appears even the Germans thought so. Unsure of what to do with him, they persuaded Casement to return to Ireland to 'continue the good work.' The prospect of an Irish uprising held obvious appeal for them. If we English were obliged to subdue a revolt in Ireland, our forces on the Continent would, of necessity, be diluted and Germany might, after all, win this endless war."

"It almost worked."

"So it did. A German U-boat landed Casement near Tralee, but he was arrested almost immediately and the uprising narrowly suppressed."

"Brutally suppressed, you might add. Yes, it was in all the papers. So much happens so quickly these days, it's hard to believe all this was mere weeks ago. Monday's tragedy is ancient history by the week's end."

He did not dispute this. "Be that as it may, Sir Roger Casement is now tried for treason by the same government that had previously knighted him."

I rubbed my throbbing temples. "Absurd." Then, recollecting myself—"And so you agreed to Sir William's plan?"

"I did. But I did point out they'd have to make me . . . presentable."

At last I understood: the black eye, the tooth, the hand, the ribs. "The Black and Tans worked you over."*

"With a will. I wasn't presented to them as Sherlock Holmes, mind, but as that Irish rabble-rouser, Gideon Altamont, so they put their hearts into it. And their boots," he added, wincing at the memory.

"And packed you off to the Tower?"

He shook his head. "Casement isn't being held in the Tower. He's in Brixton. It seems the Tower doesn't have the staff to maintain a suicide watch."

---

*    During the Irish War of Independence the Black and Tans were constables recruited by the Royal Irish Constabulary (RIC) as reinforcements. The nickname arose from the colors of the improvised uniforms initially worn, a blend of dark green RIC (almost black) and khaki British Army.

"So you went to Brixton?"

He grinned. "As you see. Black and blue instead of black and tan. My appearance as my bona fides."

"And did he remember you, the great Sir Roger?"

Holmes sat back, the old wooden kitchen chair creaking as he did so. I've jotted down as much as I can remember of what he then told me:

All prisons smell the same, Watson, and Brixton is no exception. Though modernized more than once, the place reeks of sweat and excrement no amount of disinfectant can disguise.

> *O paddy dear, O did you hear, the news that's goin' round?*
> *The shamrock is forbid by law to grow on Irish ground!*

Someone was singing in a lilting, echoing tenor. As we walked, another singer, this one less gifted but equally defiant, took up the song . . .

> *And St. Patrick's Day no more will be, His color can't be*
> *seen.*
> *They're hangin' men and women for the wearin' of the*
> *green!*

My visit, if it could be termed such, almost came to grief before it began. One of my brutish chaperones grinned when we entered the vast cell block, informing me, "We've got all sort of scum here, let me tell you! We've even got Von Bork to keep you company! Here for life he is!" You may imagine into what confusion this news threw me. Von Bork! A man, Watson, as you have reason to know, who could hardly be matched among all the devoted agents of the Kaiser.* As Von Bork's betrayer, the last thing I needed was to encounter the spymaster I had checkmated. I did not fear for my own safety but dreaded the fuss the German might make should he catch sight of me and the ruinous possibility that Casement, wherever they were holding him, should overhear Von Bork's curses and learn my identity before I was thrust into his cell. I had no difficulty, Watson, remembering his slowly spoken curse as he woke from the chloroform with which we had subdued him:

> *I shall get level with you, Altamont. If it takes me all my*
> *life I shall get level with you!*

I made light of his fury at the time, as you will recall, but now the memory of those terrible words rang in my ears. Fortunately that grotesque bit of Feydeau† did not unfold. My captors hustled me—in far worse shape than I am now, mark you—down double-storied corridors of barred cells and up cast-iron steps past yet more cells until, with an endless clinking of keys, I was heaved into Casement's small, heavily guarded enclosure, more a cage than a cell.

"Here's company for ya, Sir Roger," the second of my escorts called mockingly to him before slamming the sliding the steel door with a thunderous echo and locking us in with a final rattling of keys. "We're at yer beck and call!" he yelled after us.

---

\*    For full details of their fateful encounter with the deadly German agent, the reader is referred to the case known as *His Last Bow*.

†    Georges Feydeau, author of popular licentious bedroom farces with lovers and cuckolds popping in and out of closets and beds, too close for comfort.

The condemned man—for surely he was no less—lay on his back on an iron bedstead, sans mattress, his hands and feet shackled above and below him. He sat up, with a rattle of chains, startled by the intrusion.

"Altamont?" Casement had no difficulty recognizing me, even with my swollen eye already purple. In the dim light it was harder for me to recognize him but when I did, I could not suppress a shudder at what I beheld. It required no great powers of observation to see the transformation. The remarkable man I had so admired, the intrepid hero who had infiltrated Leopold's Belgian Congo and recorded the atrocities there before escaping and publishing his sensational exposé to a horrified world, had been, as you might say, an Edwardian knight parfait. Even when I heard him speak to Sinn Féin gatherings of Irish Americans in Boston and New York, he stood before us as a gentleman, tall, handsome, poised, and eloquent. I could not help but be impressed by his person and his passion.

"Mr. Casement!" I exclaimed as if shocked to find myself in the same cell with a man of his stature. Knowing he had repudiated his knighthood, as a fellow rebel I likewise disdained the use of it.

"Altamont!" he repeated, then, immediately lowering his voice, "Were you searched?"

I nodded, turning out my pockets and opening my empty, bleeding, hands. Casement nodded in turn. He anticipated no less. The great man was a shadow of his former self. Once meticulously groomed and clearly vain of his appearance, it was clear he had been denied all comforts and thought nothing of them now.

"Charged?" he whispered.

"With high treason, so. I'm for the next assizes. Like you, my fate is decided."

With another dismal rattle of chains, he clutched bits of my shirt front with clenched fists. "Speak softly! They listen to everything! Were you there when it happened?" he demanded, with no further word of commiseration.

"Easter Sunday—I was there," I lied, pulling free my shirt and limping to rest on the iron bed. He sat eagerly beside me, smelling like the very devil. As I had been worked over, left in fetid confinement for days in preparation for this interview, I probably smelled little better. My lips were caked with blood where my tooth was dislodged, but Casement was not interested in my condition.

"What of Shaughnessy?" he hissed, peering at me with near-sighted cobalt eyes. It was reflexive to resurrect my Irish American patois.

"Sure, Shaughnessy, McClaren, and Nolan, all dead," I told him, which was truthful enough. "Nolan hit by a stray bullet. Shaughnessy and McClaren stood against a wall off O'Connell Street and shot by a Black and Tan firing squad with no trial at all. Have you not seen the papers?"

He sagged at my news and let go my torn sleeve, which he had caught up again in his agitation. "They forbid me papers," he sniffed, wiping a grimy hand over his nose and mouth, and then in another urgent undertone—"And Michael Collins?"

"Escaped, sure enough." I swung back and forth between Irish and American patois as I had done two years before.

"Praise God." He sat back with a sigh. "That's something." Then he regarded me expectantly. Far from our cell, the tenor sang—

*I met with Napper Tandy and I shook him by the hand,*
*And said, How's dear old Ireland, and how does she stand?*

And was answered from another quarter—

*She's the most distressful country that ever you have seen.*
*They're hanging men and women for the wearin' of the*
*green!*

"Shut your face, yous!" another yelled back.

My story was ready. "They scooped me up in Limerick ten days ago. I was being cached by the Brian Malones." The name meant nothing to him, as I knew it must for I'd created the family of whole cloth. "They're for Dublin Castle now, sorry to say." I crossed myself. "Someone grassed, 'tis certain. Why I wasn't stood against the wall with the rest I've no idea, but things had calmed down by then. They knew we was finished."

Casement settled back against the cold wall behind the narrow bed. "Dr. Johnson said, 'Nothing concentrates the mind so wonderfully as the knowledge that one is to be hanged.'"

"Is Johnson one of us then?" I felt bound to ask, which provoked a burst of bitter laughter.*

"It makes no matter," he muttered at length. "Though I won't live to see it, once Germany makes the decision, the war will end in twelve weeks. Germany will win and Ireland will be free."

I did not have to feign astonishment and twisted to gape at him. "What can you be saying, man? Twelve weeks? After all this time? There's no way on God's earth. Sure, what decision are you talkin' of?"

---

* Holmes shrewdly played ignorant: Casement is quoting the endlessly quotable Samuel Johnson.

Casement stared at me, his eyes again probing mine. "Can I trust you?"

The man was no fool. It had surely occurred to him at some point that I might be a plant.

"You can't," I advised. His eyes widened at this. "If they work me over again I'd tell them everything I know. If she were alive, sure 'tis my own mother I'd sell them, so. I'd sell you if it came to that, and if I swear to the contrary this minute 'tis a liar I am."

He turned away from me then, settling the back of his massive head once more against the metal wall. I could only hope my show of candor would allay his suspicions.

"Twelve weeks," said he at length. "Twelve weeks of unrestricted U-boat warfare in the North Atlantic, sinking any and all shipping, is all it will take to starve England into surrender. Imported food, cotton, and necessaries are essential to an island nation, a truth we Irish know too well. England, 'this other Eden, this demi-Paradise,' to quote Mr. Shakespeare, cannot survive more than three months without resupply. And you know how thorough the Germans are. They've calculated English malnutrition down to the last bushel of wheat. Twelve weeks! The U-boat wolf packs are already in place, straining at their moorings like leashed hounds."

Needless to say this news stunned me. Contemplating England's imminent surrender I had to summon all my resources to stay in character as one who longed for the day.

"Only twelve weeks? Sure then you'll live to see it," I promised in a consoling voice, but then, as if struck by a thought, which in fact did occur to me, I wondered aloud, "But if the Germans start sinkin' neutral ships, for their starvation scheme to work, that must include any American vessels bound for England with supplies.

And if Germany be sinkin' ships flyin' the stars and stripes, President Wilson will have no choice but to finally abandon his pious sermonizing on holy neutrality and enter the war on the Allied side, so."

"Not necessarily," Casement surprised me by saying. "Last year over a hundred Americans died when the Germans torpedoed the *Lusitania* and still he didn't climb down from his fence. And the Lucy was a passenger liner."

"A passenger liner perhaps," I countered, "but she was British, not American, which gave the man an excuse to remain perched on his fence. But I tell you, if it's American ships they start sendin' to the bottom, it'll be another story. I lived in America and you've visited, Mr. Casement. We both know her infinite capacity. Europe may have run out of bodies to stuff into the meat grinder, but America has plenty. And if America enters the war Germany will be defeated."

My words did not surprise him. He sat in silence for a time as if trying to make up his mind about something.

*They're hangin' men and women for the wearin' of the green!*

The song was taken up again. If Casement heard those ominous lyrics, or recognized portents pertaining to himself in them, he gave no sign.

"America will not enter the war," he said finally. "There's a plan to prevent that happening."

As Holmes repeated the traitor's words, I stared at him, open-mouthed. "Do you mean to say Germany is planning unrestricted U-boat warfare?"

The detective nodded wearily. His recital had tired him. "According to Casement, it's only a question of when. The choice and timing is being hotly debated among the German high command as we speak. Many moderates are opposed, but Casement's source is convinced that in the end the decision will be taken in favor of sinking all vessels bound for England, regardless of flag or nationality. They've no choice. It's the only way to break the stalemate. As Casement described it, before Germany releases the U-boats, they will implement the plan to ensure America stays out of the war long enough for Germany to win."

"What is the plan?"

He sighed, now at the end of his long tale. "Aye, there's the rub. Casement doesn't know it."

"What? Then all this"—I gestured to his injuries—"was for n—"

"I tried to wheedle it out of him but was obliged to be circumspect so as not to arouse his suspicions. He said he didn't know it, only that it was said to be foolproof. Either he's telling the truth or he didn't trust me enough to confide it. The man had been worked over and bore unmistakable signs of ill-usage, but it seems unlikely his interrogators knew what they were looking for, only that they hoped to pop some secrets out of him. He didn't divulge anything to them and was not about to say more to me. In sum I'm at a cul-de-sac. I dared not return to Baker Street just now as I could not risk the possibility of 'Altamont' being followed through tonight's pea soup when 'he' was tossed out of Brixton, so I called on a doctor—you—instead. But as you now understand," he concluded, "Big Ben is ticking. Any day now, the Wilhelmstrasse* will imple-

---

\*      The Wilhelmstrasse was the location of Germany's foreign office; the equivalent of Britain's Whitehall, or the US State Department, give or take.

ment whatever fiendish plot they've concocted to see to it America stays clear of the European chessboard, and once that objective is achieved, the U-boats will be loosed like so many arrows at Agincourt. And twelve weeks from that date . . ." he trailed off. "And now, my dear fellow, if you've no objection, I'll trouble you for that bath and ask you to restrap my ribs when I'm dry."

"Of course, and you'll stay the night and get some rest."

"Alas, as I've pointed out, the clock is ticking. After I've had a wash, will you come with me?"

"Of course. Where?"

"Whitehall. M is waiting."

**3 June 1916.** Had I given the matter any thought I might have imagined Whitehall would be mostly deserted at half past one—as though the war, like a shop, had shut down for the night. But being escorted by police with Sherlock Holmes through piled sandbags and two security barriers where I was required to sign something called the Official Secrets Act, in which I swore never to record, divulge, or otherwise disseminate anything His Majesty's government deemed secret without express permission,* I was quickly disabused of such a notion, for the place was as busy as morning on market day. There were no idlers to be seen. Uniformed army and naval officers, as well as a sprinkling of civilians, some clutching sheaves of papers, others talking in urgent whispers, trotted down echoing corridors, passing innumerable offices within which (when doors were ajar), I spied hornets' nests of activity. Our steps were

---

* Watson's casual admission of this violation still startles. Possibly he was old enough to be indifferent to any possible consequences or never imagined his diary might be made public.

punctuated by ringing telephones and the clacking tattoo of telegraph keys. In these precincts, as much as at the Western Front,
the war was a twenty-four-hour affair.

"Of course His Majesty's government wishes to express its gratitude for the injuries you have suffered in its service," Sir William
Melville began, addressing Holmes as though he was remarking on
the weather. With the heavy door to his office closed, all noise was
eclipsed. "Naturally, you will be decorated, though due to the nature
of your work, it is understood such decorations can never be displayed."

With a drawer filled with medals and decorations he was
never permitted to wear, the detective contented himself with a
casual rejoinder: "With the current shortage of metal and cloth,
I'm sure His Majesty's government has better use for both than
creating decorations for one who only performed his duty."

Sir William, or M, as I must henceforth call him, forgetting
his proper name and title (as I must everything that follows),
sat behind a large desk, lit by a sole downward-facing goose-
neck lamp with a luminescent green glass shade. He stiffened
imperceptibly at the rebuke, his lips compressed into a thin line.

"To be sure," he amended. "And now to business," he said, as
one who has dispensed with a tiresome formality.

I sat silently next to the detective as he delivered the information he had previously shared with me. Holmes had bathed, shaved
that miserable tuft from his chin, and changed his clothing but
nonetheless looked as knocked about as he actually was, while I
must have appeared little better, my collar and tie forgotten, in
want of my own shave, bags sagging beneath my eyes on a day
that refused to end.

M listened to Holmes in silence, interrupting only on occasion
with short, pointed questions that the detective answered equally

succinctly. I judged M to be in his mid-fifties. In the sparse light
I could not make out the color of his eyes, only their gleaming
intensity. It was as if the man never blinked. He wore mufti but
had about him the squared shoulders and rigid posture suggestive of a military background. I later learned he had begun as a
policeman. Below a pugnacious nose and a set of bushy eyebrows
was an equally imposing mustache, cultivated, I suspected, to
compensate for his head of thinning brown hair. When he spoke I
was surprised to detect the faintest Gaelic lilt. Another Irishman!

As Holmes made his report, I squinted at the darkened wall behind
M where an enormous world map was displayed, pockmarked with
pins and tiny flags denoting positions, units, and nationalities. From
the profusion of markers, it looked to be indeed a world war.

"Did the prisoner make mention of any names?" He always
referred to Casement in this fashion.

*Sir William Melville, Mycroft's successor as the first M*

"Someone in Washington called Count Bernstorff."

M grunted. "The German ambassador. Not a bad sort, as these
things go, though with a weakness for the ladies."

Rummaging on his desk, he produced a folder bound by a scarlet ribbon and sealed with wax of the same colour. With a vigorous motion, he broke the seal and handed the folder to Holmes, who took it without comment. After glancing at the contents, he passed the folder to me. Within I beheld a photograph of a smiling, middle-aged gentleman in bathing costume, his arms around the waists of two laughing young women, also dressed for the seaside.

*Count Bernstorff with friends*

"I think I see what you mean."

"Casement met with Bernstorff in Washington, trying to persuade Germany to send weapons to Ireland."

This news did not astonish M. "His premise being that 'the enemy of my enemy is my friend.' Anything else concerning Bernstorff?"

"Only that Bernstorff was somehow connected with the plan."

"Interesting." M brushed his mustache thoughtfully with the knuckles of one hand.

"Anyone else?"

"Someone called Zimmermann."

"German foreign minister. Bernstorff's superior in Berlin."

A chair squeaked in a darkened corner of the large office and I became aware of a figure sitting motionless in the shadows, silently attending to every word. Before I could stop myself, I asked, "Who is that?"

"That is no one," M said curtly. Then, turning back to Holmes: "And the prisoner refused to divulge anything regarding the actual plan to ensure America's nonparticipation in the European theatre? Think carefully."

"He claimed not to know the scheme, though that it is not certain," supplied the detective, ignoring the veiled critique of his thinking. "Only that once implemented it was certain to prevent the Americans entering the war."

M leaned forward slightly. "Is that the phrase the prisoner used? 'Certain to prevent'?"

"That was the phrase."

M moved his lips soundlessly and gave the briefest look in the direction of the man who wasn't there. "Anything else?"

Holmes furrowed his brow, searching his memory for the all-important details by which he himself set such store. "At one point he appeared pleased that the American president's willingness to engage in armed conflict seemed limited to dispatching a certain General Pershing and twelve thousand troopers into Mexico where they were playing hare and hounds with someone named Villa, though I may have misheard the name."

"A trifling affair. Three months ago a Mexican bandit by that name dashed across the border into Columbus, New Mexico, with four hundred men and seized a cache of US weapons stored there. President Wilson felt compelled to respond militarily, though the effort by General Pershing and his small army to recover the arms and apprehend Villa has to date proved a wild goose chase."

"And you know this because . . ."

M hesitated momentarily, casting a glance into the shadows, before deciding to answer. Evidently Holmes's reputation and service justified his confidence.

"We routinely intercept telegraphic communications between the American ambassador in London and his superiors in Washington." M smiled. "The Americans use a letter code that is absurdly easy to crack."

"Spying on your allies?" Holmes raised his eyebrows.

"They are not our allies yet," M responded sternly.

"If this is, as you term it, a 'trifling affair,' I wonder then why Casement troubled to mention this Villa," Holmes persisted.

I recalled the detective's dictum that trifles can assume great importance.

In response, M clipped a cigar, lit it carefully, and blew contented smoke. "As our American cousins might say, we have bigger fish to fry. The question now before us is: Ought we to alert their president to the existence of a German plan to prevent America's entry into the war?"

The question hung in the air between the two men, broken when Holmes quietly wondered, "Would it be helpful to learn what Admiral Hall has to say?"

It is impossible to describe the effect these words produced. Both M and the man who lurked in the shadows started violently, the one with an oath, the other banging his fist upon his desk.

"How the devil do you come to know my name?" the man in darkness demanded in an irritable, high-pitched voice.

"It is my business to know things," the detective replied smoothly. "Have you formed an opinion, admiral?"

"Damnation," the voice muttered. A muddled silence ensued during which M gnawed at his mustache before reminding himself to leave off. Finally the same voice, now in a calmer vein as its owner regained his self-possession, spoke once more. "We will say nothing. For now. We've nothing concrete to offer the Americans, merely speculation. Their isolationist lobby will accuse us of fabricating a bogeyman to trick the United States into joining the conflict and it would not be . . . politic at this juncture to acknowledge our—"

"Eavesdropping," Holmes supplied.

"Just so. We need to learn the German plan and be able to prove what we have found out before revealing it. We—"

At this moment the room convulsed, walls buckling as though punched by a giant fist. This was followed almost immediately by the sound of a tremendous explosion, which, though distant, nonetheless had the effect of further rattling the entire building and cracking M's windows facing King Charles Street. As I flinched, plaster motes dislodged by the force of the blast trickled down from the ceiling.

"Zeppelin," M commented in a flat tone. He had not moved. Neither had Holmes.

We now sat silent amid those plaster snowflakes, each of us wondering what part of the city had been hit and if there was more to come.

Moments later a brisk knock was followed by the entrance of a major who saluted smartly without waiting to be admitted.

"They've hit Saint Paul's, sir." His voice was unsteady. "And some nearby structures."

"In this fog?" I found myself demanding.

M turned to me. "They're above it," he explained in the same flat voice. "Besides, it doesn't matter what they hit. Civilians are fair game to the Hun." He turned back to the major. "Get the details."

"Sir." The man saluted again and departed, snapping the door shut behind him.

Another silence followed as we pondered the desecration of the famed church, interrupted at length by the invisible admiral, who, like M, spoke as though nothing had occurred.

"This Bernstorff in Washington must be our key to the whole business. If he is part of the plan it must have been communicated to him. The question is how."

Taking his cue from the determined resumption of our agenda, Holmes replied promptly. "By coded cable, surely."

"Impossible," M said, relighting his cigar, which had gone out.

"Oh?" Again M threw a look to the shadows.

"Tell him," said the voice.

Now sirens, wailing like banshees, could be heard from White-hall. After waiting for the shrieking fire trucks to pass, M turned back to Holmes.

"It is not generally known, but at the start of the war the Royal Navy severed all transatlantic cables connecting Germany with the Western hemisphere. Coded or not, Germany can no longer com-municate by telegram with North America. And if they attempt wireless telegraphy, they may be sure we will pluck their transmis-sions from the ether."

"Leaving three possibilities," the detective said after the briefest pause for reflection. "Either coded messages are carried by some sort of courier or perhaps a chargé d'affaires from an allegedly neutral country—Sweden, perhaps?—using his diplomatic pouch to deliver mes—"

"A cumbersome method at best," interposed the hidden admiral, "especially if a set of instructions must be modified or clarified. What is your second possibility?"

"A U-boat landing in some secure cove or inlet on the East Coast with the message to be picked up and relayed by a local saboteur . . ."

"Again such a scheme allows for no reply." The admiral made no pretense of patience and continued in a hectoring tone, "And how to let your hypothetical 'local saboteur' know when and where to rendezvous with your hypothetical U-boat? If the Hun could do that, they'd have no need to risk one of their precious submarines in the first place."

"Which brings us to the third possibility," Holmes directed his words solely to M. "Namely, that German telegraphic communications to Washington are now routed across the Atlantic using another country's transoceanic cable. But searching the rest of the Continent to determine their point of dispatch would take forever."

"Correct," agreed M. "You've done well, Holmes. You've got more out of Casement than I imagined possible." He had finally uttered the traitor's name.

"And we did subject him to"—here he pressed his palms together—"encouraged conversation."

"Encouraged conversation," Holmes repeated without emphasis.

M paused once more, "In light of your success, we should very much like to extend your commission."

"Oh?"

"We should like you to entertain the idea of traveling to America and investigating the matter from that end."

Holmes sat forward in his chair before leaning back again. This was the only moment in the interview that had taken him by surprise. "America?"

"It is a great deal to ask, but I needn't tell you the dire straits in which we find ourselves. Every possible avenue to success must be explored, even the most remote. We realize you are officially past the age at which most men would be capable of such an undertaking, but your abilities, alas, are unique."

Holmes said nothing. M cast his eyes in the direction of Admiral Hall before resuming. "Needless to say, you would be given carte blanche."

I stole a look at Holmes and for a change was able to read his mind. Carte blanche from a bankrupt treasury was as sure an indication of desperation as could be imagined.

Still the detective did not speak. He sat, his features in the low light as inscrutable as those of the Great Sphinx. He remained motionless for so long I could almost imagine he was asleep with his eyes open. M must have wondered along similar lines, for his shifted in his chair, again exchanging looks with the admiral. He was indeed on the point of speaking when Holmes appeared to emerge from his trance.

Aloud he said only, "I should like Dr. Watson to accompany me."

There was an audible sigh of relief from both men and probably an exhalation on my part. I had attended this meeting entirely unprepared for this turn of events, but before my own surprise could be expressed, an objection was lodged from another quarter.

"To continue your biography?" scoffed Admiral Hall. "Such a notion is out of the question as you must surely know. It is enough we admitted the doctor to this interview on your say-so. Kindly remember, doctor, that you have just signed the Official Secrets Act."

Holmes appeared unruffled by this. "Two heads are better than one," he responded. "And four legs better than two. Dr. Watson brings out the best in me, and doubtless you will agree that you will need my best. It will surely not tax your memory to recall that I was just offered carte blanche."

So surprised was I by this unexpected testimonial that it did not occur to me to point out that four legs between the detective and myself was an exaggeration; with my old injury we boasted more like three.

"You will need more than your best," the voice in the shadows declared. "You smashed Von Bork and his ring but you may be sure he and his gang, like Hydra heads or dragon's teeth, have been supplanted by others. Wherever you go, in whatever guise, there will be a target on your back."

I understood now why Holmes had he asked me to accompany him to Whitehall. Whatever its origin, the detective's invitation had been no mere caprice. Why else that merry reminiscence about the old days in Baker Street? Always ten steps ahead, had he intuited that my days of use as a surgeon were at an end?

"If I'm to be in danger, surely a doctor will come in handy," Holmes said. "Watson here has practiced medicine in America and speaks the language fluently," he added dryly, then turned to me. "What do you say to one last jaunt, my dear fellow? The game is clearly afoot."

**10 June 1916**. Sherlock Holmes had made my participation a condition of his employment and his prospective employers were in no position to deny him. Had the detective taken my own acquiescence for granted? There was little doubt he had, but honesty forces me to admit Holmes would not have volunteered my services had he not had a fairly shrewd notion I would once more succumb to the old narcotic. Did this disturb me? On reflection I was surprised to find that it did not. While my days of usefulness as a surgeon were numbered, here was another capacity in which I might prove valuable, and the detective had no difficulty or qualms putting his finger on what it was. It was impossible not to grasp his reasoning, both from his point of view and my own. In any case, the decision to go to America was never discussed between us. As patriotic (if elderly) Englishmen, we could do no less. And somewhere—also unspoken—was the lure of being in harness once more.

Later, I found myself wondering if the detective had not in fact foreseen M's invitation before we'd ever set foot in Whitehall. Was that why he had brought me with him to M's office? I wouldn't put it past him.

Frenetic preparations were now underway for us to sail to the United States and much was to be done before either of us could embark. It is no simple matter to book transatlantic passage amid a world war. A neutral ship with passenger accommodations must be found. Holmes had to recuperate from his injuries and have his tooth replaced. As he anticipated, this proved a cumbersome and painful procedure, prolonged by the fact that there were wounded whose teeth took priority. I had my practice to dispose of, which I suspect might be a relief to some at the Royal Marsden who had begun to be apprehensive of my stamina in the operating theater. Then there was the Pimlico house to let on month-to-month terms, (for there was no telling when I should return), and fending off the advances of estate agents, eager for me to sell. Maria was sorry to see me go as we had certainly become accustomed to one another over the years, but her family needed her and I understood her need to be needed. I shall miss her comforting presence and only hope I won't have time to dwell on it.

Finally there was the vexing business of remembering where I had cached my service revolver. I knew without his saying so the detective wished me to bring it, but it had been so long since I had need of that ancient weapon, it required a determined search before I found it, almost out of reach on the top shelf of our bedroom cupboard. This was followed by the oddly familiar process of checking and oiling its parts. What varied memories handling the sleek dark barrel and worn grip summoned forth!

Throughout all these mundane but necessary tasks, the war ground on, each day bringing word of fresh bloodlettings in unfamiliar locations with foreign names. *Ypres* was generally pronounced *Wipers*. St. Paul's, as we feared, had been badly damaged, causing me to wonder, as I ordered my affairs, how the feeble and ill-defined efforts of the detective and myself in America could possibly affect the outcome of this unending folly. Was Holmes, rail thin, like Quixote, madly tilting at windmills, and was I, heavier now than heretofore, his credulous Sancho Panza?

The morning after our nocturnal interview at Whitehall with M and the man called Admiral Hall, too famished to wait for Holmes, I tucked into a breakfast at Craithie's, where we were to meet. Eggs were rationed here as elsewhere. There was bacon, but alas, no butter. For thin black coffee there was neither milk, cream, nor sugar. The elderly pensioner who waited on us moved with exasperating slowness, but no one younger performing such duties was any longer to be found on this side of the Channel. Everyone left alive is heartily sick of the war, though we attempt to conduct "business as usual" and obey the ubiquitous wall posters that exhort us to *"Keep Smiling."* These, I note, are every-where plastered over their predecessors, the tattered remnants of which advise one and all that *"Lord Kitchener Wants YOU!"*

The detective arrived twenty minutes late, out of breath and apologetic. "Forgive me, my dear fellow. I had several errands to run."

"You are forgiven. How is it you know Admiral Hall?" I asked him when our waiter had shuffled out of earshot.

"I assure you, my dear fellow, until this morning, I didn't know him in the least."

"But last night you knew his name and rank. How in the world of all that's wonderful did you manage that? I thought the fellow was ready to explode when you identified him."

Holmes smiled, clearly pleased with himself, and helped himself to the remains of the coffee. He could be as vain as any girl over his accomplishments.

"There's a deaf yeoman called Briggs who helps about my cottage on the Downs," he explained. "Mrs. Hudson's lumbago is advanced, as you know. Briggs does the windows, the gardening, and tends the hive when I am not there to see to it, as Mrs. H won't go near the place. Briggs can speak but not hear, the result of scarlet fever when a child. But he has learned to read lips, a gift I thought might prove useful one day and so I prevailed upon him to teach me. Last night, when I saw M move his lips and look in the direction of our phantom eavesdropper, I discerned the words 'Admiral Hall' when he silently addressed that mysterious individual. Of course now that I've identified him, this morning I was able to look him up in naval records and satisfy my curiosity. After a lengthy and distinguished career at sea, our admiral is now director of the DNI."

*Admiral "Blinker" Hall*

"DNI?"

"Department of Naval Intelligence. Admiral Hall was in fact responsible for the capture of Roger Casement. For some reason I've yet to learn he is nicknamed 'Blinker.' 'Blinker' Hall. Doubtless I shall discover why."

"You don't sound much like a retired detective to me," I observed.

"I might say the same of you, my boy, still wielding your scalpel." He swallowed the last of his unsatisfactory coffee and set down the cup more loudly than he intended.

Following breakfast we strolled along the Embankment in the direction of Waterloo Bridge. The fog had dissipated and the sun shone brightly. Save for a lone barrage balloon tethered above Lambeth and the welcome paucity of traffic due to petrol rationing, there was no sign of the war, but as an old serviceman I knew the smell of cordite when I encountered it. Holmes recognized it as well.

"The hospital at Lancaster Gate was hit last night," he informed me.

"Churches, hospitals," I muttered, "M was right. They don't care what they strike."

Holmes did not speak for several moments, striding with his hands thrust deep in his pockets, before he stopped and appeared to address the sky. "In war, morality becomes a luxury few can afford. I daresay if we grow desperate enough we should be capable of similar barbarism. Perhaps we are guilty of similar atrocities but word has not leaked out."

Here was a cheerful thought. "It doesn't take a war to dispense with morality," I felt obliged to remind him. "Remember what we saw in Kishinev."*

---

\*      Watson alludes to their experience in Russia in 1905, set down in *The Adventure of the Peculiar Protocols*.

With these pessimistic exchanges, we walked in gloomy silence, each thinking what it must be like to slip into harness again after so long out of practice, yet thrilled, I knew, to contemplate the prospect of action and of making ourselves useful.

"Who will you be in America this time?" I wondered, hoping to change the subject. "You daren't use 'Altamont' again."

"No, 'Altamont' is quite exploded. I shall have to dispense with him," the detective agreed. "I discussed it over much better coffee this morning with M and believe I shall go as myself."

"As Sherlock Holmes?" Had I heard him correctly?

"And why not? Do you know Congreve? *'No mask like open truth to cover lies, as to go naked is the best disguise.'* What could be more natural than Sherlock Holmes attempting to drum up support for England in her time of trial, with my faithful Boswell in train to spread word of my efforts? 'According to your late brother,' M assured me, 'thanks to Dr. Watson's accounts of your exploits, you are very popular in the States. Mycroft was most proud of your accomplishments,' he added."

Holmes colored slightly as he related this and I could see how much that posthumous compliment meant after a lifetime of fraternal rivalry, but he rushed on rather than dwell upon it. Whenever possible the detective eschewed displays of emotion.

"The Mercantile Bureau will arrange a lecture tour for me, starting first in Boston, thence heading south to Washington via New York. Once in the capital, we can attempt to learn Count Bernstorff's secrets."

"The Mercantile Bureau? I've never heard of such a thing."

The detective carelessly poked a pebble with his shoe. "I daresay no one has, but formally designating themselves a secret intelligence service rather defeats its raison d'être, wouldn't you agree?

Mercantile Bureau sounds suitably and flexibly anodyne. 'Blinker' Hall has given his blessing to the project," he added.

"Do we need his blessing?"

"Apparently M does."

Something about the detective's plan caused me uneasiness, but I couldn't say why. "You are not alarmed by the prospect of Von Bork's successors, eager for revenge?"

He considered this. "It's a risk," he admitted, "but on the other hand, it might flush more Hydra heads from cover."

"That is a very mixed metaphor, Holmes."

"Right you are, Watson."

**19 June 1916.** Our course of action decided upon, locating a ship with passenger accommodations proved more difficult. Neither the Cunarders nor White Star lines were operating, and a Swedish vessel that appeared promising refused to book us passage on learning our nationality. A week has passed and a feeling of anticlimax is setting in. My hospital duties discharged, I was alternately pacing my drawing room, trying to read, or taking too many naps before my telephone finally rang. It was the detective.

"Our ship has come in," he declared without preamble. I knew, without his having to specify, this was no metaphor.

**26 June 1916**. The *Norlina* is a freighter of five thousand tons, with enormous American flags painted on both sides of her hull toward the bow. In addition, a tall sign reading AMERICAN is displayed amidships and the stars and stripes fly from her taffrail. Declaring herself emphatically neutral, she was returning to Boston from Southampton, where she had delivered a cargo of corn and bolts of cotton from New England mills. Heading home, she was laden with jute, which would be turned into burlap for packing tobacco leaves in the South.

Norlina

We stole out of Southampton in darkness, pursuing a zigzag course once past the Isle of Wight. While such a route would extend our Atlantic crossing from eleven to fourteen days, Captain Davenport was taking no chances with U-boats.

The sea was calm our first night out, for which I was thankful. As a young man, I chose the army and not the navy for good reason, and I earnestly hoped for a tranquil voyage. As we would not weigh anchor till after ten, Holmes and I dined ashore before-hand at a picturesque old pub called The Cowherds and thus had no opportunity to encounter our fellow passengers before daylight. Making our way to the ship afterward proved more time-consuming than either of us had anticipated. Because of the blackout, sounds and smells were curiously amplified. The uncertain creaks of carriage wheels, the nervous honks of car horns, the smells of tar, smoke, horseflesh, and flowers inter-mingling, we became anxious about locating the *Norlina* before she cast off. Once gratefully aboard, our cramped quarters more surely resembled those of the troopship I had sweltered aboard years earlier on my way to India than anything like the appoint-ments on today's luxury liners. Holmes is tall and thin. I am . . . not thin and we were constantly bumping into one another as we attempted to arrange ourselves and our belongings in darkness, for we were forbidden to use any light.

"So sorry."

"Mea culpa, old man."

And so on. Holmes felt his way to the lower berth and slid into it with a satisfied sigh, obliging me to clamber into the upper.

"Upper and lower, Watson," said he with a chuckle. "The dif-ference between genius and talent."

"Tell me, Holmes, if you had it to do all over again, would you fall in love with yourself a second time?"

This produced a guffaw from below. "Touché, Watson."

After which I slept, lulled by the thrumming of the screw, for the passenger accommodations were situated more or less above it, producing a continuous vibration not unlike a pleasant massage.

**27 June 1916**. Daylight found us literally at sea and seated with our fellow passengers at the captain's small table, where we were served by Caleb, a silent Negro messboy in a frayed white tunic that was less than pristine. The fare was unremarkable but there was plenty of it. I had porridge and Holmes an omelet with yellow peppers and scones.

"Before I read the news off the wireless," Captain Davenport began in a peculiar accent I later learned was termed New England, "perhaps you'd all care to introduce yourselves?"

Travel always throws one into contact with all sorts and the *Norlina*'s passengers were no exception. All told we were seven. There was a jovial, middle-aged couple from Zurich called Bechmesser. He worked for Patek Philippe (of course it had to be watches), and the couple intended to visit a married daughter in Boston, attending the imminent birth of their first grandchild. They proposed to wait out the rest of the war (how long?) in the New World. "My daughter says in America there is very much good beer," Otto Bechmesser advised us with a boisterous laugh. In this he was joined by Frau Bechmesser. ("You *muss* call me Hildegarde!")

The third passenger was a Monsieur Vindelman, a Belgian salesman for the French dictionary Larousse. "Now in Les Etats Unis," he declared, "many peoples must to understand the French." The mere mention of neutrality infuriated him. "La Belgique was 'neutral' as you say—and look where that has got us! Les Boche thought to marche right through us! 'It is only a leetle violation,' the Kaiser says. Pah!" He boasted a mustache so small it was almost impossible to detect. I resisted the temptation to inspect it closely, to determine if it was painted rather than grown.

The fourth passenger, Miss Violet Carstairs, a fetching if delicate Welshwoman, had been engaged as a governess and singing coach by a wealthy family in New Jersey, for their allegedly talented daughter. "I have not yet had the pleasure of hearing her sing," Miss Carstairs confessed, her own voice pleasantly laced with Welsh accents, when M. Vindelman asked if her charge was in fact gifted. The young woman, herself a recent graduate of the Royal College of Music, could not have been much more than twenty and appeared apprehensive, though perhaps this was due less to anxiety over her forthcoming duties than the possibility of U-boats.

"You are not a soprano," Holmes observed, in response to her husky voice.

"A contralto, Mr. Holmes."

"Ah. A rarer breed."

At this moment Herr Bechmesser proffered the salt to Holmes, but in her nervousness, Miss Carstairs knocked the dispenser from his hand, causing it to spill several grains on the tablecloth between them.

"I'm so sorry!" she exclaimed, reddening and hastily tossing the spilled salt over her shoulder. "Forgive me, Herr—"

"Bechmesser," the other answered with a trace of irritation, fussily brushing more salt crystals from his waistcoat.

"May I keep this?" she inquired of the table, holding up the saltshaker. "At night I shall use it for my throat." No one raised any objection to this.

"Is it indiscreet to ask if you remain fond of Wagner these days?" Holmes inquired in an effort to alleviate her embarrassment.

"I know it is no longer fashionable, but confess I still adore him," Miss Carstairs admitted, coloring once more.

"Do you agree *Eine Prophète* is his masterpiece?" the detective asked, setting down his fork. His teeth, eye, and rib had by now all been restored to reasonable facsimiles of what they had been, and Sherlock Holmes once again resembled his old self.

"Without question, Mr. Holmes."

The rest of us, not being musically knowledgeable, listened to this exchange without comment, though the Welsh, we all knew, made great singers.

Ronald Jerome, a taciturn professor of comparative anatomy returning to Yale University in Connecticut after a yearlong stint at Cambridge, was the fifth passenger. He dressed in well-tailored seersucker and was the possessor of a monogrammed silver cigarette case. For a scholar to be so handsomely provided, I inferred money from an outside source, his family or wife, and made a mental note to compare my conclusion with Holmes's. Before the arrival of porridge he informed us that he was a pacifist. This news was greeted with awkward silence. Privately I imagined it is easier to stake out such a claim when one's country is not at war. Holmes and I introduced ourselves as succinctly as possible, though the mention of his name caused an appreciable stir among the rest, and I confess I basked in reflected glory as the detective's amanuensis.

After these preliminaries, Holmes appeared to mentally take the temperature of the room as the table was being cleared. "Captain Davenport," he startled us by saying, "are you practicing a deception on us?"

"Meaning what, Mr. Holmes?" the captain asked in turn, casually tossing his spoon after the departing messboy, who deftly plucked it from the air and set it on his tray.

"This is a British ship," Holmes declared, pointing. "All her fittings, cabinetry, all the doorknobs, wiring, light fixtures, and switches are British, not American."

At this revelation, all eyes fastened on the captain. Were we, notwithstanding the imposing signs painted on her hull, in fact a British ship and therefore a legitimate target for German torpedoes?

Davenport scowled before rearranging his features into a smug expression. "Very smart, Mr. Holmes. I can see that you merit your reputation. The *Norlina* was indeed built in Liverpool and launched as the *Harfleur* back in oh-five. But last year we Americans took her over and renamed her. I hope that allays your concern."

"Ve hope it allays German concerns," Frau Bechmesser said, her laughter joined by her husband's. They seemed to agree on when to display their amusement.

Davenport now extracted a paper from the breast pocket of his dark blue uniform, the fabric shiny with age and bereft of one gold button. "Folks, here's the news, hot off the wireless." In a monotone, he regaled us in no particular sequence with dispiriting tidings from the Western Front (the use of mustard gas by the Germans), gossip about Lady Randolph Churchill, some American baseball scores featuring a prodigy with the colorful name Babe Ruth, and word that the jury had found Roger Casement guilty of treason and that he had been sentenced to death. Also receiving the death sentence was a fellow terrorist, Gideon Altamont.

The group digested these tidings in solemn contemplation and then proceeded to finish breakfast. The weather continued fine and Holmes and I went topside to take in the fresh sea air.

"So it seems I'm to hang," he commented, packing his pipe and attempting to shield his match from the stiff wind with a cupped palm.

"A good thing you've gone abroad," I said. "You'll miss your funeral."

The detective made no reply to this, but his expression led me to understand he remained unhappy and unreconciled regarding the fate of a man he had once held in such high esteem.

"Treason is merely a matter of dates," he mused at length. "Had George Washington been defeated, he would surely have been hanged. As he was victorious, he is canonized. The same posthumous fate would doubtless hold for Roger Casement were Ireland ever to become free."

**28, 29, 30 June 1916**. Up until today our crossing has proved uneventful, giving Holmes and myself a few days respite from recent upheavals. As I'd hoped, the seas remained calm and as a result my stomach was on its best behavior. Settling into an agreeable routine, we sunned ourselves in rickety deck chairs by day (there were but four and one was no longer serviceable), where Holmes perused documents supplied him by M. Once memorized, he tore them to shreds, dropping them from the taffrail into our churning wake. Nightly we were lulled to sleep by the reassuring revolutions of the *Norlina*'s engines below us. The Bechmessers played evening rubbers of bridge with Monsieur Vindelman and Professor Jerome. One couple's tricks were accompanied with much merriment while the other team played in determined silence.

I had brought three or four books I'd always meant to read, but found it hard to concentrate on *The Red Badge of Courage*. By now I'd had a surfeit of red badges, yet it was equally hard amid such pleasant surroundings to ruminate on future difficulties. With no land in sight, the realities of war appeared as distant as terra firma. Amid balmy salt-scented breezes, searching for Germany's secret plan to preserve America's neutrality became a curiously insignificant undertaking. At best we should be seeking a needle in a gargantuan haystack. It felt as though—

"U-boat!" screamed a voice from the foremast. Then—"Two points off the starboard bow!"

All lassitude abandoned in an instant, Holmes and I, together with our fellow passengers, scrambled or fell out of our deck chairs and raced forward, where we were soon crowded at the rail by much of *Norlina*'s small crew, some of them standing behind us atop the cargo hatch for a better view.

"Where? Where is it?" voices cried.

"There!" Holmes extended an arm and jutting forefinger.

Sure enough his eagle eye had detected a submarine, rolling amid gentle swells, off the righthand side of the ship. Even as I caught the number U-88 on her conning tower, she disappeared into a trough and submerged.

*U-88 outside New York Harbor (Statue of Liberty on the horizon)*

"Bloody hell!" we heard the captain cursing within the open windows of the wheelhouse on the bridge above us.

In the next instant, there was a clanging of bells from the same location as the *Norlina* banked hard to starboard, her engines thudding more loudly with exertion as the captain had obviously demanded more speed.

But none of us could tear our eyes from the place where the U-boat had been sighted, even though there was no longer anything to see. Nonetheless we stared at the spot, hypnotized in frozen attitudes.

"Where is it, where *is* it?" wailed the young governess.

"Getting ready," Holmes murmured in my ear.

Professor Jerome, the pacifist, made strange noises in his throat.

The *Norlina* had two lifeboats and I instinctively swung round to look at them. Situated on either side of the aft superstructure, neither inspired confidence. The white paint on their hulls was chipped and the davits appeared corroded from disuse. Could these flimsy things on which our lives might depend even be lowered? And if we managed that feat, were they watertight? They did not appear—

"*Torpedo!*"

The cry was succeeded by a chorus of gasps and exclamations as we crowded the bow to gape slack-jawed as a white streak just below the smooth surface churned furiously in our direction.

"Sweet Jesus!" whispered the steward, Caleb, next to me, his hands clutching the railing beside my own. His sentiments articulated my own. It is said that in the sight of death one's entire life passes before one's eyes, but I cannot claim to have experienced that phenomenon. My vision contained nothing other than that approaching livid streak, the concentrated epitome of malevolence.

*"Gott im Himmel!"* prayed Herr Bechmesser as the streak now ran parallel to us, not a hundred feet distant to the left of us.

I stole a look at Holmes, who watched the torpedo impassively. He had discerned before the rest of us that the shot would go wide.

As the projectile crossed our bow, like spectators at a tennis match, all heads turned in unison to follow its trajectory behind us. The realization of the miss was followed by collective exhalation as the wake of the deadly torpedo dispersed in the distance, leaving only the tranquil ocean and our throbbing engines.

*"Gott sei danke!"* exclaimed Herr Bechmesser, mopping his brow with a large handkerchief. He saw no cause for laughter now.

"Will they try again?" wondered Monsieur Vindelman. He still grasped the railing as though clutching it would ensure his remaining afloat.

"Why wouldn't they?" whispered Professor Jerome hoarsely. Despite the breeze, he, too, was perspiring freely.

"They will not," Sherlock Holmes informed us. "By turning hard to starboard, Captain Davenport shrewdly made us a narrower target, but in any event their purpose was to frighten us, not sink us."

"They daren't attack an American vessel," I assured the trembling steward beside me. "To do so would provoke America's entry into the war. Miss Carstairs?" I turned to ask, just in time for the poor woman to crumple into my arms.

What happened next was such a cluster of bizarre events (seemingly unrelated at the time), that I can scarcely manage to recall all the details in their proper order, let alone make sense of them. But I shall try.

Supper that night was a monosyllabic affair. Violet Carstairs remained in her cabin, two doors down the narrow passageway from ours. Blackout shades were scrupulously secured over every porthole. Dining by candlelight, we had little to say to one another, but Monsieur Vindelman could not resist one jab.

"How do you like your pacifism now?" he felt obliged to taunt Professor Jerome.

Before the anatomy professor could reply, a crisp "Belay that!" from Captain Davenport cauterized the possibility of conversation degenerating into a row and the meal concluded in chastened silence, after which all retired for the night, still unsure whether Holmes's logic would hold.

Not able to see the time, I have no idea at what hour I was roused from a restless sleep by a woman's scream. I sat up sharply, striking my forehead on the ceiling directly above me.

"That's Miss Carstairs!" Holmes cried. "Come, Watson!"

Fumbling with our robes in the wretched blackness, we tripped into the corridor, met by Professor Jerome, Monsieur Vindelman, and Hildegarde Bechmesser, all emerging from their rooms in various states of undress. With portholes blacked, the corridor was safely lit by a lone overhead light, and there we were greeted by the unearthly spectacle of Violet Carstairs staggering toward us, her white satin nightgown besmirched with blood.

"Help!" Shaking with sobs, the young woman flung herself into the arms of Sherlock Holmes. It took but moments to realize that the blood on her nightdress was not hers. With an outstretched arm waving distractedly behind her, she indicated her cabin.

Holmes made to help her back to it but she shrank from the place in horror.

"*Wo ist Otto?*" Frau Bechmesser suddenly wondered.

That question was soon answered. Feeling first to ensure the blackout curtain was fastened, I clicked on the light in Miss Carstairs's cabin.

Otto Bechmesser, formerly in the employ of Patek Philippe, lay on his back, sprawled across the bed in his nightshirt, his jovial features contorted and teeth bared in a hideous snarl. An effusion of blood, sticky and already turning brown, blossomed in all directions below his heart.

Hildegarde Bechmesser, at my heels, clamped a hand over her mouth in an unsuccessful attempt to muffle her own screams. Holmes pulled her gently but firmly from the small room while I proceeded to examine the body. It was no great matter to determine the cause of death: the man had been stabbed near the heart with a very slender blade. There were no other signs of injury, save for a tear at the collar of his nightshirt, which suggested some sort of struggle before the fatal blow.

"Stiletto, by the look of it." Holmes, rejoining me, peered over my shoulder. I knew the treacherous, retractable blade to which he referred. Now in general use, it was originally favored by the notorious Red Circle.*

"Whoever it was knew exactly what they were doing. They deftly bypassed the ribs to hit the aorta." I turned to him. "Did she manage to say anything?"

"Only that she heard a thud against her door, rose, turned on the light, and went to answer it, at which point Herr Bechmesser fell against her, collapsing atop her on the bed before expiring. That would account for the blood on her nightgown." He examined the room as he spoke, working methodically in his search, accompanying himself as he typically did with muttered exclamations and

---

*    See *The Adventure of the Red Circle*. The crime organization was also known as the Black Hand, and, more recently, the Mafia.

low whistles. "No trace of the weapon," he remarked at length, "and no evidence of a third party. The killer was left-handed," he added.

"Doubtless the killer has thrown the knife overboard," I sniffed, sitting on the edge of the berth beside the corpse and wishing ardently for some black coffee.

"Unless the murderer has a further use for it," Holmes rejoined, rising from his examination of the floor and cabin door. "Stilettos have only one purpose," he noted grimly.

I prepared syringes of laudanum for Frau Bechmesser and Violet Carstairs, both distraught, the former with a hand still clamped over her mouth and the latter shaking as with palsy, a ship's blanket wrapped about her as she threatened to go into shock. She did not react as I swabbed her upper arm and planted the needle.

We were now assembled with our fellow passengers and crew in the crowded captain's lounge where there followed the necessary business of taking detailed statements from everyone on board. These were conscientiously entered in the log by the first mate, (there was no second), a Portuguese named Amendola. A strange group we made, passengers and crew glimpsing one another at close range for the first time.

Two crewmen were sent to wrap the unfortunate Bechmesser's body in sailcloth and stow the remains in the galley's refrigeration unit, a gruesome but unavoidable juxtaposition with our food supply. The nine-member crew was housed in the forecastle, (but for Caleb, our steward, who being Black, was not allowed to sleep where they did). Excepting Caleb, the crew had no access to the passengers' quarters. No more had the stokers, who dwelled below us. They would have been conspicuous had they wandered, covered in coal dust, above their hellish domains, though between eight-hour shifts, they were permitted to air and sun themselves at the taffrail.

"Someone murdered a passenger on this ship," M. Vindelman stated simply. "But who?"

"And why?" wondered Professor Jerome.

No speculations or theories were advanced.

"Ladies and gents, we're in a pickle," the captain announced, looking up after he'd finished reading our transcribed testimonies. "Unless we find the perpetrator by tomorrow, the *Norlina* will arrive in Boston and all on board will disembark. How long can they hold all of us with no charge? The murderer will walk free."

"We could choose to remain at sea until the murderer is discovered," the professor offered.

"We could not," Davenport returned. "The *Norlina* doesn't have enough coal or food to sustain her, and sitting in the mid-Atlantic only prolongs our status as a sitting duck for German U-boats whose skippers might have itchy trigger fingers."

"A very pretty problem," Sherlock Holmes commented, lighting his briar. I could tell from his tone that it was one he had not encountered before and that he was intrigued by the fact.

"Which is why, if you've no objection, I'm asking you to conduct this inquiry, Mr. Holmes," the captain faced him squarely. "You're the great detective," he threw in.

"No objection whatever," Holmes answered at once. "But as I must be numbered among the potential suspects, I cannot be at liberty to tamper with potential evidence."

"What do you suggest?"

"I should like two of your crew to inspect all rooms, passengers, and crew quarters alike, while we remain here, so as not to interfere with or inhibit their search. They're to catalog and bring back anything they deem of interest, bearing in mind the smallest trifles may be of supreme importance."

Caleb and Amendola the mate were dispatched to carry out Holmes's directive. The rest of us were too exhausted by now to offer any objections, so more time passed as we sat, dozed, stood, or stretched as hours crept by.

Matters were briefly enlivened when my service revolver was produced but as it was unloaded, had not been fired in eons, and had played no part in the crime, it was returned to my bag.

"It's a handicap my not being able to see things for myself," Holmes acknowledged, lighting yet another pipeful of Balkan Sobranie, "but waiting must be a detective's specialty."

It was late afternoon when Caleb rushed in, followed by the mate, brandishing a bloodstained stiletto.

"See what I found, captain!"

"Where did you find it?" Holmes asked, coming to life at once and tapping out the pipe on his heel. Seizing a napkin from the captain's table, he took the knife, which he held before the light. There were rust-colored stains on the sliver of steel and ivory handle. The weapon was a common one. In my time with the detective I had seen many like it.

"It was in Cabin C," Amendola said.

There was a silence before Professor Jerome broke it. "Cabin C is mine," he stated, realizing all eyes were now upon him.

"The *pacifist* did it?" Monsieur Vindelman could not refrain from saying.

"We know only where the weapon was found, not who wielded it," Holmes corrected quickly. "Where exactly?" he asked Caleb.

"On the floor near the berth, sir."

"Any traces of blood elsewhere?"

"No, sir. None."

The others watched as Holmes considered this. "Was anything else found? Anything unusual?"

"Only this," Amendola held up a saltcellar. "It was in Cabin B."

"My cabin," Miss Carstairs slurred, the narcotic having done its work.

"The saltshaker was full as it is now?" Holmes regarded the object, then looked at Carstairs, who remained listless and did not reply. "Captain, it will now be necessary for me to question everyone individually with Dr. Watson here as witness. I will except the crew, whose depositions, already recorded, are sufficient for the moment."

"Mr. Holmes, look at this bunch. They're spent. They need sleep."

"Captain, with every hour, the *Norlina* draws closer to Boston."

"I know that, but you can see for yourself, man. Two of your witnesses are so drugged they couldn't give straightforward answers if they tried."

Holmes frowned, conceding Davenport's point. The detective may have been tireless on the hunt but the rest were only human.

"Very well, we will desist for four hours with a crewman posted outside each passenger cabin to prevent exit or entry. Giving time for the laudanum to wear off, I will question Miss Carstairs and Frau Bechmesser last."

"Agreed. Questioning will be commence at eight bells," Davenport declared.

"Eight bells?"

"Midnight, Dr. Watson."

Thus we retired to our cabins, staggering with fatigue after the events of the previous twenty-four hours, beginning with a close encounter with a German torpedo. As I lay in my berth, too exhausted to sleep, I could hear occasional chat in low undertones exchanged among the crewmen posted in the corridor outside our door.

"Holmes, are you awake?"

"Wide awake, my dear fellow," came the detective's voice from below. "What do you make of all this?"

I scratched the back of my head, my elbow scraping the nearby ceiling as I did so.

"I confess I've no idea what to make of it. Have you a theory?"

"As you know, it is a maxim of mine not to form theories in advance of data, but, as it happens, we do have some facts at our disposal."

"Which ones?"

"To begin with, there are at least two personages aboard this vessel who are not what they seem."

"The murderer and his victim."

"Good, Watson. Let us begin with the victim, Herr Bechmesser. He never worked for Patek Philippe."

"How can you possibly know this?"

"Because he was so imprudent as to wear a fake Patek Philippe watch."

"What's that, you say?"

"A Patek Philippe bezel is a gold-platinum alloy. Platinum, whose atomic number is seventy-eight, mixed with gold, does not tarnish as that which Herr Bechmesser has on his wrist—or I should say *had*. Herr Bechmesser's bezel looked to be fashioned of brass, a copper-zinc alloy that oxidizes a verdigris patina, especially in proximity to salt water, as we find ourselves.* Someone is on a budget, and Germany's is tight at present."

---

\* Recall Holmes was first and foremost a chemist.

"I did not notice."

"Noticing is everything, my dear fellow. You observe but you do not see."

How often had the detective chided me for this failing, and try as I might, how often had I failed to overcome it? Here we were, falling once more into our old habits as the years disappeared.

Below me, I heard the sizzle of a match. The dark room was briefly illumined by a flare of light, succeeded by the agreeable smell of Balkan Sobranie wafting from the detective's pipe.

"Details, Watson. For want of a nail, et cetera. Ergo, Otto Bechmesser, if that is even his true name, was not employed by Patek Philippe. The question now becomes whom does he work for? Or rather did," he amended, "since the murderer has shortened his hire."

"What of the murderer, then? Left-handed, you say?"

"Ah, yes. There are some interesting features about our murderer. I draw your attention to the curious detail of the saltcellar retrieved from Miss Carstairs's cabin."

"The saltcellar was full," I remembered.

"That is the curious detail. Miss Carstairs appropriated the shaker at our first breakfast, saying she needed it for her throat, a natural requirement, one might imagine, for a singer. Gargling with salt water requires a great deal of salt. Yet after several days the shaker remains full as when she first commandeered it." The detective's voice was soft in the darkness.

"Perhaps she replenished the contents of the shaker," I suggested. "And we didn't see her do it."

"Perhaps. But these cabin partitions are thin and gargling is not a quiet exercise. Has anyone been disturbed by her vocalizing?"

I had certainly heard no gargling.

"And if our faux Swiss watchman were as bloody upon entry to her cabin as she claims," Holmes went on in the same quiet voice, "why was there no trace of blood on the outside of her door when, in extremis, he allegedly thudded against it?"

"To be sure. So," I added, after a second's thought, "she is not a singer nurturing her throat?" Holmes's observations nettled me, for I had found the young Welshwoman sympathetic.

The detective made no answer. In the gloom, my mind continued racing. "But the weapon was found in Professor Jerome's cabin," I mused aloud. "And as I recall, the man is a professor of anatomy. He would doubtless know where to thrust home."

"Very good, Watson. A professor of anatomy, I would agree, would certainly know where to plant the blade. Let me embellish your argument: The professor is left-handed, or had you not noticed?"

I confess I had not, but Holmes was not satisfied. "But what possible motive could provoke a conscientious objector to murder an employee of Patek Philippe whom he has presumably never met before?"

"Perhaps they had met, but under very different circumstances. We have dealt with cases of that nature in the past."

"True, but, you will admit, unlikely in this instance. We are left with the question of what lethal enmity could have erupted between these two in only a week's time, to cause Professor Jerome to abandon his foremost principle?"

"Perhaps the professor is no more a conchie than Bechmesser worked for a Swiss watch firm. Perhaps, like your former client Shaw, the professor's pacifism is . . . flexible.* Did you notice

---

*    In *The West End Horror* we learn George Bernard Shaw was a client of Holmes.

Jerome has pronounced calluses on his left forefinger and thumb? I observed those! Certainly indication of manual employment must be counted unusual in a man who teaches?"

I thought I heard a chuckle. "That is certainly a suggestive detail, Watson, though there are doubtless repetitive motions besides murder that can produce callouses on the hand. Tennis, for example." This appeared to put him in mind of something. "You will recall Dr. Freud's comments about the phenomenon he terms *paranoia*, the conviction that imaginary foes are bent on one's destruction?"*

"What about them?"

"Merely that I wonder if I am being what Herr Doktor would term paranoid to suspect that Bechmesser's death is in some way connected with our mission? We've all been instructed to leave our doors unlocked in case we need to escape in the event of a torpedo strike. Was someone else's door mistaken for ours?"

"Why call that paranoid?" I retorted. "You recall Admiral Hall warning us that in Von Bork's wake, his successors would be on your trail?"

I heard a sigh. "Correct, Watson. I listened but did not hear." Before I could answer, he went on. "These are indeed murky waters, and U-boats may not be all that is lurking below the surface."

"I begin to see what you mean."

"I wish I did" was the reply, followed by a yawn. After which silence reigned, broken when I started at the sound of eight bells.

---

\*      A little-known fact: Freud was a tennis player with a strong backhand, as
       Watson recounts in *The Seven-Per-Cent Solution*.

**1 July 1916**. It is after midnight and Holmes and I are ensconced alone in Captain Davenport's cabin, placed at our disposal for the purpose of our interrogations. We spoke first with the fussy Monsieur Vindelman, Larousse salesman from Brussels, who, upon request, produced his passport. Four hours of allotted repose had not improved his humor and his tiny mustache bristled with irritation. Holmes questioned him about his background, his business, and his family. His answers were testy and brief.

"He seems rather cut-and-dried," I remarked when our interview was concluded and Holmes had thanked the man for his patience.

"I am inclined to agree with you, doctor. Poor blood-soaked Belgium has been through much and Monsieur Vindelman's bitterness is understandable. We will of course use the wireless to verify the details which he has provided, his employment, family, three children, and so forth, but I doubt we shall be surprised. Shall we ask Professor Jerome to step in?"

The professor was likewise brief in his answers though his tone differed markedly from that of the Belgian. Rather than testy and put upon, Professor Jerome knew that the presence of the murder weapon found in his room and his inability to explain how it got there did not work in his favor.

"I tell you I was out like a light," he began wearily. "Our encounter with that torpedo had greatly excited my nerves, as you may suppose, and so I had taken the valerian drops I sometimes use to help me sleep. As a result, I heard nothing until the screams of Miss Carstairs, which would have roused the dead." He scowled, realizing his infelicitous choice of words.

In further conversation the professor averred that he had never met any of his fellow passengers before boarding the *Norlina*. He looked on anxiously as Holmes examined his passport.

"Born in seventy-five," the detective noted, then looked up. "Where in the United States?"

"Vermont," the man answered promptly, evidently relieved to find himself on secure footing. "My people are Quakers, Mr. Holmes, originally settled in Indiana, where they farmed until Confederate soldiers drove them off, killing my grandfather, who refused to take up arms on either side. So you see, my peaceable antecedents are long and grim."

Holmes chose to ignore this. "May I ask," he inquired, pointing, "why you have developed calluses on your left hand? You teach, am I not correct? Surely these did not come from clutching chalk?"

I was breathless with anticipation.

Jerome held his hand before his face and examined the calluses as though noticing them for the first time. Then he splayed his fingers, smiling through them at the detective. "I garden. In Cambridge I had a small plot behind my lodgings, and in fair weather and foul I relaxed by wielding a trowel and potting. My Tudor roses this spring were much admired by the bursar. I did the same in New Haven, a passion I inherited from my mother in Brattleboro. I'm forever cleaning my nails," he added.

Holmes studiously avoided looking in my direction. He stared at Jerome's American passport some moments longer before he handed it back.

"Thank you for your time, professor. Will you ask Miss Carstairs to step in?"

"I'd be happy to." Relieved, the professor pocketed his passport, then turned at the door. "You will find who did it?"

"I already have," said Sherlock Holmes.

The professor's eyes widened at this but since Holmes volunteered no more, he left, closing the door behind him.

It was almost two when Violet Carstairs entered the cabin and seated herself. Still agitated from the night's earlier events, she remained attractive, running her fingers through luxuriant dark curls in an effort to subdue them.

"Are you somewhat recovered following your ordeal?" Holmes began solicitously.

"I will be," the young woman responded in a breathy whisper. She was still deathly pale. "I feel the drug still in my system. Do we need all these lights?"

Holmes nodded in my direction and I clicked off one of the lamps. I was startled to behold him unsure of himself, as if he did not know how or where to begin.

"Did you ever make use of the salt in the shaker you took from the breakfast table?" was his opening.

I could see the question surprised her.

"I did not," she answered after a pause.

"May I ask why?"

"I found I didn't have need of it after all." She passed a hand over her forehead, once more pushing back a lock of rebellious hair. "Mr. Holmes, what does that saltshaker have to do with poor Herr Bechmesser?" She ended the question on an upturned interrogative as though unsure if she was pronouncing the dead man's name correctly.

Again, Holmes seemed to hesitate. "But you didn't return the saltshaker."

"I forgot." Her voice was scarcely audible now. She could see the detective was not about to relinquish his preoccupation with the saltshaker.

"Really? These cabins are small. You could hardly wish to add to the clutter."

The woman swallowed and said nothing. Holmes collected himself like a horse making ready for a jump.

"Miss Carstairs, a singer who professes a love for Wagner ought to know that he never wrote an opera called *Eine Prophète*, whereas Giacomo Meyerbeer, a Jewish composer whose music Wagner despised, did."

The detective's gaze was cool and appraising; the woman's eyelids fluttered in response.

"I begged them not to make me a singer," Violet Carstairs sighed.

Holmes kept his voice steady. "And the salt crystals?"

"Potassium cyanide. Odorless and tasteless. Undetectable. Had you seasoned your omelet at breakfast, you would have died within seconds. An autopsy would have suggested you succumbed to natural causes, a stomach rupture, or perhaps an aneurysm. I kept hold of the crystals to turn over to the authorities."

Holmes passed a hand over his mouth. "It appears I owe you my life, Miss Carstairs."

It was impossible to tell from his tone how Holmes felt about his debt to the woman. Her shoulders briefly rose and fell.

"It's why M sent me, to keep an eye on you both."

So Holmes had not been paranoid!

"Stop a bit! *You* killed Bechmesser?" I ejaculated.

Violet Carstairs smiled again, looking suddenly older in the dim light. "It was him or me. Once I intercepted the salt intended for Mr. Holmes, your assassin knew I was onto him. He'd have to dispose of me before he could try again. Recognizing his preference for the indirect, I knew he'd try to make my death look natural. Perhaps he'd smother me with a pillow, but however he'd manage it, I knew that sooner or later Herr Bechmesser would put in an appearance. Every night I lay in wait for him with my weapon."

"The stiletto?"

"Mother's little helper. In my haste in the dark, I couldn't locate and open the porthole to dispose of it, so when I ran into the corridor, I tossed it into the next stateroom, not recalling until later that as a professor of anatomy suspicion might fall on poor Professor Jerome." She smiled. "But I was sure he'd be cleared in due course. You must admit you find it amusing, Mr. Holmes—a pacifist suspected of murder."

Holmes stared at her in fascination. Always skittish where women were concerned, in his lengthy career he'd encountered his share, but never such a one as this.

"You'll be arrested, of course. What will you tell the authorities in Boston?" he asked.

She shrugged again, unconcerned. "A large helping of truth. 'Intent on having his way with me, Herr Bechmesser entered my cabin and I fought him off with my hat pin.' His torn nightshirt collar will offer additional confirmation of that fact and the stiletto I feel certain will be misplaced before we reach Boston. The police will turn me over to the BOI, who will contact M and I will be shunted elsewhere on another neutral vessel. Somewhere I will be of further use."

"BOI?" I asked. These endless initials.

"Bureau of Investigation, America's domestic intelligence department—their counterpart to SIS. But understand, gentlemen," she sat forward, deadly serious now, "once you are on American soil, given my altered circumstances, I can no longer function as your guardian angel. You will be left to your own devices, there's nothing for it. May I go now?"

She made to rise, but Holmes leaned forward, a hand on her arm.

"One last question, Miss Carstairs."

She sank back into the chair. Past experience had taught me the detective saved his most meaningful interrogatories for last.

"Is your name Tom?"

Her eyelids fluttered. "I beg your pardon?"

"Or Dick? Or Harry?" Holmes pressed his fingertips together as was his habit.

The woman known as Violet Carstairs twitched spasmodically. Her head snapped back as though an object of some kind had flown too near her face. Pale to begin with, in the dim light whatever color remained seemed to drain from her countenance.

"How did you guess?"

"I seldom guess," responded the detective, who regarded her with frank admiration, "but I doubt a woman such as yourself could have fended off the advances of a man the size of Herr

Bechmesser, and when you later threw yourself into my arms, your cheek against mine was rougher than it should have been. Afterward, I discovered traces of face powder on my dressing gown. In my limited experience, women remove unguents and beauty nostrums before they retire, but given your need to maintain your disguise, such habits were denied you." He opened his cigarette case, lit a cigarette, and offered her one, which she accepted gratefully.

"I take my bonnet, or rather my hat, off to you, Mr. Holmes. You're the best."

"But wait!" I cried again. "The murderer was left-handed, yet you hold your cigarette with your right hand."

She smiled prettily. "I am ambidextrous, doctor. It is useful in my line of work."

"But I injected you with laudanum, and when I took hold of your arm it was—"

"Thin as a woman's?" Carstairs exhaled a satisfied stream of smoke. "Some of us are made that way, doctor. Surely you have encountered many such in your civilian practice."

"Well, I'm blessed." Now it was I who felt the air taken from me. "So you are—" I stopped, remembering with consternation that I had been drawn to this woman.

Carstairs stubbed out the cigarette. "An actor. Why not? Occupations for men of my type are . . . limited. It's an old tradition, isn't it, Mr. Holmes? In Elizabethan times all the women's roles were played by men, were they not?"

It must be said that now that I was aware of her true sex, I could not see her as anything but male and wondered how she had managed to deceive so many of us for so long. Now even her husky voice sounded masculine to my ear.

And yet, I continue to refer to her as *she*.

"What of Hildegarde Bechmesser, the Swiss widow of Herr Bechmesser? Was she part of his crimes?" Holmes wondered.

"They're as Swiss as I am female," Carstairs responded. "Of course she was. Take her in and she'll sing better than I ever could."

"May we know your real name?"

"You may call me Reilly."

Yet another Irishman!

We heard a yell from outside. "Land ho! Boston!"

**15 August 1916**. After six weeks, our trip has yielded little of value. More truthfully, it has been something of a disaster from the moment we disembarked in Boston Harbor. Our timing was unfortunate as we arrived on 1 July, days before Americans celebrate their independence, and people were in no mood to listen to Holmes when he addressed a gathering at Quincy Market, pleading the cause of a country whose dominion their ancestors had fought and died to escape. To complicate matters, the city turns out to have an enormous Irish population, and, preceding our arrival, news of Roger Casement's hanging had unleashed a firestorm of outrage. One "Honey" Fitzgerald, the city's former mayor, a peppery Celt the size of a leprechaun, delighted in heckling Holmes as he attempted to speak.*

---

\*    John Francis "Honey Fitz" Fitzgerald, a congressman and twice mayor of Boston. His grandson was elected president of the United States in 1960.

Compounding his difficulties, here and there in the audience
I spied men sporting deerstalkers and copies of Holmes's distinctive houndstooth overcoat. Were these sartorial items displayed in
mockery or emulation? Were the wearers what we now term "fans"
or fanatics? It was impossible to say. In England it is true that, as
his fame grew, Holmes was recognized and sometimes accosted
by admirers, but in the aftermath of the recent attempt on his
life, encounters with strangers, more especially on foreign soil,
now filled me with alarm. M had predicted the detective would
constitute a target, a prophecy that had been borne out before we'd
even set foot here.

At the end of his talk Holmes was besieged by autograph
seekers. At least that is what they appeared to be, though I kept a
wary eye on each. Though none seemed intent on doing him harm,
the fact that they sought out the detective's signature, rather than
his opinions regarding England's plight, was cold comfort.

America was noisier and bigger than I remembered and I could
not escape the contrast between this enormous place, with its limitless resources, protected from attack by two vast oceans, and poor
England, with its rationed provisions and decimated manhood.
Where London's streets once boasted omnipresent iron railings
before each house, these had long since been smelted for weaponry,
the nubs mute testimony to a desperation unknown in America's
horn of plenty.

Holmes, who had lived here more recently than I, found the
country little changed.

"America keeps becoming more itself" was his only comment.

Surprisingly I had never heard Holmes speak in public and I
was discomfited to find he was no orator. In private discourse or
addressing a small group while elucidating the steps that led him

to solving a puzzle, he had no peer, but as a fundamentally private individual, happiest motionless contemplating a "three-pipe
problem," puttering with his chemicals, cataloging his books,
or (lately) cultivating his bees, the man was at a disadvantage
addressing a hall of intoxicated Irishmen hurling silly questions and insults. "What color is my necktie?" "Where's my old
lady tonight?" and other such taunts. It is true, as I have noted
elsewhere, that the detective was a versatile actor and master of
disguise, but it must be remembered that his performances never
took place in any location where his voice had to carry over foot-
lights. In Boston, gibes and catcalls from red-faced listeners served
to drown him out.

At least at Quincy Market we had only to contend with rowdies,
not assassins. But in America we no longer had Miss Carstairs,
or Reilly, as he designated himself, at the ready to intercept fatal
saltcellars. That curious individual, still uncannily presenting as
female (albeit with handcuffs on his wrists), had been escorted
briskly down the gangway from the *Norlina* by police in full view
of passengers crowding the rail and onlookers gaping on shore. (I
could not then imagine the sensational circumstances under which
we would once again encounter that remarkable personage.)*

"Hardly a propitious beginning," the detective remarked as he
picked at his supper after his dismal debut. We ate near Faneuil
Hall at Durgin Park, a boisterous establishment, ignoring hostile
glances from fellow diners and ignored in turn by surly barmaids.
For my part, I confess I was more preoccupied by my evening
newspaper, which trumpeted still more inconceivable fatalities

---

* This parenthetical was clearly inserted later in a shaky hand that nonetheless still looks like Watson's.

in Europe. If the figures were to be believed, sixty thousand Englishmen had perished on the Somme in a single day.

"And any minute the U-boats may come to finish us off." Holmes did not look up from a red lobster so large it overflowed the platter on which it nestled. "I can't possibly eat all this," he added. At home it would have fed four people. "Oh, look, Watson." He gestured with his fork to the back of my newspaper, "The Boston Symphony is performing. Wagner and Stravinsky, what a curious program." I could not help detecting his wistful inflection. "I don't suppose Wagner is on offer in England these days, though he does help me introspect. As for *Le Sacre du Printemps*, in my view, it is merely ahead of its time."

I knew Holmes missed hearing and playing music. Though I cannot entirely understand his infatuation, yet I perceive its importance. Music is his remaining drug, the habit he cannot surrender. And why should he? Ever since the destruction of his priceless Stradivarius by Russian thugs, he has pined for it.* These days music might have consoled him, but we had neither time nor—til now—the opportunity to listen to any.

And to crown all our disappointments, our clandestine meetings with M's agents in situ yielded no information on the subject of Germany's secret plan to prevent America's entering the war.

"Haven't heard a smidgeon," a beefy, scabrous individual who introduced himself as O'Higgins volunteered later that evening. A member of the Ancient Order and Brotherhood of Hibernians, he affected a bluff demeanor that vanished when he set down his glass of Jameson. The Order, he said, made no secret of its loyalties, but if plans were afoot to prevent America's entry into the war

---

*       See *The Adventure of the Peculiar Protocols*.

beyond opposing it, he'd not heard or learned them. His mottled complexion turned a dusky red as the whiskey did its work.

"And 'tis plugged in deep I am, so," O'Higgins added with a touch of pride, smacking his moist lips before wiping them with the back of his hand.

Subsequent attempts on Holmes's part to rally support for England fared little better elsewhere. If it weren't Irish sympathizers shouting him down in Boston and Buffalo, Americans of German descent did so in New York. Holmes's reputation proved of little use where feelings ran high.

I tried coaxing him to speak more loudly but he shook his head. "It's no use, Watson, we are all of us as God made us—and many of us rather worse. Were I to shout, they would only shout louder. The American Revolution was a great mistake," he added as an afterthought.

"The Americans do not appear to regret it," I felt bound to point out.

"A mistake on *our* part, my dear fellow. Had we managed things better at the time, the colonies, with their stupendous resources, would have come to our aid today with no bones about it."*

At Western Union offices in both cities, Holmes was obliged to report our lack of progress to M. "Aunt Abigail still sick," "No improvement Aunt Abigail," and the like. The silence from London was its own reproach.

In New York City, Herr Feldenstein, M's plant in the district known as Yorkville, was only slightly more helpful than his counterpart in New England. To ensure discretion, we sat with him

---

* Holmes expressed similar sentiments in *The Adventure of the Noble Bachelor.*

in the back of a noisy bratwurst tavern south of his own neigh-
borhood, near the hulking Queensboro Bridge, which towered
above us. Not for the first time I was reminded that everything in
America is outsized.

The ferret-looking man was well up on labor agitation in the coal
mines of West Virginia and Pennsylvania, and factory sabotage in
the Northeast.

"There was an explosion last month in New York Harbor that
killed four and destroyed twenty thousand dollars' worth of war
materiel bound for England," he informed us in a heavily accented
whisper. "We believe a 'Swiss' who calls himself Emil Gasche was
behind it, but have no proof."

While antiwar sentiment was vehement among the local population, Feldenstein had obtained no intelligence regarding a secret
plan to prevent America's coming to the aid of the Allies. The most
he knew was the ongoing effort to sabotage America's munitions
factories against the day when circumstances might find America
contemplating joining the fray. With insufficient ammunition and
other supplies, the United States would be of little help.

"If there is such a scheme, it must originate higher up and they
are keeping a tight lid on it," Feldenstein declared. Beyond this the
man could say little that was of use or news to us.

We met with several such informants, all of whom, despite
superficial differences in face, form, or attitudes, struck me as
displaying the furtive similarity of men who live much of their
lives in shadow and, it must be said, drink. Holmes himself had,
not so long ago, been one of these, but seemed over time (and
tending his bees in Sussex) to have largely shed the effects of living
a double life.

We watched impatiently as Feldenstein downed a gargantuan lager before we collected our bags at the Knickerbocker Hotel and headed for the Pennsylvania Station.

"No scheme may be needed," Holmes conceded as we sat in our compartment on the express bound for Washington. "With the mood in the country as it is, one begins to understand the president's dilemma. Mr. Wilson can hardly snap his fingers and plunge his constituents into a war the majority oppose."

I stared at the appalling headlines and murmured, "One can hardly blame them."

"What's that you say?"

"I was complaining of the humidity."

Certainly, the atmosphere added to our sodden spirits. The damp was bad enough in Boston, but as we drew near the nation's capital, it became unendurable. "I feel as though I were in a swamp."

"How true," the detective agreed. From his tone I judged he was not alluding merely to the weather.

"Union Station!" bellowed the conductor. In America, everyone walked faster and talked louder.

**20 August 1916**. "My situation is not much better than your own," Cecil Spring Rice, the British ambassador, confided. "In fact, I daresay your popularity—thanks to Dr. Watson's accounts—far exceeds mine. At present I am persona non grata in Washington."

Arriving at the Willard Hotel, we were greeted by the ambassador's invitation to take tea that afternoon, but could not escape the impression that the invitation was more in the nature of a summons. In London, M was growing impatient.

Holmes gratefully discarded his coat and deerstalker with the concierge ("I could not have packed a less appropriate wardrobe"), to be deposited in our rooms with the rest of our luggage while we struggled through muggy, mosquito-laden air, arriving at the embassy just in time. Neither Holmes nor I had visited the nation's capital before, but despite its symmetrical beauty, the oppressive heat caused us to wonder why the city had been situated in what felt like the Grimpen Mire.*

---

* The treacherous bog Watson experienced in *The Hound of the Baskervilles*.

"Accomplishing anything here," Holmes remarked in the taxicab, dabbing at his brow with a handkerchief, "must feel like doing it underwater."

This difficulty, I later learned, was solved by the Congress going into recess during the month of August. No such relief was granted the city's residents, most of whom were Negroes. Washington was essentially a southern city and as such I beheld more dark-skinned people here than I had seen anywhere excepting India.

The British embassy offered some relief from heat and mosquitoes. The windows were open but ingenious wire mesh screens kept the pests at bay while overhead fans helped circulate the damp air within.

Ambassador Cecil Spring Rice I judged to be in his sixties and was surprised to learn afterward he was ten years younger than my estimate. Although trim (he had rowed for Oxford), the man appeared haggard. His bloodshot eyes bulged slightly behind his glasses, which he kept removing to pinch the bridge of his nose with his thumb and forefinger. His dark beard and mustache were streaked with a gray that almost matched his pallor.

"Over the course of my diplomatic service, I have labored in Japan, Korea, Russia, Persia, and Sweden," Spring Rice informed us, "but all my life, this was the posting I coveted. Amity between our two English-speaking countries seemed to me the most natural thing in the world." He sighed, nodding to the factotum to pour. "And see where it has got me!" His expression was now crestfallen. "Americans are dead set against coming to England's rescue. The Gaelic among them are outraged by Casement's hanging and in total sympathy with Irish demands for independence, which makes for common cause with the Hun. As I am myself of Anglo-Irish ancestry, it is impossible to be insensible of their grievances, but the prospect of a German victory must remain unthinkable. And yet it is fearfully close! Both England and Germany are effectively bankrupt, but if the wolf packs are turned loose on shipping in the Atlantic . . ." He left the sentence unfinished.

*Sir Cecil A. Spring Rice*

I allowed myself an inward sigh of relief and sensed Holmes letting out a shallow breath. The ambassador's comment was the latest information we had received that the U-boats were as yet in their pens.

"But your own influence here is said to be enormous," I struck in. "Were you not the best man at President Roosevelt's wedding?" I had read that somewhere.

My remark provoked another sigh, another removal of the glasses, and another pinch of the bridge above the nose.

"Former president. Alas, that too now counts as a black mark against me. Theodore's—that is, President Roosevelt's—intemperate remarks about the White House's current occupant have done my mission little good. You must understand," he added with what would have been vehemence had the man not been so spent, "everyone in Washington *knows* America must join the Allies. All it would take is America's thumb on the scales!"

"Everyone knows but President Wilson." Holmes's tone was neutral. He was stating a fact.

"All his aides and advisors! Even Gerard, his own ambassador to Berlin, has tried to tell him! Half of Congress! That's another plan that has come to grief," Spring Rice added bitterly. "I was on the point of obtaining an invitation for you to address a joint session of the legislature."

"Sherlock Holmes speaking to Congress!" I exclaimed. "Holmes, what a coup—you could have presented our case to a respectful audience." And would not have had to shout above the mob, I thought to myself.

The detective smiled faintly but kept his eyes on the diplomat, who pinched his nose and rubbed his red eyes yet again, leading me to wonder if he suffered from Graves' disease, which I later learned to be the case.

"But protests from Count Bernstorff put paid to that idea."

"The German ambassador here in Washington?"

"You are well informed."

"M saw to that," I explained.

"I beg your pardon?" Spring Rice peered at me, replacing his glasses.

"Sir William Melville," Holmes interposed, realizing before I did that the ambassador knew nothing of Melville's incognito and probably less of SIS.

But the ambassador understood enough. "The embassy has been instructed to assist you in any way we can," he said. "But Whitehall, as you may understand, craves results."

Holmes shifted uncomfortably in his chair. "Originally I had thought to infiltrate some of the Irish societies here to learn more of their German sympathies and activities, but it turns out I am too well-known. In every audience we see men dressed in facsimiles of my wardrobe. Thanks to Dr. Watson's accounts, we've seen fat Sherlocks, dark Sherlocks, even one Chinese Sherlock—"

"I had no way of foreseeing—" I began, but the detective cut me off with a reassuring pat on the knee.

"The fault is none of yours, my dear fellow, but rather the law of unintended consequences. Who could have anticipated the price of notoriety? What can you tell us of Count Bernstorff?" he asked the weary diplomat before I could respond.

"Ah, Bernstorff," Spring Rice shook his head with a trace of amusement and cleared his throat. "At one time we were colleagues, by which I mean respectful members of the diplomatic corps. Now, if through some hostess's oversight, we encounter one another at functions, it's as if we were society belles, caught wearing the same gown by Worth. One of us is obliged to scurry away."

"What do you know of the ambassador personally?" Holmes asked. "I'm told he has a weakness for the fair sex?"

Spring Rice smiled more broadly. "More a strength, I should say. The count's . . . proclivities are common knowledge. There's no denying the man's an attractive specimen, good-looking and charming after the German fashion," he added is if to subtract from overpraise. "At any rate, many Washington doyennes find him so. It is certain the count gets around," Spring Rice concluded.

"And is he generally accounted an able representative of German interests and policy?"

Spring Rice eased back in his chair and pulled a face. "A predecessor of mine remarked that an ambassador's function is to go abroad and lie for his country. Whatever Count Bernstorff truly thinks of the Kaiser's folly, in public he represents Germany's position to the letter and carries out his instructions with Teutonic diligence. Were he to do otherwise, Foreign Minister Zimmermann would have recalled him long since. I'm not sure any of this is much help, Mr. Holmes."

Holmes set down his tea. "On the contrary, Mr. Ambassador. Most helpful. Doubtless you will hear from us."

Shortly thereafter we took our leave. Holmes, too, had been diplomatic; in reality our mission appeared moribund as ever.

"As Blinker Hall said, Bernstorff must remain our key to this whole business," he reflected in our taxicab afterward. "But how to crack him open?"

"No matter what his private views, he will never agree to see us. Our countries are at war."

"His views are not the point, Watson, his instructions are." Holmes lowered his voice out of the driver's earshot. "Since the German transatlantic cables are severed, how and from whom does their prepossessing representative receive his marching orders? Does he know when and under what circumstances the U-boats are to be loosed?"

Our difficulties were shortly overcome through an unforeseen series of events that spun everything upside down.

As our taxicab deposited us before the Willard Hotel, it was impossible to miss a large crowd milling outside, within which a cordon of police struggled to maintain order. Cries of "Oh no!" were heard among onlookers.

Holmes leaped from the car and I followed, hastily pressing a dollar into the driver's hand and not waiting for change.

"What's the matter?" I asked a nearby bystander.

"Sherlock Holmes is dead," the man responded without turning.

While I stood rooted to the spot, Holmes sprang into action. He had, over time, perfected the art of public disappearance. Hunching his shoulders, lowering his head, and pulling his hat (a straw boater purchased along with a seersucker ensemble at Gimbels in Manhattan) over his eyes, he explained to a struggling policeman that we were stopping at the hotel, whereupon we were admitted through the improvised barrier. I had only the briefest glimpse of the tragedy as we entered the building, but it was sufficient. On the pavement was splayed the body of the detective in his houndstooth coat, a widening starburst of blood emanating from his head and permeating the porous concrete that soaked up the dark liquid like a sponge. Beside what remained of his face, his deerstalker was absorbing more gouts of the viscous scarlet, now turning dusky brown. The frightful likeness was so persuasive it required a force of will to shift my gaze from the corpse to that of the real Sherlock Holmes as I followed him into the lift.

"What in the world—?" I began, but indicating the lift operator, the detective lay a forefinger over his lips.

On entering our suite we found several men examining the premises, turning over chairs and peeking under antimacassars, which they tossed aside rather than troubled to replace.

In mufti, they wore fedoras, but Holmes and I knew them for police of some kind. Their movements were altogether directed by a diminutive youth, who handed Holmes his card. Stout and putting me in mind of a fireplug, he wore a dark, tight-fitting wool suit, which must have felt oppressive in this heat, and a fedora of his own that he removed but once during the exchange that followed.

"You gentlemen may leave," he addressed his underlings in a low growl.

Touching the brims of their hats, the men departed in silence, whereupon the young man turned his attention to us.

"I knew it wasn't you," he began. His voice was that of a frog with a slight Southern accent.

Holmes glanced at the card and handed it to me.

*Special Agent John E. Hoover, BOI, Baltic Hotel, K Street.*

*Special Agent Hoover*

"BOI?" I remembered those initials from someplace.

"Bureau of Investigation." The youth could not have been twenty-five but his manner was that of an older man, born to command. Meticulously groomed, his features in combination were not unpleasant, but in motion I could not help imagining a bulldog. Beneath his high domed forehead was a pug nose, a thick neck, and eyes that furthered the resemblance. Only a firm and graceful mouth redeemed the canine impression.

"Apparently, one of your enthusiastic admirers, of whom I am one"—(here he nodded stiffly in my direction)—"managed to gain entry to these rooms, whereupon, likely prompted by a height and build similar to your own, sir, he put on items of your wardrobe and paraded about in them, doubtless enjoying the effect of his transformation in the mirror . . ."

He jerked a thumb over his shoulder to indicate a full-length mirror in the open cupboard door behind him, pausing to allow us to follow his reasoning.

"Ah, yes," the detective murmured. I could see his eagle eye taking in all the room's details.

"My guess," continued the fireplug, "was that the disparity between his true identity (an unremarkable one, as I'm sure we'll learn) and yours, plunged him into despair, at which point, still dressed like yourself, he flung himself from the window."

"Unhappy man." Holmes stared at the scrum surrounding the body eight floors below. On land I have a strong stomach, but one look was sufficient for me.

The special agent gave the detective another moment in which to take in the scene before clearing his throat to regain our attention. "We knew you were in Washington, of course," he croaked. "I hope my men didn't make too much of a mess," Hoover gestured to a chair, "but I'm training them to be thorough."

"As you should," Holmes righted one of the overstuffed arm-chairs and sank into it, gesturing to another for me. "I take it you are in touch with M?"

"Have you had any luck in gaining support for the Allied cause?" Hoover asked rather than answering the detective's question.

"What can you tell us about Emil Gasche?" Holmes parried. The mention of Gasche's name broke their verbal impasse.

"Oh, Gasche," responded Hoover with a snort. "Von Bork's replacement. We know all about him. Another unsavory specimen. Gasche has set up several dummy corporations to pay his dyna-miters and done some damage, I'll allow, but so far we've not managed to discover how he communicates with Berlin, and we'd like to learn before we bring him in."

"Perhaps via Count Bernstorff?"

The special agent favored us with a show of curiously unpleasant teeth. "We keep both men under close surveillance and there's no evidence of contact between them. Gasche doesn't venture near Washington. His mission appears strictly limited to labor unrest and factory sabotage."

"In that case, what can you tell us about Count Bernstorff?" Holmes stretched out his long legs. The two men now regarded one another intently. Standing, Hoover was only slightly above eye level with the seated detective.

"My loyalties are split three ways," Hoover offered with an attempt at humor, after he judged they'd savored sufficient silent communion. "My father is of English descent and my mother German." Then, knitting his brows once more, he said, "But always and above all, I represent the interests of the bureau."

"And of the United States," Holmes said softly.

Hoover appeared nettled by what he took to be a reproof. "To be sure."

Holmes extracted his cigarette case and proffered it to the special agent, who waved it off, wrinkling his nose in distaste. "I trust you've no objection? Like Dr. Freud, tobacco helps me think."

"Dr. Who? Never mind. I'm sure your public expects it," came his gruff reply.

Hoover removed his hat, allowing a brief glimpse of what looked to be a thatch of crinkly hair subdued with brilliantine. With the heel of his hand he smoothed a portion of this at the temple before resuming the fedora, adjusting its brim at an aggressive angle. Affability was not his forte. Eyeing me, his expression abruptly changed. "May I trouble you for my card, doctor?" Extending a pudgy hand, he tore the card to pieces when I returned it to him. In an offhand manner, he dropped the scraps into the wastebasket below the writing desk.

"You were about to tell us about Count Bernstorff," I prompted, eager to defuse what was threatening to turn into a confrontation.

Holmes threw me a grateful look as he struck his match.

"Was I?" The special agent appeared to give the matter some consideration, at which point something close to a smile creased his pug-like features. "Very well. I believe the individual who might provide some intelligence regarding Count Bernstorff is Mrs. Nicholas Longworth."

"Mrs. Nicholas Longworth," repeated Holmes, jotting down the name in his notebook.

Hoover's countenance assumed an almost mischievous cast. "Alice Longworth is . . ." Here he regarded the ceiling. "What shall I say? An intimate acquaintance of Count Bernstorff." His intonation leered at the phrase.

"An intimate acquaintance," Holmes echoed, without writing.

"And something of an eccentric. Wife of Congressman Longworth of Ohio. I daresay Nick Longworth will be Speaker of the House one day. He's angling for it—if his wife doesn't trip him up." Hoover snapped a look at his wristwatch. "Is there anything else I can do for you gentlemen? I've got to wrap up this business downstairs."

Holmes got to his feet and I followed his example. "Special Agent Hoover, may I ask one additional favor?" he added as the young man turned to go.

"A favor?" The special agent was not accustomed to granting favors.

"As people now suppose Sherlock Holmes is dead"—Holmes smiled—"might I propose that we allow that supposition to linger?"

"May I ask why?"

Holmes smiled. "You may ask."

Special Agent Hoover was no more accustomed to rebuffs than favors. He hesitated, then proffered a stiff bow. "I can ensure confirmation of your death appears in the papers and add some official expression of commiseration."

"What about your men?" I asked. "They will have seen Holmes."

"My men are mine," was the curt reply, "but even assuming their discretion, I cannot guarantee its duration. It can only be a matter of time before word of your survival leaks out. Leaving the capital might buy you some time, but not a lot. Truth will out," he concluded sententiously.

Holmes's face was a mask. "I will bear that in mind."

The little man looked from one of us to the other as if weighing what else he might say, but apparently decided against it.

"Good day, gentlemen." With that he shut the door smartly behind him, leaving us to our disheveled rooms.

"Regardless of nationality, they do make a mess of things," Holmes sighed, referring to the police. "But there's no quitting the city at present." He lit another cigarette with the remains of the first, the only sign of his upset.

"Some of the clutter may have been created by your late devotee." I pointed to the detective's strewn-about clothing and picked up a shirt collar that belonged to me. "Unhappy man." I echoed the detective's words.

"Special Agent Hoover?" Holmes resumed his chair and blew what I can only describe as an introspective smoke ring.

"Of course not. I refer to the suicide of your deluded admirer. I can imagine him wandering about in your clothes, then catching sight of himself in the mirror and overcome by the disparity between his appearance and your own, in a fit of despair at the difference, flinging himself—"

"Ah, yes, all very persuasive, my dear fellow. I can easily follow your act of sympathetic imagination. Except that none of it happened."

"What?"

He blew another smoke ring. "Well, some of it. But my admirer was no suicide."

"What are you saying?"

"You know my methods, Watson. As is my wont, I look for clues. Granted, the special agent's minions, in the manner of police everywhere, have managed to obscure them, yet I note the twin furrows in the carpet, leading from the wardrobe to the window. Yes, they are briefly interrupted near the chesterfield by police footwear, but here they resume their fatal trajectory." He pointed to the tracks. "The furrows are the shoes of a man dragged across the carpet toward the window. My unhappy imitator went to his death quite against his will, tugged there by his killer."

"Great heavens." I could plainly make out the parallel tracks in the rug. They spoke as plainly of the man's fate as if they had been written on the front page of a newspaper. Yet I was compelled to ask, "Can you be certain?"

"As if I had been there." Bending over the wastebasket, the detective now began retrieving and patiently piecing together the scraps of Hoover's engraved calling card.

"So the man was murdered."

Hunched over his task, Holmes continued my thought: "Undoubtedly. Our demented intruder was the victim of an assassin concealed in this suite, who, understandably mistaking a man wearing my clothes for me, threw the man he believed to be Sherlock Holmes out the window to his death. Defenestration. Had I entered the room instead of him, I should doubtless be lying on the pavement where he is now."

This chilling thought brought forth an involuntary shudder. "That being the case, why didn't you share this information with Mr. Hoover? Without being aware of it, he is certainly correct about one thing: if the public learns you are alive, your would-be assassin will learn it as well."

Holmes was arranging the scraps of white cardboard, face down.

"Hence my request to confirm my demise, Watson. For the moment, my would-be assassin believes himself successful. Such confidence may make him careless. Though," he added before I could speak, "sometimes I do find I outsmart myself."

"I beg your pardon?" I could not remember his ever expressing such sentiments before.

"It was a blunder to visit America in my own persona, perhaps the biggest of my career." Now another thought seemed to occur to him. "Am I past my prime, Watson? Like one of those celebrated tenors who make repeated farewell tours, have I outstayed my welcome, or, in this instance, my usefulness?"

In truth I had been thinking along these lines, now recalling my initial uneasiness when Holmes had first proposed going to America as himself. But rather than allowing him to succumb to a debilitating attack of melancholy and self-doubt when our mission remained crucial, I determined to effect a diversion.

"Holmes, your 'usefulness' has changed police work for generations to come, but even the best detective can sometimes—"

He stopped me with a languid hand. "To be sure, as young Hoover implies, the art of detection has benefitted from my methods, but what effect on the wider world do public personages exert, and is their influence a good thing? This unfortunate man, seeking to emulate or absorb my persona, stole into this hotel in the confused or desperate hope of looking or becoming like one whose character has been popularized in your accounts. Granted, he paid more dearly for his idolatry than most. But what of others? Has my notoriety been in any way beneficial outside of police work? If you told your readers I was able to fly, would some be so foolhardy as to try? Am I, in short, partly responsible for an innocent man's death, as Agent Hoover suggests? I worry that I am."

So surprised was I by this speech that I had to grope for an answer, but the best I could muster was "Holmes, by your reasoning, if anyone is to blame for our intruder's fate, the burden must fall on me, who created your fame, not you."

Still not looking up from his task, he smiled sadly. "That is typically selfless of you, my dear fellow, but it was my vanity—what Herr Doktor Freud would term my ego—that allowed you to publish your 'case histories' in the first place. I may have criticized your penchant for embroidery but it cannot be denied that I tolerated, no, enjoyed and encouraged your accounts. It is my actions, therefore, not your own, that must be reckoned with."

In the wake of these morose sentiments I could only fumble for more of my scattered wardrobe. Following my awkward movements and sensing my distress, he mercifully changed the subject.

"What do you make of Special Agent Hoover?"

"Hoover? A trifle officious?" I hazarded, grateful to be speculating about someone other than ourselves.

"Trifles are important. The Baltic Hotel address on his card certainly suggests an improvised headquarters for a 'Bureau of Intelligence,' and I find myself wondering if 'special agent' is not an honorific of Mr. Hoover's own devising. Something to create additional . . . stature?"

As always, the detective chose his words with care. As if manipulating the pieces of a jigsaw puzzle, he was approaching matters in his familiar circuitous fashion. "But why go to the trouble of handing me his card, only to reclaim and tear it up?"

"I thought it curious."

"Curious and suggestive. As the engraved face of the card is surely identical to others the man doubtless dispenses ad lib, I am compelled to wonder what is on the back of this particular card that Mr. Hoover belatedly felt the need to conceal. Did you not observe his sudden change of expression before he asked you to return it?"

I had seen the change but attached no importance to it.

"He saw something he had not expected to see." Contemplating his work, the detective's face now broke into a rare, satisfied grin. "As for revealing I was the target of an attempted assassination, I confess I am not inclined to confide in a man who admits to having three loyalties. Especially one who still lives with and under the thumb of his Germanic mother."

"What's that, you say?"

Holmes gestured to his handiwork spread on the desk. On the back of the now reassembled fragments I saw scrawled in a tiny, almost indecipherable hand: *Edgar—eggs, butter, bacon, bread, don't forget strawberry preserves! Mutti.*

"*Mutti* is the German familiar of *mother*. Young Hoover, for all his aura of command, like our unfortunate intruder, seems tied to his own choice of apparel, to wit, apron strings."

"And now we know what the E stands for," I said, turning a piece of the card face up to reveal the man's middle initial. "Do you seriously imagine Mr. Hoover is one of Von Bork's Hydra heads, working for the Kaiser?"

Leaning forward, Holmes scooped up the shards of white stock with slender, nervous fingers and slid them into an envelope from the desk drawer's supply of stationery. In answer to my question, he allowed himself a mirthless chuckle.

"He is certainly working for his mother. But rather than speculate on Frau Hoover's strawberry preserves, let us endeavor to see if Mrs. Nicholas Longworth will be 'at home,' to the late Sherlock Holmes."

The detective was regaining his spirits.

I was sorry to inform him my revolver was missing.

**22 August 1916**. "How could I refuse to receive a man whose calling card is his obituary?" Mrs. Nicholas Longworth began, setting aside her afternoon paper with its outsized headline proclaiming Holmes's demise. American newspapers were not subtle.

"My death has occurred on more than one occasion," Holmes acknowledged. "Thank you for finding the time to see Dr. Watson and myself."

"I wouldn't have missed it for worlds." Alice Longworth drawled with a smoker's rasp. "Though I confess I don't really care for mystery stories. Someone called them the recreation of second-rate minds. May I offer you gentlemen some sherry, or do you not drink on duty? Have I read that somewhere?" She gestured to the book-filled room.

"Perhaps later," said Holmes.

Having received us in the library of her elegantly furnished home on Dupont Circle, the congressman's sultry wife settled back on a pale gray divan. Ever-present fans whirred and tall screened windows were open, but the place remained a hothouse. Sitting stiffly on two unforgiving Biedermeier chairs, Holmes and I felt as though we were paying a call on a queen bee at the center of her hive. Behind her above the mantel, a tall painting of a dark-suited man with a mustache and pince-nez seemed to preside over the room.

"Is that a likeness of the congressman?" I ventured, attempting to fill the silence.

Mrs. Longworth appeared amused by my question but offered no reply.

"We've no desire to trespass on your valuable time, Mrs. Longworth. We are indebted to Special Agent Hoover," Holmes said in an effort to direct the conversation where he wished it to go.

"Try not to be," the lady advised. "The 'special agent' is a score-keeper." She placed Hoover's title in scornful quotation marks.

Holmes chose not to dispute the newspaper's account of his death. Not precisely an obituary (that was yet to come), it was merely a condensed—and sensationalized—summation of his achievements and the regrettable accident that had taken his life. He was content instead to study Alice Longworth. Sheathed in green satin, she bore his scrutiny as one accustomed to admiration. Without question she was an extraordinary creature, a woman in her prime, with an imperious nose, full lips, a rose-tinted complexion, and a crown of golden hair, coiffed by someone encouraged to take their time. As a physician who has seen many women patients over the course of a lengthy practice, I knew from her recumbent posture that she wore no corset. I wondered only at the glistening, patterned fur draped about her neck, which must have been uncomfortable in the heat.

"My boa," she said, catching my look. "Pinocchio keeps me cool."

Even as she spoke, the garment undulated. It took us a moment to realize Mrs. Longworth was in fact wearing, or somewhat enveloped by, a fat, dark brown snake, whose immense length trailed over her shoulder and down the back of the divan to the parquet floor.

Not a boa but a boa constrictor.

"They make lovely pets for those of us allergic to dander," Mrs. Longworth went on, evidently enjoying our surprise. "They are calm, feel wonderfully cool on the skin in weather such as this, and require little maintenance, only a rat or mouse now and then." She stroked the reptile fondly. "And, like me, Pinocchio despises hypocrisy, n'est-ce pas, Pinocchio?"

The snake did not speak French, for it did not answer. Beside this singular pair I noticed a rust-colored bolster. Its gold needle-point inscription was displayed so any caller might read:

> *If you can't say something good about someone,*
> *Sit right here by me.*

Holmes eyed the needlepoint but determined to push forward. "I take it Congressman Longworth is not 'at home'?" he began.

"Congressman Longworth is in . . . recess."

"In Ohio?"

"A safe distance."

"And you?"

She smiled. "Always in recess. Never in Ohio. I love to watch—and there's more to watch here. One finds one's amusements where one can. Are you sure about the sherry? What was it you've asked to see me about?"

"Do you find Count Johann Heinrich von Bernstorff amusing?" Holmes began again.

Now it was Mrs. Longworth's turn to be surprised. She stiffened momentarily, but recovered, reclining once more, and proceeded to take renewed inventory of the detective through heavily lidded eyes, as though realizing she had missed something earlier.

"Count Bernstorff?"

"You know the count?"

"*Know* is a peculiar verb, Mr. Holmes. There's *know* as in general knowledge of a subject or place, there's *know* as in 'to be acquainted with a person and then, to be sure, there's *know* in the Biblical sense. . . ." She trailed off, lacing her hands together in her lap as the snake shifted its position slightly, its large, flat head now coyly visible behind her left ear.

Holmes waited, his gray eyes unblinking. If Mrs. Longworth thought to intimidate her guest with protracted silences she had again misjudged her visitor.

"The Count and I take . . . tea from time to time," the lady finally allowed.

"At his embassy?" I inquired.

This produced a laugh more nearly approaching a guffaw. "Ah, Dr. Watson, you are just as I imagined!"

Holmes waited until her merriment subsided. "As you and Pinocchio despise hypocrisy, I will put my cards on the table, face up. You may not like what I have to say."

Mrs. Longworth abandoned striking attitudes designed to startle visitors and listened with attention, her formerly languid features now alive with intelligence.

"There is a German scheme to keep America from joining the war on the side of the Allies," Holmes informed her. "We have been dispatched to learn what that plan is and are convinced Count Bernstorff must know it, though how and from whom he presently

receives instructions is a mystery, as Germany's transatlantic telegraph cables are severed."

"No mystery," Mrs. Longworth answered promptly. "He receives
telegraphic communications nonetheless."

"Oh?" Holmes was careful to sound offhand.

"Berlin's original solution to the severed cables handicap was to
route its communications through Sweden and thence to Brazil,
whence they were forwarded via south Atlantic cable to Washington. In code, to be sure."

"But Sweden is neutral!" I couldn't for the moment remember
what Brazil was.

My expostulation was met with a shrug. "Neutral is as neutral
does, doctor. Neutrality inevitably requires serving both sides."

Holmes and I resisted the temptation to exchange sidelong looks
but were in fact overjoyed. After almost two months, this was the
first break in our undertaking. Mrs. Longworth, whose antennae
were on full alert, caught the look that did not take place.

"You say Sweden was the original solution, implying there must
be another, possibly simpler, expedient. Do you know what that
might be?" Holmes's tone implied he understood this was likely
too much to hope, but more surprises were in store.

"Everyone in Washington knows," Mrs. Longworth returned,
"for it is no secret. In the name of neutrality, our grotesquely naive
president has granted Germany permission to use State Department cabling facilities to communicate around the world."

"*What?*" we exclaimed simultaneously.

"Stipulating only that Germany promises to, quote, 'not transmit
any material inimical to American interests.' Close quotation
marks. Do you enjoy those apples, gentlemen?" Her words dripped
with contempt.

"I can't believe it." I could not refrain from raising my voice.

Holmes did not speak, but his habitual self-possession momentarily abandoned him and his features registered dismay.

"Neutral is as neutral does," the lady repeated.

"Do you mean to say," I persisted, "that President Wilson has knowingly turned over American cabling facilities for the use of German coded messages?"

"*I* don't mean to say it," Mrs. Longworth specified. "*He* does." Like M, she refused to dignify the object of her detestation by name, regarding the detective with something like a smirk as Holmes passed a hand over his brow. "Coded messages from Berlin to Washington are helpfully forwarded by our own Ambassador Gerard in Berlin to Walter Page, our ambassador in London, who cheerfully sends them on to Johann—Count Bernstorff—here."

We sat in stupefied silence, aware of our hostess's amusement. "I assume this is of some help?" The smouldering purr had returned, accompanied by the grin of a Cheshire cat.

"It is a great help." The detective strove to keep his voice steady. "May I ask, did Count Bernstorff ever—" Here he hesitated.

The feline smirk broadened. "I believe the subject you are reluctant to broach is referred to by Hamlet as *country matters*, but less subtly known in these parts as *pillow talk*. Washington runs on pillow talk, Mr. Holmes." Mrs. Longworth grinned, displaying gleaming teeth somehow more alarming than Hoover's. "There are sentiments a diplomat would never express upright in daylight, but on the horizontal after dark, things are different. As you surely know, one four-letter word for intercourse is t-a-l-k. At the end of a long day, men complain about work to a sympathetic ear. The count finds his position most frustrating. His diplomatic position," she amended serenely.

"Frustrating in what way?" Holmes persisted.

As if in response, Pinocchio uncoiled and reconfigured himself, slithering downward. A gigantic speckled band, the bulky reptile seemed endless, the library a veritable garden of Eden with Eve and her slimy companion placidly reposed amid all that knowledge—some of it, as we were learning, forbidden.

"And if it is still on offer, I believe I would enjoy some of that sherry," Holmes said.

Silence reigned while the butler was summoned and sherry served. Servant and serpent appeared accustomed to each other. During this solemn interval, Mrs. Longworth removed the top of a black-lacquered box on the table before her. Within its voluptuous, Chinese-red satin interior were nestled orderly clusters of cigarettes. With a languid arm, she extended the box in our direction. When we declined, she sighed and addressed her pet.

"Oh dear, Pinocchio, I think the gentlemen were anticipating hashish." She plucked a cigarette for herself and struck a match, not waiting to see if Holmes would oblige her.

I confess the sight of women smoking still irritates me. I remember coming upon Juliet and Maria in the kitchen, red-faced and coughing as they experimented with tobacco, which Juliet defiantly asserted was the prerogative of the New Woman. Today a certain class of woman smokes brazenly in Oxford Street. The war has changed everything.

"Thank you, Bertie." Mrs. Longworth waited until the factotum had withdrawn before answering the detective's question. "Count Bernstorff is desperate for peace, thinks the Kaiser mad as a hatter and this war the height of insanity. On this point we were in accord, though not as to the remedy. There I am firmly in my father's camp. Unless America joins the Allies, the war threatens Europe's manhood with annihilation. Meanwhile," the lady went on, her complexion reddening at the thought, "our pusillanimous chief executive remains so firmly impaled on his palisades he risks contracting hemorrhoids."

Mrs. Longworth's talent for invective was so great I wondered if she herself had embroidered the needlepoint on that bolster. To cover my shock at language I did not expect from this quarter, I merely repeated, "Pusillanimous?"

"Timid and lacking courage." Mrs. L was the reader in this library. "The president has given the term *rail splitter* new meaning." She stumped out her unfinished cigarette. I wondered if she'd lit it simply in hopes of shocking us.

Outside the open windows, it began to rain heavily and noisily. Without separating her gaze from that of the detective, the congressman's wife clicked on a nearby table lamp and waited. The ball was in our court.

"Are you still on friendly terms with Count Bernstorff, Mrs. Longworth?" Holmes returned to his chosen topic.

The lady stiffened. "I am not a spy, if that's what you're proposing, Mr. Holmes."

"I'm afraid it is, Mrs. Longworth. Are you in touch with the count?"

"Another awkward choice of words, Mr. Holmes."

"Could you be?" the detective persisted. Before she could reply, he went on. "You have said you despise hypocrisy, that you share your father's view that America must join the Allies. Owing to circumstances regrettably beyond my control, I find myself presenting you with an opportunity to help stanch this endless slaughter. We must learn what plot Germany has concocted to ensure America doesn't enter the war."

Mrs. Longworth continued studying Holmes for some moments. "In this country that's called saying a mouthful, Mr. Holmes."

"Pillow talk," Holmes responded, gesturing to the inscription on the adjacent bolster. "Intercourse, as you have defined it."

Mrs. Longworth stared into space for the better part of a minute. Her silence on this occasion was not another attempt to intimidate the detective but was plainly indicative of her conflicted feelings. There could be no mistaking the disagreeable nature of the mission Holmes was proposing. With automatic gestures, she lit another cigarette and exhaled with something like a sigh.

"Poor Johann," she said finally. "One must remember La Rochefoucauld: 'It is not enough to succeed; a friend must also fail.'"

Mrs. Longworth must have read every book in the large room.

"Will you see that friend?"

For the first time the woman spoke in an unaffected voice.

"Count Bernstorff is a decent man."

"His superiors are not."

"He is only following orders."

Holmes's gray eyes allowed no escape.

"Some orders are wrong."

In response to this Mrs. Longworth murmured a soundless reply.

"I agree," said the detective. "It is a revolting task."

She stared at him. "Can you read my mind?"

"I can read your lips," Holmes replied. "It is a skill I have lately acquired. Mrs. Longworth, you have said you like to watch. All I am asking is that you listen as well."

It was seldom, I think, that Alice Longworth found herself outgunned. As far from lassitude as could be, she was unable to meet the detective's steely gaze. She looked down and stroked a portion of Pinocchio as though for reassurance. She did not raise her eyes when she spoke again, her voice a bare whisper.

"What is it you wish me to learn, Mr. Holmes?"

The detective suppressed a sigh of relief, ready with his list. "Everything about the code you can, and most particularly where the count forwards any instructions. When he forwards telegrams, what does the embassy do with the original messages? Are they retained? Are copies made? If so, where are they kept? Also, is the embassy wiring money to anyone? Is the ambassador in contact with a so-called Swiss named Emil Gasche? I know what I ask is difficult and even repugnant," he went on before she could object, "but I am certain your views in this matter closely align with your father's."

"You don't know my father," Mrs. Longworth's smile was for once devoid of irony. "In these matters he is very much a prude."

"But as former president of the United States, Theodore Roosevelt has always known clearly where America's best interests lie."

The silence that followed was filled by the rain pelting down outside. The air within had begun imperceptibly to cool.

"You knew?" Mrs. Longworth said at length.

Holmes gestured to the tall picture above the mantelpiece. "I don't imagine a husband would tolerate an image that size other than an ancestor or family member so prominently displayed in his home. The style is modern, as is the wardrobe, ergo not an ancestor. It looks to be the work of Repin or Sargent. Repin, in faraway Russia, is less likely. It is a good likeness or you would not have chosen to display it."

Gazing at the painting more attentively, I realized it could be none other than Theodore Roosevelt. I had observed but not seen.

Mrs. Longworth also glanced at the picture. "Under the circumstances, I think you'd better call me Alice."*

*Alice Roosevelt Longworth*

"Alice."

"Sherlock."

"Sometimes called Princess Alice?"

"I've been called many things."

"As have I."

I studied the gilt-wood traceries at my feet.

Later, in the metered taxicab, a subdued Holmes directed the driver to take us to the nearest office of Western Union.

---

\* Alice, Theodore Roosevelt's eldest child, was named for the president's first wife, who died shortly after giving birth. Of his wayward daughter, TR said: "I can run the country or I can manage Alice. I can't possibly do both."

"M will be glad to learn 'Aunt Abigail' may be getting better at last," I said.

The detective said nothing, having lapsed into a pensive silence. "Mrs. Nicholas Longworth," he said at length, shaking his head. This was followed by a mirthless chuckle. "The effrontery of the man."

"Which man?"

"Special Agent Hoover, who must be enjoying his little joke."

"But shouldn't you be pleased? For the first time since we came to this country, we appear to be making real progress."

"We are asking a woman to perform an odious task," he mused, pursuing his own train of thought rather than responding to mine. "*Revolting* was the word she mouthed."

"Delilah was a patriot, Holmes. Desperate times . . ."

He looked over at me. "What a cold-blooded creature it is," he commented.

It took me a moment to realize he was not referring to Pinocchio.

"There are circumstances where men can't always do what is necessary," I protested.

"Violet Carstairs could," came his curt reply. "But Delilah will serve," he added. "Mrs. Longworth's true foe is not hypocrisy but boredom. All her antics are designed to ward off its effects."

Not for the first time I realized that Holmes's experience in Vienna with Dr. Freud had not been limited to overthrowing his addiction to cocaine. In Vienna, the detective had learned there were forms of observation besides the physical.

Holmes again appeared lost in thought before clearing his throat. "You continue at the Willard, doctor. You are remaining in America to plead the Allied cause. M will of course foot the bill."

"And you?"

"I shall go to ground."

**22 September 1916**. Once again there are no geraniums in the box on the first-floor balcony on Dupont Circle.

"That makes six days," I complained. "What can she be doing?"

Sherlock Holmes said nothing, but I took his silence to mean it was better not to ask.

"But this is like pulling teeth!"

"More like hairs." The detective hailed a taxicab. "But if our Delilah cuts too close or soon, Samson may feel the scissors."

It had in fact had been much longer than six days, and the incremental pace at which Alice Longworth succeeded in extracting information from her "teas" with Count Bernstorff and passing the intelligence to us was maddening.

Among the tidbits we gleaned was the knowledge that Bernstorff's superior in Berlin, Foreign Minister Zimmermann, fancies himself an authority on the United States, having spent time in America some twenty years ago. Count Bernstorff regards the foreign minister with condescension. Though Zimmermann has the requisite dueling scar on one cheek, the Junker insignia of class and rank, yet there is no von attached to his name, and this was considered a bad sign.

*German Foreign Minister Zimmermann (with dueling scar)*

More encouraging was word that the foreign minister, passionately in favor of the U-boat—lately regarded as Germany's weapon of last resort—has so far been unable to convince the Kaiser's high command to risk provoking President Wilson by unleashing submarines to torpedo all shipping bound for England regardless of flag or freight. The debate in Berlin, we were informed, remained ongoing and heated, though for now, cooler heads have prevailed.

But for how long?

Further impeding our progress, Congress was back from its August recess, and Delilah was obliged to be more circumspect. While the Longworths were tolerant of each other's fondness for afternoon refreshment, understandably neither wished to know what beverage was consumed by the other and where.

As if the foregoing were not sufficient, there was the issue of Mrs. Longworth's temperament. As she told us plainly at our first meeting, the woman despised hypocrisy. Dissimulation of any kind was foreign to her. Alice Longworth was accustomed to say the first thing that came into her head. Candor was her stock (or shock) in trade. Giving listeners a piece of her mind was reflexive. Holding her tongue was an unfamiliar exercise. Over time this necessity would exact a toll.

And there were other complications, some of which would have qualified as hilarious had our errand not been so desperate.

We lost an entire week due to fastidiousness on the part of a maid in Dupont Circle, who, worried her mistress's geraniums were getting too much sun, kept moving the plants indoors. In consequence, no afternoon meetings at Boulder Bridge in Rock Creek Park were signaled and Mrs. Longworth cooled her heels there daily, no doubt fuming in her own colorful lexicon at what she took to be our ineptness. Being "stood up" did not qualify as the lady's idea of amusement.

On another occasion, the same zealous servant set out the pot for some rain. It thus became our turn to loiter near the picturesque bridge, sheltering under an adjacent gazebo during a sweltering downpour, worrying about the fate of our spy who, as it proved, remained at home, dry and oblivious throughout.

When we were not engaged in retrieving intermittent scraps of intelligence and passing them on to Cecil Spring Rice at the British embassy (whence they were cabled—always in code—to M and Admiral Hall in London), Holmes and I existed in separate worlds. I remained at the Willard, proselytizing on behalf of England and the Allied cause to anyone who would listen, but for safety's sake I did not know how or where the detective was living.

The press, however, remained keen. Holmes's formal obituary appeared in the Washington *Times* and the *Herald*. Both cobbled together summations were riddled with exaggerations and errors in the way of newspapers everywhere and I was besieged by reporters with questions unrelated to the war but regarding the Great Detective, as he was termed. How long had I known Sherlock Holmes? (Since 1881.) What was his greatest case? (Impossible to say, there were so many.) Had he ever erred? (He had, though I felt it injudicious to specify when and where.) Was it true that His Majesty, learning news of Sherlock Holmes's death, had donned a black armband? (His Majesty had many reasons to wear mourning these days.) I did my best to answer these and a hundred other inquiries, some bearing no relation to Holmes or the European conflict that I could make out. As a reputed "man of the world," what did I think of American women? (Words failed me.) Most frequently I was asked what my personal reactions to the tragedy were. (I stated that in my view, Sherlock Holmes was the best and wisest man I had ever known.)

I could not begin to imagine with what merriment Holmes, wherever he was concealing himself, read these pieces, though in short order the papers were obliged to retract much of what they had printed, beginning with the obituary itself:

## Sensational News—
## Sherlock Holmes Not Dead!

It is with astonishment we have learned the body presumed to have been that of the famed detective, killed by accident in a fall from his rooms at the Willard, was not in fact that of Sherlock Holmes, but of a deluded admirer. According to Special Agent Hoover of the Bureau of Investigation, the unfortunate man, Oswald Smith, a shopkeeper from Arlington and devotee of the detective's, had stolen into the rooms of his visiting hero, dressed in clothes found in the closet of the famed sleuth, and then, in a fit of despair, flung himself to his death.

Truth, as the Special Agent had prophesied, will out—or at least some of it had.

Now the number of reporters deluging me with questions multiplied. Had I known the true identity of the dead man? For how long? And, most insistently—where was Sherlock Holmes now? To this I could truthfully answer I had no idea. (I only saw Holmes, when, summoned by the geraniums on her balcony, we made our separate ways to Rock Creek Park, there to be joined by Mrs. Longworth with her gleanings.)

Aware the press was watching my every move, it took all my ingenuity and several modes of transport to throw off my pursuers each time I left the hotel. The reporters were easy to spot, for they made no attempt to conceal their presence or motives but chased me like foxhounds. Hoover's men from the BOI were more subtle though ultimately just as obvious. I worried most about German agents, whom I judged more sophisticated than either flock, as I knew the capital must be crawling with them. But I had been taught by the best and always began by taking the second taxicab or leaving through the hotel kitchens and rapidly switching vehicles thereafter. My task was simplified by the ubiquitous black Model T Fords that were conveniently indistinguishable from one another. But forgetting that cars here drove on the wrong side of the road, I was almost run down on several occasions, endeavoring to elude my pursuers.

**4 October 1916**. When Mrs. Longworth and I finally succeeded in meeting at Boulder Bridge, convinced we had given any possible pursuers the slip, we were dismayed to find ourselves accosted by a policeman who inspected us at his leisure, insolently twirling his truncheon and demanding to know what we were doing in the park at midday.

"Holmes!" I was first to recognize the detective's slender form, but Mrs. Longworth was taken totally unawares. It was one of the few times that unflappable individual exhibited surprise.

"Well, officer, you had me," she said, snapping open a parasol either to protect her delicate skin from the sun, or perhaps to suggest her annoyance.

"Let us walk," the policeman responded, gesturing with his baton. "I shall appear to give you directions."

"You asked about someone called Gasche," Mrs. Longworth began as we set out. "He's no more Swiss than Chief Sitting Bull. He's Captain von Rintelen, in the pay of the Wilhelmstrasse, and it seems that last year Captain von Rintelen, directed by the German embassy, funneled a great deal of money to President Huerta."

"So much for Special Agent Hoover's expertise," Holmes murmured. "And I take it von Rintelen was acting on orders from the foreign minister?"

"That was not volunteered."

"Who is President Huerta?" I asked.

Mrs. Longworth looked from one of us to the other in disbelief. "Do you gentlemen not read the newspapers?" she demanded, not troubling to conceal her irritation. Our many false starts in obtaining this rendezvous doubtless contributed to her ill humor. "Victoriano Huerta was, until recently, the president of Mexico. He was driven from office and deceased in Fort Bliss as of June. Fort Bliss is in Texas," she added for our benefit.

It stupidly occurred to me there must be worse places to die than one named Fort Bliss, but Mrs. L had not finished.

"Huerta was a dissolute, bloodthirsty tyrant, and gossip in Washington says he may have been poisoned after he was hounded from Mexico. Good riddance, in my view, but the count was scandalized. 'All those marks spent to no effect!' he fumed. Oh, and in answer to your other question, copies of all communications received or forwarded from the embassy on instructions from Berlin are burned."

Holmes received this intelligence with an unhappy frown. "And the money?" To any bystander it would have appeared the policeman was chatting amiably with strolling visitors. "What was it for and what became of it?"

"I shall endeavor to learn," Mrs. Longworth replied. "But I must do what you ask in my own way and at my own pace. Now if you will excuse me, it is Wednesday and Pinocchio eats his mouse on

Wednesdays, and he does not enjoy dining alone." Before Holmes could object, she held up a gloved hand. "Good day, officer."

"Her pace may not be ours," I remarked when she was out of earshot, but Holmes was following his own train of thought.

"What possible motive could the Germans have in sending vast sums to the ousted president of Mexico and a scoundrel, at that?"

"Possibly because he *was* a scoundrel?" I suggested, but a look from my friend made clear he was dissatisfied with my reasoning.

A policeman was merely the first of many guises in which Holmes presented himself to hear Mrs. Longworth's news. On other occasions, in response to the potted geraniums, he variously appeared as a tatterdemalion vagabond, a Unitarian clergyman, a park gardener, and once, quite convincingly, an umbrella-wielding suffragette. I had no idea where and how he procured his disguises and made it my business not to learn. Holmes had previously been in America undercover for two years and though this was his first experience of Washington, I imagine "Altamont" had a great many associates and resources from his previous mission. When Mrs. Longworth quizzed me on the subject, I sagely implied I knew more than I could reveal.

**31 October 1916**. "0075," Mrs. Longworth informed us when she arrived, late as usual, at Boulder Bridge. "Each and every telegram sent has its own number," she explained. "The code itself uses numbers in preference to letters—these are apparently more difficult to decipher."

Hearing this, I recalled M remarking on how easy the American alphabet codes were to crack.

"Well done, Mrs. Longworth," the priest on the bench did not look up from his breviary.

Pleased by the cleric's praise, but unsure how to acknowledge it, Mrs. Longworth gave an exasperated look at a coven of witches, hobgoblins, and small pirates shrieking and racing in swarms about the park.

"It's Halloween," she explained. "At the end of October in America, children dress in costume and frolic. It makes one long for the Salem witch trials."

Sometimes it was difficult to tell if Mrs. Longworth was serious. By this late date, the weather had finally broken. Red and yellow leaves were swirling and falling about us in mercifully cool air.

Still the priest did not raise his eyes. Everyone in the park today was in masquerade. "And what does 0075 signify?"

"0075 is the designation for the German diplomatic code."

Holmes shot me a look and I jotted down the numbers. Spring Rice would forward them to M, who would evaluate their importance.

"And the money Zimmermann ordered sent to the former Mexican president?" He slowly turned a page in the book of psalms. "What was it for?"

"The topic has not come up again," the woman answered shortly.

"How much was it?"

"I repeat: the topic has not been referred to."

"Have some more tea."

Mrs. Longworth blanched. "You have no right to speak to me in that fashion, Mr. Holmes."

"The situation is desperate, Mrs. Longworth."

Bristling with indignation, Alice Longworth turned to leave. Sherlock Holmes made no move to stop her but after she had taken no more than a dozen steps she recovered her poise and turned to face us.

"When he's ordered to forward messages, Count Bernstorff employs a different code. I gather it is more sophisticated."

"The superior code must have its own designation. What is it?"

"I knew you'd ask me that." With another of her sighs—sighs that were becoming increasingly common—Delilah used a rolled umbrella to thread her away through a gaggle of prancing leprechauns. She was unceremonious in wielding the device, ignoring the appalled protests of several nannies.

"Our spy is not happy," I observed.

The priest still had not moved. "I know."

The difficulty emerged when Delilah failed our next rendezvous. Or rather, the geraniums, when next they appeared on the balcony on Dupont Circle, were dead.

"When shall we three meet again?" Holmes muttered. "In thunder, lightning, or in rain?"

I had no notion why he was referring to the weather as there was not a cloud in sight.

**15 November 1916**. The lovers, it appears, have quarreled. Their falling out has proved ruinous. At Mrs. Longworth's last report, those in Berlin who favored submarine warfare were in the ascendant, convinced by Zimmermann's vaunted knowledge of America that nothing would induce its president to abandon neutrality, while my presence at the Willard Hotel was becoming less plausible by the day. Arguing England's cause at local book clubs and libraries where I was heard in noncommittal silence, or writing to various newspaper editors, my seeds were landing on arid soil. The papers indeed stopped printing my articles, an altogether novel experience for an author long accustomed to publication, but that disappointment paled compared to what I read on their front pages each morning. I perused the headlines through half-closed eyes, afraid to bring into focus the remorseless numbers staring back at me. Nowhere in history had such a war been fought. Nowhere in history had there been less to show for superhuman effort on both sides, with no territory won or lost by either, yet the bloodlet-ting continues unabated. The origins of the carnage are by now obscure, absurd, and forgotten. Europe has become its own Red Sea. Although I know it is impermissible to say so, the only reality is that two mighty empires will deplete themselves to extinction rather than lose.

And what was I doing while Europe burned and America bustled about its business? Stopping at a luxe hotel, eating sump-tuous, non-rationed meals, and going for rambles in the park where I conversed with a beautiful woman—all at bankrupt England's expense.

"He's hopelessly in love with me," Mrs. Longworth fretted when we eventually managed to reconvene. On this occasion we assembled at Fort Stevens, summoned now (ironically) by a pas-sionflower, its purple blossom in place of the homely geraniums. "I cannot continue to lead him on. He talks of my leaving Nick and our getting married! And Nick with the House Speakership within his grasp!"

"I assure you," said a busker adroitly juggling four tennis balls nearby, "such men thrive on what is unobtainable. Raised on Goethe, they sorrow with young Werther and would fly your presence were you to become truly available."

I had not known Holmes could juggle. With people's emotions or tennis balls. Nor, after all this time, had he lost his skill with either. For the latter, passersby dropped coins into his flannel cap, so busking was turning a profit. I wondered if his horde should technically fall into Whitehall's empty war chest.

Mrs. Longworth wanted to believe what the detective was telling her, but there was no gainsaying that the triple roles of American wife, German mistress, and English spy were taking a toll. Once confident of her powers and person, Alice Longworth now often smelled of the sherry she had first offered us.

"Spies do not last long" was Holmes's sidelong murmur as he continued tossing balls into the air. This from the man who had recently found me cold-blooded! "Mycroft once endeavored to explain their lifespan," he added, his hands ceaselessly in motion, "but it took two years working undercover in America before I had an inkling of his meaning. After which I gratefully returned to my bees."

"Have you learned the designation of the second code?" were his only words to Mrs. Longworth. Holmes's dexterity was not limited to tennis balls. I confess I marveled at my friend's ability never to lose sight of his objective. Confronted by the woman's evident distress, I am not sure I could have followed his example.

"Do you know how patient I must be?" Our spy's complexion was flushing a splotchy, disagreeable red. "I cannot ask questions! He must supply the answers unprompted, while I pretend I that I am uninterested, that I do not understand—! Me! Have you the least notion of how galling it is to feign stupidity? And he knows me better! Do you know what I've become? *Whom* I've become? Not Alice Longworth. Alice in Wonderland! Alice Through the Looking Glass!"

"Have you learned it?" Holmes repeated the question.

Mrs. Longworth gnawed her lip. "13040 designates urgent and most secret," she finally answered in a low voice. "I tell you he is in love with me."

"And you . . . ?" Holmes continued to juggle as I wrote down the new code number, my notepad on my knee.

"That is no concern of yours," Mrs. Longworth said.

"Can you not make him see things between you are better as they are? A scandal at this juncture would do neither of you good."

"He loves me," the hapless woman said in the same tone of resignation. "He is losing his mind. The strain is relentless. Now he talks of asking me to spy for Germany!"

Hearing this, Holmes almost fumbled one of the balls and emptied the rest into his canvas bag before leading the distraught woman to the nearest bench and sitting beside her.

"What did you tell him?"

"What I'm telling you. That I cannot do this anymore. Read my lips," she concluded emphatically.

The busker looked over at me before lighting a cigarette and handing it to her. She accepted the gift without looking at him.

"One final inquiry, the last, I promise." She gave no sign of having heard. "When he is directed to forward messages using code 13040, where do they go?"

Without a word, she rose and left us.

"Will she do as you ask?" I wondered.

"She will," the detective replied without embellishment.

"What makes you so sure?"

"Dancers are always desperate to please the choreographer."

**10 December 1916**. "Do you know of someone called Edward Doheny?"

The British ambassador removed his glasses and pinched the bridge of his nose.

"Who wishes to know?"

I said nothing. It was my job to report on Holmes's behalf, and not to divulge information unless specifically instructed by the detective to do so.

"I will rephrase my question," Spring Rice said. "*Why* does He Who Shall Not Be Named wish to know?"

"Because our source assures us that is where cash and telegrams from the German embassy have lately been sent in the unique 13040 numerical code, which is employed for only the most secret communications."

"I see." The ambassador unscrewed the cap of his pen and jotted down the number. "May I know your source?"

"I am not at liberty to say." My answer did not surprise him. "In any event the question is moot as our source is no longer available."

Behind his formidable desk, Spring Rice stared unhappily into space.

"Come, Mr. Ambassador, this cannot be so difficult a question. Your expression tells me the man's name is not unfamiliar to you."

"Ah, doctor, you've been acquiring some traits of your—" he hesitated over how to refer to the detective.

"A number of telegrams," I pressed, ignoring the implied compliment. "And a great sum of money forwarded by a saboteur on instructions from the Wilhemstrasse. This busybody calls himself Gasche and claims to be Swiss. The BOI knows of him, but not his true name, which is von Rintelen."

"You have been busy," murmured the ambassador.

"The money forwarded in pesos," I added, hoping to sweeten the pot.

"Sent to Doheny in Tampico? In Mexico?" The man was now idly scrawling designs on the desk blotter, circling the number 13040. I sensed the dam would shortly give way.

"Using State Department cabling facilities, yes. Who is Edward Doheny?"

"Edward Doheny," he sniffed, "is an American of Irish extraction who recently made a fortune in Los Angeles pumping oil out of the ground."

"Oil?"

"Automobiles continue to proliferate, doctor, and they require petroleum. Wherever oil is to be found, in America, in Arabia, in the Antarctic, if such a thing were possible, you will find men groveling for it—and making fortunes in the process."

"And Tampico?"

"Doheny's newest refineries are in Tampico. The Mexican government is leasing claims and stakes in the province of Veracruz. Mr. Doheny has bought them all up and is doing a massive business in Mexico."

There it was again. Mexico. Why on earth could Germany be sending messages and money to Mexico?

Spring Rice had not the faintest idea. But it was certain the money hadn't stopped with the death of the villain Huerta. "And Mr. Doheny, loyal to his homeland, has contributed funds to the rebellion in Ireland. I wish someone would offer *us* money," the ambassador concluded bitterly. "Without another bank loan from America, England is done."

With this unhappy news, I took my leave.

ᴥ

"We are drowning, Watson," said Sherlock Holmes, after I made my report regarding the oilman Doheny.

"Drowning?"

"In data. Too much information is almost as perplexing as too little," Sherlock Holmes reflected when we met that evening on Chain Bridge at its halfway point across the Potomac. "We are faced with too many clues."

The detective lit his pipe, which I knew signified an involved discussion. After several rapid puffs, he shook out his match and flicked it into mist-shrouded water too far below us to hear it sizzle. The December night air was chilly and our breath showed as we spoke, but at this hour traffic was light and, leaning over the parapet, we could talk undisturbed. "We have facts, we have clues, we have suspects. We even have two murder victims."

"And two different murderers."

"Which only compounds our difficulties."

"But how does all we've learned or experienced relate to Mexico?" I knew all the words to this chorus.

"Precisely. At this point, all is conjecture."

I lit my own pipe and we smoked in familiar, companionable silence. I saw the detective struggle to find his way in a labyrinth of possibilities. Sherlock Holmes had a mind like a steel trap but on occasion was unable to escape its confines.

At length he spoke again. "As you know, Watson, crime, not politics, is my métier."

"Do you not consider what is happening on the Continent a crime? As I recall, some years ago, you pointed out that in the twentieth century crimes seemed to be getting bigger. It seems you were right. I have been a soldier and have the hurts to show for it, but what is happening in France is not war, it is a crime. A crime against humanity," I concluded somewhat feebly.*

Holmes considered this. "I am afeared there are few die well that die in battle," he murmured, "for how can they charitably dispose of anything when blood is their argument?"

"I beg your pardon?"

He smiled faintly. "Forgive me for quoting a writer other than yourself."†

---

\*     Holmes makes his observation in *The Adventure of the Peculiar Protocols*.

†     Holmes was evidently fond of *Henry V,* as he frequently quotes another of Shakespeare's lines from the same play, which readers mistake for his own: "The game's afoot!"

So saying he knocked the remnants of his pipe on the heel of his shoe, signaling he'd reached his decision, sending a flurry of sparks into the fog gathering at his feet. "It appears we must go to Mexico."

"Mexico?"

He heaved a sigh. "Mexico, my dear fellow. If Mrs. Long-worth's reports are accurate—and we have no reason to suspect them—we will not get to read any telegrams sent to or from the German embassy in Washington, coded or in plain text, as both are routinely burned. Which leaves us no choice but to work the case from the destination of those specially coded telegrams—Mexico."

"And if they have been destroyed in Mexico as well?"

He did not answer.

The thought of traveling still farther afield from beleaguered England made me uneasy, and I had been uneasy for months. Holmes had survived no fewer than two assassination attempts. Cats may have nine lives but the detective, I knew by now, had used up many more. As if to emphasize my confusion, the mist had now risen above the bridge span and was enveloping us in its damp embrace.

"How can you even be sure this Mexican business is related to preventing America's entering the war?"

"We cannot be certain, but two facts strongly suggest it is. Primo, the Wilhemstrasse is using its most sophisticated code to transmit instructions to a wealthy Irish American in Tampico, who is no friend to England. Secondo, they continue sending vast sums when Germany is as crushed by debt as we are, ergo, Foreign Minister Zimmermann is convinced money they don't have is worth spending south of the border. As the oil rich Doheny has no need of funds, the money is clearly intended for someone else, also in

Mexico. As ex-president Huerta is dead in Texas, he cannot be in need of it either, yet still it flows . . ." He trailed off, lost in thought.

I wondered if he was remembering Mrs. Longworth's "gossip" that Huerta had been poisoned in Fort Bliss. Why? Because he declined to involve himself in some scheme but had become inconveniently privy to it? The prospect of journeying to Mexico was an undertaking that, even under ideal circumstances, would consume time we did not know whether we had. Months were passing. At any moment, the U-boats could be loosed, and England's fate sealed in twelve weeks, if the late Roger Casement's information was correct.

The detective's mind and mine were now running on identical tracks. Without speaking, we contemplated imploring our Delilah to reopen her tonsorial parlor and learn where Mexico fit into this puzzle. Was it, as now seemed likely, to do with oil? Tanks and aircraft as well as cars required it. But again, without any need to discuss the matter, we knew this avenue was closed to us. Delilah had definitely broken with Samson, who was pulling out his own hair without any scissors, under the strain of the U-boat argument raging interminably in Berlin.

"It is quite a three-pipe problem," said Holmes quietly. Separated by less than ten feet, the mist had now resolved itself into a fog so thick I could scarcely make out the shape of my friend. "Get a good night's sleep, my dear fellow, and I will emerge from my incognito and join you at the Willard for breakfast."

"As you like."

"Goodnight, Watson."

"Goodnight, Holmes."

I remained where I was as his slender form disappeared into swirls of cold smoke, his footfalls growing fainter as he made his way toward the Virginia shore. When his steps were no longer audible, an eerie silence reigned. It was late and almost all traffic had either gone or been curtailed by what was now a dense fog such as I knew in London, a place and time that lately seemed a dreamlike world away. As if it no longer or never had existed. All that remained at this hour were flaring streetlights here and there, beaming like lighthouses perched on invisible shoals, with an occasional distant car honk punctuating the stillness like a foghorn. Finally even these faded to silence.

I turned to face Washington and began hesitatingly retracing my steps, my left hand groping the parapet for guidance, while tapping my stick on the pavement with my right like the blind man I had suddenly become.

I had not gone thirty paces before I became aware of other steps. Between the hour, fog, and my fatigue, it was difficult to discern from which direction they originated.

"Holmes?"

Rather than departing, these steps were approaching.

I stopped, irresolute, but the other steps did not. They echoed in the stillness as they drew closer.

After what seemed an eternity, a tall, erect form appeared out of the fog. The face, when I could make it out, was not the detective's, yet it was familiar. The poet's phrase "the sneer of cold command" popped unbidden into my mind. But in these strange surroundings I could not place the proud, aquiline features, thick mustache, and hideous dueling scar, fifteen paces from where I stood.

"Dr. Watson, I presume?"

The stranger smiled with grim satisfaction before he shot me.

Only as I fell did I realize the identity of my assassin.

"Von Bork!"

And the weapon which he fired.

**25 December 1916**. "Watson?" a voice I knew reached me from a hazy distance, amid repetitive noise and a rhythmic undulation that felt like being rocked to sleep; certainly I could not wake up.

"Watson?" the voice repeated, more insistently. I tried to open my eyes, then realized: they *were* open.

"Happy Christmas, my dear fellow."

As I struggled to focus, the sounds resolved themselves into the clacking of a train.

"Holmes?"

It was indeed the face of the detective peering anxiously down at me. I looked about, though I found the slightest motion ached throughout my body.

"Where am I?" My voice squeaked like a machine in need of lubricant.

"Aboard the Twentieth Century Limited, bound for Chicago. There we are obliged to change trains again, which I fear will cause you some difficulty."

Again, I strove to understand. "Is it day or night?"

"Would you care to see for yourself?"

I followed his movements with my eyes alone as he raised the wide green shade slowly, giving me time to adjust to the light that streamed through the huge window.

"Not so much!"

Obligingly he tugged down the shade, admitting just enough light to answer my question. The sun appeared to be setting or possibly rising. In my condition it was impossible to say which and I am not sure it made much difference to me.

"What has happened?"

The detective sat carefully on the edge of my berth. As my vision improved, I could see he was relieved to find me able to converse.

"A great deal, Watson. A very great deal. In Washington I was totally enveloped by that wretched fog when I heard the gunshot, sharp as the crack of a whip in the stillness. Unfortunately by that time I had left the bridge, but without the help of the railing was unable to retrace my steps and so was unable to locate you, or indeed much else. You may imagine my consternation. I called your name but you did not answer."

"Von Bork . . ."

"Lie back, there's a good fellow. Yes, Von Bork, as I shall explain."

"He could have killed me as easily as he dispatched poor Mr. Oswald Smith."

The detective shook his head. "Killing you was the furthest thing from his mind. He had already bungled his errand by throwing the unfortunate Smith to his death at the Willard instead of me. Had you died, I should now have been free to leave the capital and pursue my quest. Only with you wounded could he be certain I would stay where I was until sooner or later he succeeded in locating the real me. He knew I would never abandon you. Can you ever forgive me, Watson?" His eyes gleamed with intensity. "God knows I can never forgive myself!"

"For what?" I was still not in possession of all my faculties.

"My selfishness! Dragooning you into this fraught enterprise. Placing you in harm's way."

"You hardly had to do that," I recalled without difficulty. "I was a lonely widower and a surgeon at the end of my usefulness. If you hadn't knocked at my door—"

He went on as though I hadn't spoken. "I told myself I was thinking of England in her hour of peril, but I must own that was a lie"—he held up a hand—"or at any rate a bit of self-deception. I knew only that I needed you. Not that I was, as I once said, lost without my Boswell. No, the truth, my dear fellow, is that I am lost without *you*. You bring out the best in me and the best is what I knew I would need. And this," he sighed, "overcame my scruples and my common sense. Two elderly men on a fool's errand. With this unhappy result."

It is not possible to describe with what joy I heard these words. Holmes guarded his emotions more zealously than the Bank of England its bullion. His simple declaration on this occasion was worth more to me than all that gold.

Seeing and perhaps fearing the expression on my face, the detective rushed on, intent as always never to acknowledge any display of feeling. "It is hard to separate all the strands of this tangled skein. You were found by a copper on his rounds, who applied a tourniquet to your leg—it's the same leg as Maiwand, I'm sorry to tell you.[*]

---

[*]   Site of the dreadful battle during the Second Afghan War (1880) where Watson received his original leg wound.

As you are a British subject, Spring Rice was notified. Thanks to his intercession, you were cared for at the Walter Reed Military Hospital, where the doctors are accustomed to bullet wounds. Fortunately, though painful, they assured Spring Rice your injury was not a serious one. In this instance, the femur was not touched."

"Dear God." So that was the throbbing sensation I was experiencing. The knowledge that the wound was in the same leg where a Jezail bullet had found me all those years ago in Afghanistan prompted a groan unrelated to my injury. A hand on my shoulder prevented my attempt to sit up and the detective continued.

"When I failed to see your copy of the Washington Herald waiting for me two days in succession on my bench in Lafayette Park, I knew for a certainty something untoward had occurred. You are so reliable, Watson."

"Predictable."

"Dependable. You will always sell yourself short. For security's sake you were admitted to Walter Reed under the name Sebastian Undershaft."

"Sebastian Under—what sort of name's that?"

"About as likely as Sherlock Holmes, I'd wager. I was thinking on my feet, my dear fellow, not where I do my best brainwork,* and chose the name of a deceased client—one of my failures, I regret to say, though not without its interesting features. It involved another infernal orangutan—" Seeing my expression, the detective hurried on. "At any rate, Von Bork had succeeded in his aim of keeping me in the capital. It was only a matter of time before he would run me to ground and exact his revenge. You recall his curse at the time

---

\* Smoking a pipe, nestled amid an improvised pile of cushions, like Alice's Caterpillar, seems to have been the detective's preferred locus for brainstorming.

we chloroformed him? *'I'll get level with you, Holmes, if it's the last thing I do!'* or some such braggadocio? It maddened me to think he had succeeded in rendering me a stationary target in Washington when by rights I needed to be in Mexico City. Here, take some tea before the pot grows cold."

On the folding table hinged below the window I spied a gleaming silver service, the escutcheon of the celebrated express emblazoned on the pot and aromatic steam issuing from the spout. I watched dully as Holmes poured the brew into a white china cup which likewise boasted the train's crest.

As he made my tea, I attempted to marshal my thoughts. "But Von Bork was in Brixton! You said as much when you came to me in London that first night—"

"So I did. And so he was." Holmes covered one hand with the other as he squeezed in lemon, remembering how I preferred the drink. "But two months ago, on November fifth, to be precise (Guy Fawkes Night, Watson!), a zeppelin over London dropped an incendiary bomb that landed on the prison. Whether this was deliberate or happenstance, there's no way of knowing, but in the ensuing mayhem several prisoners made their escape, Von Bork among them.* According to M, he boarded a Swedish ship for New York, where Gasche (or Captain von Rintelen, as you please), helpfully directed him to Washington in pursuit of his vengeance."

"Nice of M to send us warning," I lamented with some bitterness as I now beheld a set of crutches stacked beneath the luggage rack.

"Statecraft seems a pragmatic affair. I take it M subscribed to Mycroft's dictum that three can keep a secret only if two are dead."

---

\*       Twelve prisoners escaped Brixton Prison in the confusion on the night in question. All but three were recaptured within days. Von Bork was not among them.

"In other words, we did not need to know."

"On this chessboard, you and I appear to be little more than pawns." The detective hunched his shoulders philosophically and resumed his narrative. "Von Bork was unable to locate me, but as you were daily in plain sight at the Willard, he followed you and executed his plan, firing point-blank. To ensure there could be no misunderstanding, he left your service revolver where you lay—minus the one bullet in your leg—as a sort of calling card."

Holmes produced my weapon with a conjurer's flourish. In my present state it was as if I had never seen it before.

"And so the man could be anywhere by now—in any disguise."

"Not quite." Holmes tapped his left cheek. "The one thing he cannot conceal, even with a beard: that livid saber cut those Heidelbergers with vons before their name insist on etching as though it were a prerequisite."

"His dueling scar?"

"Their badge of honor."

"That's something, I suppose." I could not prevent my dubious inflection.

"The only thing he didn't anticipate was my persuading Spring Rice to spirit you, wound and all, from the hospital onto a train bound for New York. You must promise not to scold when I explain how you were extricated from Walter Reed."

"Holmes—oh, very well." I was too spent to argue.

"Sebastian Undershaft was narcotized with opium, identified as a pneumonia victim, and placed in a coffin bound for burial in the family crypt in Forest Hills."

"In a coffin! Why not embalm me while you were about it?"

My friend favored me with an injured look. "My dear man, we drilled air holes for you beforehand and the medicos at Walter Reed knew how much of the drug to administer to render you inert for eighteen hours. I received you at the Pennsylvania Station and transferred you to Grand Central, where I facilitated your resurrection, and here we are, flying at a veritable seventy miles per hour, though I daresay Von Bork will learn our whereabouts soon enough."

"But why are we going to—did you say Mexico City? I thought Doheny was to be found in Tampico—"

"I was just coming to that. While you were being patched up, I was at loose ends, always in disguise, but wild with impatience as you may surmise. Imagine my stupefaction when, wandering out of habit near Dupont Circle, I was greeted by the sight of a potted geranium flourishing on Mrs. Longworth's balcony."

"Mrs.—"

"Precisely. Not knowing what to make of this, but hoping against hope, I betook myself to Boulder Bridge, site of our original rendezvous, where I was perplexed to find a band concert in progress beneath that elegant nearby gazebo. There were dozens of concertgoers swathed in overcoats and mufflers, enjoying the afternoon winter sunshine and Christmas music performed by a naval ensemble.

"I took my place in a canvas folding chair and listened to the performance. I am not normally an aficionado of band concerts—someone once remarked that military music is to music what military justice is to justice—but that, after all, was not why I had come."

The detective tenderly held up my throbbing head and with difficulty I swallowed some tea. It was amazing how restorative a mere few drops were. My head began to clear almost at once.

"Go on."

First he managed to get some more tea down my throat. "Looking casually about me, I soon spotted Mrs. Longworth. She was seated beside a bored-looking man."

"Bernstorff?"

"Unlikely, in public. Besides, her companion looked nothing like the photograph M showed us of the ambassador, trim in his bathing costume, with two bathing beauties. With his paunch in his astrakhan coat, this prosperous gentleman was a businessman or politician. In Washington, probably both."

"Congressman Longworth."

"Bravo, Watson. You are clearly on the mend. Yes, Delilah's husband. Not Uriah—I'm surely mixing my begats—but Nicholas Longworth in his too-too solid flesh. At all events, catching my eye, Mrs. Longworth made a discreet gesture with her hand, signing me to stay where I was, and sure enough, within five minutes the congressman closed his eyes, as indifferent to cacophonous music as myself, and let his head loll on the top rung of his chair."

"But surely she did not dare speak to you with the possibility of her husband waking?"

"She was cleverer than that, my boy, and had no need to utter a word, only to face me and form words one at a time, like a hesitant teleprinter at the stock exchange."

"You read her lips? Astounding. What did she say?" In my excitement I managed to prop myself up on one elbow.

Holmes doled out the words as he had deciphered them. "He. Telephoned. Yesterday. While. Husband. In. Congress. Ambassador. Ready. To. Blow. His. Brains. Out. Said. Had. Been. Ordered. To. Send. Telegram. Number. One. Five. Eight. To. Ambassador. In. Mexico. City. Called. It. Telegram. From. Hell."

I managed to rub a hand over my face, startled to realize I was badly in want of a shave.

"The ambassador in—?"

"Mrs. Longworth mouthed the name several times but it was not in my lip reader's vocabulary. I fretted that a single error on my part and this whole affair would degenerate into a calamitous game of Chinese Whispers,* but Spring Rice came to my rescue, confirming the German ambassador to Mexico is one Heinrich von Eckardt."

"All these vons . . ."

"I wager your ambitious German doesn't get to be a diplomat without one. My hypothesis is that Doheny in Tampico was merely an obliging relay point or cutout for telegram 158. She repeated the number. Which is why we are bound for Mexico City, where additional funds from Spring Rice are on deposit for us at the Banco Nacional."

"The telegram from hell," I echoed. "You are certain those were her words?" I was unable to stifle a yawn. The benefits of the tea had begun to wear off as quickly as they had appeared.

"Without question. She quite evidently wondered if she had made herself clear because she repeated the phrase until I nodded in acknowledgment, at which point, as if on cue, a crashing chord from the ensemble caused Congressman Longworth to start from his sleep and look about him, blinking in confusion."

The detective peeked under the window shade, revealing darkness outside. Satisfied, he raised it entirely. I could just make out a large body of water glimmering in the black.

"The Hudson River," Holmes explained.

We sat in silence as I tried to absorb all the detective had said. My powers remained under a cloud.

---

\*    The politically incorrect name for the game now known as Telephone, where a message becomes unaccountably distorted as it is whispered from ear to successive ear.

"Did I understand you correctly? Has Count Bernstorff actually forwarded telegram number 158 to Mexico City? The telegram from hell?"

"I was unable to ask, as only one of us could read lips. But extrapolating from his previous conduct I theorize that your German may procrastinate but will ultimately do as he's told. It's the Teutonic mind. Theirs not to reason why, and so forth. Tennyson applied it to the English, but as you know, I am seldom burdened by the same trait. Bernstorff is ardently opposed to the U-boat faction but sooner or later he will obey orders. Whatever this telegram says, it's somehow to do with freeing the U-boats."

My drugged brain tried to make sense of what I was being told pell-mell. There were no U-boats in Mexico. Now overcome with drowsiness, I shook my head in a futile effort to clear it. "And who are you this time?" I managed to croak.

He smiled down at me. "Lionel Undershaft, brother of the deceased. And now, my dear Watson, you're all caught up. I suggest you go back to sleep and I'll wake—" Before he had even finished his sentence I felt my eyes rolling upward in their sockets.

**31 December 1916**. Opium is deceptive in its effects. Hours pass without one being aware of time, thus I remember little of the last few days. I have dreamlike recollections of changing trains in Chicago, sleepwalking on crutches (or was I carried?), but it is now New Year's Eve and we are presently aboard the rather less luxurious Golden State, chugging through the arid American Southwest, bound for Los Angeles, though we will disembark before reaching that terminus. Holmes has explained that we must change trains yet again in Texas.

"Can you manage a short walk to the dining car?" he asked, seeing I was once again conscious. "The gong has sounded for the second sitting." I grunted by way of reply and fumbled for my medical bag when my friend laid a gentle hand on mine. "I know morphine eases the pain, my dear fellow, but this sort of thing is a slippery slope."

He had every reason to know. Our roles were now reversed.[*]
I nodded grudgingly and released my hold on the bag. "Perhaps
you'd best take charge of it, Holmes."

"Capital. Here are your crutches, Watson."

Outside, omnipresent greenery had given way, first to endless
wheat fields and now to unforgiving desert.

It goes without saying that American trains are much larger
than their English counterparts, though it was still a struggle
for me to make my way. In the dining car, minus the Twentieth
Century Limited's nosegay of roses at each table, I stared at the
desolate, tawny landscape, where the only green to be found were
intermittent stalks of cacti.

Holmes, as oblivious to change of scenery as he was to scenery
in general (unless it bore on a case), peered at the menu before
writing his choices on the notepad provided by our Negro steward.

"El Paso, Las Cruces, Rio Grande, Santa Fe, Agua Dulce,
Corpus Cristi—everything in these parts is Spanish," he murmured.

"And so it should be," I informed him. "Did you never hear of
the Alamo?"

Holmes cupped a hand to one ear. He had not.

"All this part of the world—Texas, Arizona, New Mexico, and
most of California besides—was settled by the Spanish. All that
territory was seized and annexed by the United States following
the war with Mexico."

"War with Mexico?"

"In 1848. Holmes!"

---

[*]     Years before, in Vienna, it was Watson who helped wean Holmes from drug
        addiction.

All this came as news to the detective, whose understanding of matters outside his own specialty meant little or nothing to him. "What does it matter if the Earth revolves around the sun or vice versa," he once said to me in the early days or our acquaintance, "so long as it does not affect my work?"*

When our inevitably huge repast was served, Holmes remained lost in thought.

"Holmes?"

"Not a pyramid in sight," he commented, finally reacting to the lunar terrain. "Much less a sandstorm."†

For which I was profoundly grateful. And the so-called Rio Grande, when we reached it, could in no way be compared with the mighty Nile.

The detective remained uninterested by the topography. Overwhelmed by a limitless sky whose expanse crushed the horizon, the Golden State became a mere centipede wriggling its way on the sand beneath the cerulean firmament.

"Holmes, your food is here."

When he finally turned from the window to look at me, his countenance bore a puzzled expression.

"What are you thinking?" I asked.

"I confess I'm not quite sure. It's on the tip of my brain, Watson. Something you said moments ago. Most vexing." With a shrug, as if giving up the matter, he tucked into luncheon with a will. But I knew my friend; if he once got hold of a thought, he would not easily part with it.

---

*      Uttered in their first case together, *A Study in Scarlet.*

†      Holmes refers to the khamsin that almost killed the pair in Egypt, 1911.

**2 January 1917**. Incredibly, the war has entered its fourth year. Laredo, when we reached it at last, I deemed an outpost with little to recommend it. A dusty thoroughfare through the center of the town (if it could charitably be called that, for it boasted only the one street) was devoid of anything that resembled commerce save three or four shops and something called a general store. The wind blew withered plant remains along the avenue of dried mud, which a casual glance told me would be impassable in rain. These mysterious rolling twigs were called tumbleweed by the inhabitants. The faint jaunty tinkling of a piano within what looked like swinging window shutters beckoned visitors beneath a sign identifying the Gold Nugget Saloon. Here and there horses and wagons were tethered to crude posts, submissively awaiting their next labor.

The contrast between trains could not have been greater. Rail travel made a steady declension from the grandeur of the Twentieth Century Limited in New York to the Golden State, emanating from Chicago, and now in Texas to a sorry-looking string of desiccated carriages with flaking paint and markings that bore nothing so aspirational as a name at all. The gauge of the track was narrower heading into Mexico than that on which we had glided from Washington to this remote place.

The only thing attractive to my eye was a string of well-fed horses being herded up a wooden ramp to take their places in a gondola, fenced in by ropes to prevent the handsome animals spilling out in transit.

"The cavalry," Holmes murmured beside me as we listened to a deal of shouted Spanish and rumbling hoofs as preparations for our departure were underway. I followed the detective's jutting forefinger and beheld a company of booted, blue-uniformed troops climbing aboard the car adjacent to that which bore their mounts.

"Why is the United States Army on a train bound for Mexico?" I wondered aloud.

"To kill or capture Pancho Villa," said a tall officer in blue trimmed with gold braid who stood beside us surveying the loading. "Excuse my eavesdropping, gentlemen, but I could scarcely help overhearing your talk. It's a question I have to answer each time a new company arrives to join General Pershing." He shifted his weight and his spurs jingled as he touched a yellow-gloved hand to the broad brim of his hat. "Chauncey Owen, colonel, First Ohio Cavalry."

I had a dim recollection of Villa's name from our nocturnal conversation at Whitehall with M months earlier, before the commencement of our American odyssey.

"... a trifling affair... a Mexican bandit by that name dashed across the border into Columbus, New Mexico, with four hundred men and seized a cache of US weapons stored there."

"You mean they still have not apprehended the rascal?"

Colonel Owen acknowledged as much with a taut smile. "We've been trying for the better part of a year," he said, "and Black Jack's fit to be tied, but the president had no choice. It boils down to Mexico invaded the United States, and he has to respond. Incidentally, they'll be passing out Winchesters or Remingtons to all the male passengers about now. I take it from your looks you gentlemen know how to shoot?"

"What are we to shoot at?" Holmes inquired as we now beheld the weapons being distributed.

"At Pancho Villa, to be sure. It's in this way, gentlemen. We've not been able to corner that bandit, but he or his muchachos do have a record of attacking this train. They can't get close enough in the mountains to do much damage, but it's best to be prepared. You surely saw the notice?"

"I did not," the detective said.

Colonel Owen's scowl betrayed his annoyance. "It's posted in English and Spanish. I'll wager they've torn it down or hidden it again, as it does tend to discourage business. 'Passengers to Mexico on this line are advised they travel at their own risk.'"

I recalled similar warnings in newspapers cautioning passengers proposing to sail aboard the *Lusitania*: "Vessels flying the flag of Great Britain, or of any of her allies, are liable to destruction." It was not a comforting memory.

Holmes's next comment broke in on my thoughts: "You must be familiar with this sort of work, colonel, as I perceive you have spent time similarly occupied in Cuba."

The colonel's eyes widened at this. "Stationed there for the last ten years. How do you come to know that, sir, may I ask?"

Holmes smiled. "Your legs are bowed, indicating lifelong equestrian employment. You are a professional soldier, aged close to fifty,

I should judge, and your lock-jawed speech suggests your New England origins. It is an accent with which I have lately become familiar. Your deep tan is more the humid, tropical shade than what I see produced by this southwestern sun, which is windblown and ruddy. Now where in the tropics might an American cavalry officer of your age and Bostonian background have served? Were you, in younger days, a Rough Rider?"

Colonel Owen grinned and removed his hat, smoothing close-cropped steel-gray hair. "That's mighty impressive, Mr.—"

"Holmes."

"Mr. Holmes. Truth is I was at Daiquiri Beach and San Juan Hill with the former president back in ninety-eight, though of course he wasn't president then. There was a bunch of us from Harvard or North Dakota or wherever, that joined up when Teddy put out the word, though wouldn't you know it, we didn't get to bring any of our horses on that fly-bitten campaign—except Teddy of course. Being Teddy. These days I play nursemaid, ferrying recruits and mounts back and forth on the Águila Azteca."

"Águila—"

"Azteca. The Aztec Eagle, to you gents."

So the ramshackle train did in fact have a name.

"All aboard!"

**4 January 1917.** A fateful day. Seated on frayed red velvet in our private *camarín*, Remington carbines across our laps, we crossed the Rio Grande into Mexico. There followed endless stretches of straight track on brushy plains abutting mesas. Amid chaparral and swirling dust devils, animals stared at us as we passed. At length we wound our way into the craggy Sierra Madres where we were rejoined by Colonel Owen, who either did not know who Holmes was or saw no need to acknowledge it.

As the train twisted and leaned into corkscrew curves, imperceptibly climbing, the agreeable officer proved a most useful source of information. Something of a botanist, he pointed out the omnipresent agave from which the potent, indigenous drinks pulque, tequila, and mescal are brewed.

"I make this trip with fresh troops every twelve weeks and bring back the spent ones, for it's hard work trying to corner those characters. We'll debark when we reach Querétaro and join the general. <u>Once in country,</u> we'll try to get the locals to point us in Villa's direction, though most are unwilling to give us the time of day. Fear, you understand. Mexico more or less fell to pieces after the revolution of 1910, when the dictator Díaz was overthrown. Imagine, after thirty-one years of calling himself president, the rascal fled to Paris! Mind you, Díaz modernized the capital, but since then the government's been more or less a case of revolving doors, or maybe more like musical chairs," he added after a moment's reflection. "Only if the music stops and there's no chair, you're dead. After Díaz, there was Madero, who was killed, then there was Huerta, who suffered a similar fate, and now it's Carranza, for who knows how long? Obregón's breathing down his neck, plus we've got Zapata raising hell in the south and Villa carrying on here in the north. Being president in Mexico seems on a par with fighting on the Western Front. Chances are you won't make it out in one piece. Word is they're writing yet another constitution. God knows how many that makes, but I'm guessing these dagos will never figure out which way is up."

Out of the corner of my eye I saw Holmes stiffen at the casual use of the epithet.

"Yours seems rather a thankless assignment" was all he said.

"Oh, you'd be surprised at the competition to volunteer." Colonel Owen smiled. "You see, gentlemen, once the redskins were subdued on the plains and Cuba was over, there were no chances for a young man to see action, let alone obtain promotion in our tiny peacetime military. So coming down here to chase wily Pancho is not without its appeal."

"That view of the matter had not occurred to me," the detective said, though harking back to my own youthful days in the army, I had an intimation of what the colonel was referring to. War always looks promising until you're fighting one.

"Nowadays the place they test their mettle is college," the colonel was saying.

"College?"

"What you call university. It's on the gridiron today's youth meet their destiny. I'm a proud son of Eli myself, Skull and Bones,* by the way, though I never got to play the game, more's the pity."

He might as well have been speaking Chinese.

"What game? What is the gridiron to which you refer?" I asked.

"Football, gentlemen! A game which has the advantage over war of being completely without rules. Teams are so desperate for opponents, the army has even taught the Indians to play."

"You don't say," murmured Holmes.

"I do!" Owen shook his head at the memory. "And the army lived to regret it. Right before the present European war, it was. The undefeated Carlyle Indians routed Army at West Point. Jim Thorpe!"† he shook his head again at the name, which meant nothing to either of us. "It must have made those redskins feel grand, trouncing the sons of those who had driven them off their land."

Having nothing intelligent nor knowledgeable to say in response to this, a silence fell on our *camarín*. I was suddenly conscious of the heavy rifle on my lap.

---

\*   This is either an indiscreet boast or pure invention on someone's part. If you're really Skull and Bones at Yale, you don't tell people.

†   The famous game took place in 1912. Thorpe, the greatest athlete of all time, faced off against four future generals in the West Point backfield, two of whom included future five-star General Douglas MacArthur and future Supreme Allied Commander (and President) Dwight D. Eisenhower.

"We don't seem to be in a particular hurry to get anywhere," I observed, regarding our leisurely speed.

"We have to go slow through these mountains," the colonel explained. "Too many curves, and the banditos like to pull up the tracks or explode 'em while taking potshots." He shook his head. "But there's no need to worry, gentlemen. They say when the bullet with your name is headed your way, you'll know it's yours by the sound of it."

It was at this moment that shots rang out. I did not identify the distant popping sounds at first, but Colonel Owen knew them for what they were at once.

"There they go, wanting to get their hands on our horses, but they won't succeed! If you'll excuse me. Look for puffs of white and stay low," he advised. "This shouldn't last long."

In this he was correct, but the next few minutes were lively enough. Peering cautiously through our window, we did indeed spy intermittent puffs of white here and there, followed by the distant retorts of the rifles that created them. Bullets like angry wasps buzzed and whanged on the rocks, clanged on our locomotive, and splintered the wood carriages of the Águila Azteca, one shattering a window. Closer rifle shots and shouts came from the carriage in front of ours as the soldiers in Colonel Owen's party returned the bandits' fire.

None of this noise did the precious cargo of cavalry horses any good as the Águila Azteca swayed and threatened to escape the embrace of the curving metals. The frightened animals neighed and slid and stamped as they struggled for purchase on the trembling boards beneath them.

The same uncertain motions of the train made it difficult to steady our carbines as Holmes and I chambered rounds and attempted to shoot at the white puffs of Villa's "muchachos," but I knew our chances of hitting anything at this range were nil. In the event, as we hadn't been provided with much in the way of ammunition, our ability to return fire ended as our cartridges were soon spent. I thought of my recovered service revolver, but it contained only the five bullets Von Bork had mockingly left me, and I could not have hit anything with them at this speed and distance.

Our locomotive began to accelerate, the cars behind it yawing precariously as we rounded a series of tight bends. We could only pray we did not fly off the metals. Any malfunction of train or the track on which we squealed would leave us to the mercy of the muchachos. Something told me they would not be satisfied with horseflesh.

Holmes, rummaging for more carbine cartridges, expressed much the same sentiments. It was then we heard the shriek. I must go!

**8 January 1917**. Ciudad de México. Every afternoon at four, Markus Cronholm, the Swedish consul, makes his way to the Western Union office beside the Plaza Tolsá. In that unexpectedly palatial gallery, adorned with ceiling murals that I fancied might rival those of the Sistine Chapel (telegraph towers and wires are proudly depicted among the seraphs and cupids!), the diplomat threads a forest of pink marble columns topped with caryatids to the North American desk.

*Mexico City's Western Union office*

There, messages from the United States to Mexico City are relayed, first through Texas and then again via Tampico. The Swedish consul could have chosen any time of day for his visits, for the place is staffed by at least fifty telegraphers, clacking away behind chest-high, basalt counters, but he invariably did his business with Señorita Rondón at the North American station and always at four when the offices reopened following the siesta, during which all Mexico shuts down. The siesta, it was explained, was a response to the midday heat.

*Swedish Consul Markus Cronholm*

"What midday heat?" I demanded, for January was distinctly chilly. I saw a great many cars, Rolls-Royces, Model Ts, Pierce-Arrows, and Daimlers, all with their windows shut for warmth. These and various lorries, stacked to toppling with produce, emitted a variety of purrs, honks, and belches, but the natives on the street appeared inured to the cacophony while those behind closed shutters seemingly ignored it while they dozed.

I anticipated presenting ourselves at the British embassy but Holmes surprised me.

"I see nothing to be gained by doing so at present," he said. "Let us remain inconspicuous for as long as possible. I think it likely that sooner or later our presence will be discovered, but prefer not to involve anyone unnecessarily. As it is, I am still Lionel Undershaft and you are—"

"His deceased brother, Sebastian."

"Indubitably."

I was not sure how I felt about this, but consoled myself with the thought that if I didn't exist, I had no reason to concern myself with anything, and in my present state this was perhaps for the best.

The city itself wore a deceptively somnolent aspect. In the countryside, warlords (what else to call them?) savagely vied for hegemony as Colonel Owen described, but in the capital people go about their business and take their siestas, the quiet only occasionally disturbed by distant *rat-tat-tat*s dismissed as car backfires. But I knew the sound for what it was, the snickering enfilade of a Gatling gun, familiar to me from my soldiering days in the Northwest frontier and a noise I hoped never to hear again. The sound made plain that all is not serene in Ciudad de México and was, as well, a grim reminder of lives a world away being cut down like so much chaff.

In the Western Union emporium, amid the din of incessant telegraph clacking, Señorita Rondón, whom I judged not yet thirty, would hand the Swedish consul anywhere from two to thirty dispatches whose teletyped contents she had carefully pasted onto

Western Union forms and afterward sealed with mucilage in yellow envelopes. In addition to those addressed to the American embassy, there were coded messages from Berlin, the latter sent over State Department wires and forwarded by Ambassador Bernstorff in Washington to Ambassador von Eckardt in Mexico City, by permission of the American president with the caveat "that nothing therein is considered inimical to the interests of the United States."

Consul Cronholm then deposited both sets of telegrams into a lime-green dispatch box and, escorted by a German Oberst serving as a bodyguard, the pair marched smartly to the nearby American embassy (technically a mere legation) on Calle Londres, where both American and German messages were duly turned over to Henry Fletcher, the newly appointed American ambassador.

Under the watchful gaze of Consul Cronholm, Ambassador Fletcher would separate telegrams intended for Ambassador von Eckardt and return these to the Swede, who—again accompanied by the Oberst—would stroll from the imposing American legation to its somewhat smaller German counterpart on nearby Calle Dinamarca, where Berlin's telegrams were placed in Ambassador von Eckardt's hands.

These Byzantine maneuvers were dictated by Sweden and the United States' imperative to conduct themselves as befitting impartial players in the "European conflict," albeit neither was anything of the kind. As Holmes and I had learned, everyone in the American government, with the arguable exception of its president, was committed to intervention on the Allied side, while the Swedes, contrary to their public stance, stood firmly in Germany's camp.

Neutral is as neutral does, as Alice Longworth pointed out. At the time, I was inclined to debate this cynical observation; now I am less certain.

Much has happened. In my eagerness to set everything down, I fear I have put several carts before as many horses. We have been ceaselessly occupied since the Águila Azteca wound its way through Popocatépetl and Iztaccíhuatl, the two volcanoes with unpronounceable names that preside over the valley within which the Mexican capital is situated. The valley itself, formerly the seat of the Aztec empire, is curiously elevated over a mile above sea level, initially causing strangers some difficulty. Both Holmes and I had headaches brought on by the altitude and thinner air, though these diminished over time.

Ciudad de México, capital of this uncertain nation, continually riven by civil and international strife, is a perplexing combination of titanic structures and one-story, adobe dwellings (many of the latter daubed in brilliant blues, pinks, and yellows), at once a metropolis and a village. Among the largest structures are the pyramids built by the Aztecs prior to their Spanish subjugation. Though they did not compare with those Holmes and I experienced in Egypt, yet these ceremonial stone piles were remarkable enough, many now topped by monumental, gold-encrusted cathedrals erected by the conquistadors in a determined effort to expunge the old gods.

But there were other outsized structures of a more modern character, most created at the direction of that long-term "president," Porfirio Díaz. These included the Plaza Tolsá, a splendid square the size of a battlefield, with its adjacent rococo telegraph office. On the side opposite, a labyrinthine, gilded post office resembled Versailles with letter boxes. Near the cluster of stately embassies, consulates, and legations, Díaz erected a combined fire and police station, the building more nearly a fortress with turrets and crenelated battlements than a place intended to house servants of public order.

Our arrival in the city had been delayed by the melancholy task of stopping at Querétaro, within sight of the old Spanish aqueduct, to unload the body of Colonel Owen for shipment home to Boston. The unfortunate officer had been shot through the eye by a chance bullet during our encounter with Pancho Villa's muchachos in the Sierra Madres. At the sound of his scream, which could be heard above the fusillade in the forward carriage, I rushed to where he lay sprawled on the floor, gunfire blazing all around us, but saw at once I could do nothing for the poor man, who died in my arms without regaining consciousness. I could not help wondering if he had first heard the sound of the bullet with his name on it, as he assured us was typically the case. I did not understand his earlier reference to "Skull and Bones," but it was certain he would be now.

Understandably shaken, we finally arrived at Estación Colonia in Mexico City, or as the natives term it, Ciudad de México. From the train station, we stopped at the Hotel Geneve, another Díaz extravagance, built to lure businessmen and impress foreign dignitaries, near the Paseo de la Reforma, a broad boulevard intended to compete with the Champs-Élysées. This grand thoroughfare was not the brainchild of the ambitious Díaz but built some years earlier by Maximilian, the French viceroy imposed on the country by Napoleon III in yet another foreign attempt to subjugate the country. In the fashion of the place, Maximilian too was taken out and shot. As I recall, Holmes had once dragged me to a gallery off Pall Mall where I saw a painting of the scene.*

Poor Mexico, doomed to suffer one convulsion after another. Still, it cannot be denied that the resplendent Geneve was more

---

\*     That would be one of Manet's many depictions of the execution.

than welcome after what we had endured. Like the opulent telegraph and post offices and fire station, the hotel was situated in convenient walking distance of the tree-lined embassies.

And near the closely guarded residence of Mexico's current president, Venustiano Carranza.

Telegram 158, Count Bernstorff's telegram from hell, was not yet among the dispatches being circuitously distributed by the "neutral" Swedish consul. I know this because I had been deputized by Holmes to cultivate Señorita Rondón, Cronholm's exclusive contact at the Western Union office. "The fair sex is your department, Watson," the detective reminded me. "Why is it that the Swedish go-between always does his business at four o'clock and only with that particular telegrapher? Is he, for some reason, attracted to her fist?"

Here I must hastily explain that telegraph operators can frequently be identified by the distinctive manner in which each taps out dots and dashes on the telegraph key. This manner of identification is referred to in the profession as a "fist," though why that of Señorita Rondón should command the loyalty of the Swedish consul was bewildering to Sherlock Holmes.

"There are dozens of telegraphers in this room and the queues are invariably shorter than those for the señorita, yet Consul Cronholm will deal with no one else and always at the same hour, even if he is obliged to wait his turn."

This was one of the few occasions when I was able to solve a mystery that had confounded my brilliant friend. We were ensconced amid walnut paneling in the Hotel Geneve's foyer, taking coffee under a colorful stained glass skylight.

"Holmes, surely you have noticed that the darkly splendid señorita is the most prepossessing woman in the establishment.

She is in fact the only telegrapher at the North American desk who merits such a description. The rest are either male or matronly. As Consul Cronholm is receiving, not sending, telegrams, her fist is not in question. It is not the lady's fist but her face and figure that commands the consul's devotion and punctuality. She comes on duty at four and leaves at midnight. The long queues for her services are surely the result of her wondrous appearance and, it must be said, her flirtatious manner."

The detective stared at me as I divulged this intelligence, before his features became wreathed in smiles.

"Excellent, Watson. You have seen where I merely observed. And the fact that Consul Cronholm's telegraphic infatuation is monogamous may serve to simplify matters. What else have you learned?"

He signaled the waiter for more of the wonderfully sweetened coffee.

Proud of my accomplishments, I could not wait to regale him. "There is a bodega on Calle República de Chile, behind the telegraph mansion, where the señorita passes the time during the siesta when others are literally napping. The señorita has a fondness for tequila, no doubt hoping to steel herself before eight hours of telegraph clatter. The office is no place for anyone subject to migraines. Even with headphones to help distinguish her own incoming messages, which she first transcribes in pencil before typing them into the teletype, she likens the ambient noise to the incessant clicking of castanets. Telegraphers then paste the extruded teletype tapes onto the yellow telegram forms that messengers afterward bicycle to their local destinations. And, to answer your next question, the penciled transcripts are destroyed. Holmes, are you aware that mescal bottles contain a dead worm?"

"The things we do for England," the detective murmured. "Go on, my dear fellow."

"A fondness for tequila," I repeated, "and she is pleasantly intrigued by older Englishmen who walk with the aid of a stick and pay for drinks." I tried not to convey my satisfaction with this tidbit but was unable to conceal it entirely. "In these parts it is not unusual for young women to marry much older men."*

The detective offered a thin smile. "Walking stick or not, Watson, let us attempt to navigate a straight line. Anything else?"

I shifted uncomfortably in my chair. "I hesitate to say."

"He who hesitates is lost."

In truth my apprehensions were so vague that I was reluctant to communicate them, but my friend's silence demanded I fill it. I fortified myself with a sip of coffee.

"I have the sense that I am being followed."

He raised his gray eyes from his coffee cup to look at me. "What, you too?"

"It is just a feeling." I had felt sheepish for having mentioned it, but the detective's sharp rejoinder made me feel less so.

"A most curious sensation, is it not?" he commented, stirring his coffee with a desultory spoon. "A kind of sixth sense that triggers alarm bells in the brain."

"Exactly! Have you any sense of who—" I interrupted myself with a snap of my fingers. "Von Bork!"

"It's not beyond the realm of possibility. Lower your voice, old man."

"But can the Kaiser be so determined to—"

---

\*    In his Parisian exile, eighty-year-old ex-president Díaz married the seventeen-year-old Carmen Romero Rubio.

He shook his head. "The Kaiser has neither the leisure, the motive, nor, one suspects, the resources to attempt my assassination.\* No, Watson, we may be sure if it is Von Bork, it is entirely personal. At least you will not be his target this time."

This was cold comfort. "But if it isn't Von Bork—"

"Therein lies the difficulty. This is a coin with many sides. If we are being followed, it is so artfully done that it might as well be me that was doing it."†

"Or perhaps a team, if we are both being watched."

"Perhaps." But he did not sound like a man convinced. Our replenished coffee arrived and he broke off while it was poured. "I confess I am still thinking about what you said on the train," he murmured when our waiter had departed.

"On which train?" We had taken so many.

"The Golden State, crossing Texas. Most irritating."

"Irritating?" I was distressed to think that a chance remark of mine had annoyed him. "What was it I said?"

The detective frowned. "That's it just it, my boy. I can't for the life of me recall. I feel like a horse with a burr under its saddle, the irritant maddeningly out of reach. And yet at the time, I understood what you said as being of tantalizing significance. I am aging, Watson, and my powers are not what they were."

"Nonsense."

---

\*    Such long-distance hits persist to this day. Within twenty years, Leon Trotsky would be stabbed to death with an ice pick on Stalin's orders within walking distance of where Holmes and Watson drank their coffee. Putin's agents are successful poisoners in Europe. And recently, in the United States, Salman Rushdie barely escaped the Ayatollah Khomeini's thirty-three-year-old fatwa with his life.

†    Holmes boasts of his abilities in this department in *The Adventure of the Devil's Foot*.

He acted as though he had not heard me. "I know I'm seeing a picture, but I seem unable to connect the dots."

"Dots?"

He made an impatient gesture, expecting me to understand his reference. "Surely you are familiar with those children's puzzles sold at Hamleys that form an image when you draw lines from one number to the next."

"I was never much good at those things."

"Neither am I, of late." He smiled sadly. "However, let us not dwell on my failings. What of telegram 158?"

I breathed an inward sigh of relief, glad to have disposed of the awkward topic, though I knew it was likely to be resurrected. From the time he had limped across my threshold months ago in Pimlico, pummeled by the Black and Tans, Holmes had bemoaned his age.

"Señorita Rondón assures me a German telegram numbered 158 has not arrived. I presented myself in the bodega in the character of a Western Union representative, anticipating ciphered instructions from Count Bernstorff in Washington. I waited to pose my question until the señorita had downed several glasses of tequila. Mildly intoxicated, she insisted no such numbered communication had been received, assuring me it would have been logged in the North American receipt ledger had it been. The señorita boasts one of those curious brains that have no difficulty in remembering numbers."

"That is something," Holmes said.

"Something perhaps, but disliking the sound of her slurred replies, she ordered a double *café negro* before leaving to begin her shift. Her suspicions would doubtless have been aroused had I pursued the matter further."

Aware that the acoustics in the foyer did not favor private conversation, the detective waited to reply until we had signed for our drinks and were walking outdoors.

"You did well not to press her, Watson. But what about copies? Does the office retain carbons of the telexes?"

Attired in the nondescript cosmopolitan dress of commercial travelers, we were now strolling on the Paseo de la Reforma.

"They do not. There are simply too many incoming messages to index and file. Copies are retained at their point of origin and nowhere else. In this case, Berlin."

He said nothing, but it was clear the news did not surprise him. I was, I confess, waiting for some additional words of praise for my industry and cunning, but the detective walked beside me, lost in thought. Finally I could brook his silence no longer.

"And what, may I ask, have you been doing while I have been scalding my insides with tequila?"

"Preparing the way."

"I beg your pardon?"

The detective chuckled in his soundless fashion. "Forgive me. I realize that sounds faintly biblical," he said. "Firstly, I paid a call on American Ambassador Fletcher and revealed my identity."

"Was that wise?"

"As the Americans are in first possession of the telegrams, I judged it necessary."

This made sense to me. "And then?"

"I conveyed the respects of His Majesty's government and of Spring Rice in particular."

"Ambassador Fletcher is acquainted with Spring Rice?"

Before he could reply several loud shots rang out in quick succession, close enough that we reflexively dived to the pavement, my walking stick flying from my hand. From my street-level vantage I was surprised to see varieties of footwear, none breaking stride in response to the gunfire.

"Watson? It's nothing, Watson, a car backfire."

Crouched on the curb, we regarded one another with doleful expressions. This was the world we now inhabited. Having recently been shot, I remained on the pavement, unable to move, my heart exploding in my chest.

Not a Gatling, I told myself several times; a Mercedes coupé was my only foe.

The detective recovered his equanimity before I did. Brushing his knees as he stood, he extended a hand and helped me to my feet, retrieving then silently handing me back my stick. Choosing to ignore the incident, we fell into step once more, but I was too flummoxed to remember what we were discussing.

"Ambassador Fletcher and Spring Rice," he reminded me. "The diplomatic world turns out to be a small one. Many representatives whose countries are at odds nonetheless contract personal friendships. In this instance, both men are intimates of former President Roosevelt."

"Mrs. Longworth's father." I made a desperate effort to concentrate.

"Just so. In the name of Anglo-American amity and of the common language and history that binds us, I was hoping to learn the contents of telegrams sent for his dispersal from the German embassy in Washington."

"Then surely, in light of these sentiments—"

"I met with a polite rebuff. The ambassador has been instructed by the current occupant of the White House not to interfere with German telegraph traffic and is reluctantly obeying. I was unable to persuade him even to delay delivery of any German telegrams, which might have given us time to unseal and duplicate their contents. According to the ambassador, the Swedish consul stands before him the whole time, waiting to carry the Kaiser's correspondence around the corner to the German legation."

As the detective offered no further comment, we walked on in silence. I tried to slow my breathing and believe in the benign landscape before me, but it was difficult. Whether here, ambushed in the Sierra Madres, poisoned aboard the *Norlina*, or shot on the mist-laden Chain Bridge over the Potomac, I had simply seen too much. But I knew from long experience that Holmes was undeterred by anything that had happened. He was in the process of making other plans. At length he spoke again.

"If there are no copies to filch at Western Union from Señorita Rondón at the North American desk when and if telegram 158 should arrive, and if Ambassador Fletcher will not let us see or copy that message, it will be necessary to borrow it from the German legation after Consul Cronholm has delivered it."

"Borrow it?"

"And return it before its absence is remarked."

"And how do you propose to do that?"

"With difficulty, I fear. Once received, the telegram will be decoded immediately since it will doubtless be sent in the 13040 code, designated urgent and most secret."

"You are confident 13040 is the code that will be used?"

"Count Bernstorff described 158 to Mrs. Longworth as the telegram from hell. That would seem to imply communication of a sensational character, demanding instant attention." He sniffed. "But decoded or not, it is imperative we lay hands on it."

"And how do you propose to do that?" I demanded, my eyes still roving restlessly in anticipation of I knew not what. Another car backfire? Or a possibly a gunshot?

"It is a stratagem with which I daresay you are familiar, my dear fellow. Like yourself, I have been enjoying intercourse with a woman."

"Holmes!"

The detective laughed silently once more. "Talk, Watson. With señora Emilia Vasca, a stout widow in her sixties. She took ours to be a chance encounter, whereas in reality I followed her from the German legation, where she is one of the charwomen. I have not your gifts as a jolly wooer, Watson. In order to make the señora's acquaintance, I was obliged to join the Communist Party of Mexico."

"What?" I was not sure I had heard correctly.

"Yes! So you see, Watson," the detective added with some satisfaction before I could expostulate, "I am a political naïf no longer."

"The Communist Party of Mexico? Holmes, what can you possibly be thinking?"

"I have been thinking of access to the German legation, and Señora Vasca will be my passe-partout. At her invitation, I have become a founding member of the newly formed Mexican Communist Party.* Our meetings are held in the rear of a smoke-filled cantina on Calle Puebla. There, amid stacked crates of bottles, twenty or so men and women of varying social positions are harangued by a series of orators, some local, others imported, regarding the class struggle and the oppression of the Church. Most spoke Spanish, others in fiery German or Russian, and occasionally a phrase or

---

\*     Founded January 1917. Holmes was in at the start.

two in English crept in. 'The masses,' 'dialectical materialism,' and so forth. Dropping my *h*'s, I arranged myself as a disaffected Englishman eager to partake in the overthrow of the state while exchanging meaningful looks with the señora. Here is my copy of *Das Kapital.*" He produced what looked like a doorstop. "It is in Spanish, which fortunately I am unable to read, though I suspect it would make no more sense to my poor brain in English."

"The things we do for England," I murmured.

"Indeed. As it turns out, it isn't love that makes the world go round. It's the triumph of the proletariat."

"And the señora is prepared to enlist in the Allied cause?"

"Far from it! 'Compañero* Undershaft,' she explained to me in haphazard English, 'you do not comprehend. Germany or England? It makes no difference! We Communists view the entire war as a capitalist folly, fought by and at the expense of the workers who are dying for the benefit of plutocrats!'"

"Then why do you imagine Señora—"

"Vasca would be willing to help achieve my goal? An excellent question, Watson. The answer again comes down to the class struggle. From the disgruntled señora I learned the cleaning staff at the German legation is treated with condescension bordering on contempt."

"That is the first thing you've said that does not surprise me."

"'We are viewed as peons and paid accordingly. We are invisible to them' is the señora's complaint and the motive for her cooperation."

"Politics makes strange bedfellows," I observed.

Holmes grunted, acknowledging my point. "As the señora describes it, security at her workplace is surprisingly lax."

---

*      Comrade.

"I should not have expected that from the Germans."

"I confess I was surprised at first, but on reflection less so. Mexico is a world away from the war, and the capital—for those who can afford it—encourages indolence. Señora Vasca longs for the revolution and, prompted by my willingness to strike a blow for the lumpenprolotteariat, was happy to describe the legation, bin by rubbish bin. With a little prodding from the Good Book"—with an effort, he flourished the weighty edition of *Das Kapital*—"Compañera Vasca was induced to provide a rough sketch of the premises. Telegrams, she assures me, are kept in a safe in the ambassador's office at the back of the building on the first floor."

"A safe. That complicates matters."

"So I should have thought. But it turns out that at two, the safe is typically left open while the ambassador takes dinner at his desk in the next room. At that time, decadent capitalist that he is, he invariably entertains a certain Señora Gonzáles."

"Ah."

"Yes, your German siesta may vary slightly from the local practice."

"Or perhaps it doesn't." I failed to suppress a smirk. Holmes's severe expression caused me to press on. "And assuming you manage to lay hands on the telegram?"

He pointed across the wide boulevard where we stood to a photographic studio. "Señor Esquivel specializes in baptisms, first communions, and weddings, but is prepared to photograph what I bring him at short notice without asking questions. The images will take twenty-four hours to develop and dry."

It was no accident the detective had chosen to walk in this direction.

With hands that were still unsteady I pondered his news as I tried and failed to light a cigarette. Cupping his hands around the match, the detective completed the task and I nodded awkward thanks.

"Twenty-four hours." I forced myself to think. "But you cannot attempt to return the original 158 until we are sure Señor Esquivel has photographed a legible copy. By that time its absence may have been noticed and whoever is following us may have done his work."

The detective nodded, conceding my reasoning. "Two unappetizing possibilities, and if either comes to pass, all this"—he waved a hand to indicate our journey from England through the United States and down to Mexico—"will have been for naught. The wait indeed I had not counted upon, but there's nothing for it. We must risk retaining the original until we have possession of a perfect facsimile. Our photographer insists on payment in dollars and the price of Señor Esquivel's incuriosity is not cheap."

The detective removed his hat and rubbed the back of his head in vigorous agitation before kneeling to tie his shoe and looking surreptitiously behind us as he did so. Once again we both sensed we were being followed. The hairs on the back of my neck prickled with the knowledge, but when I turned there was nothing untoward to be seen.

I now became aware of a faint tremor in my right hand. The sight of my vibrating fingers filled me with astonished revulsion and I flexed them, hoping to make them still. Were my nerves now completely shattered? Could I ever again wield a scalpel? To that question I already knew the answer.

The detective continued, oblivious to my situation or tactfully determined to give me more time to recover from my shock.

"I have been obliged to withdraw more funds from the Banco Nacional to satisfy Señor Esquivel, but before you scold I remind you we are playing for the very highest stakes and there's many a slip 'twixt the cup and the lip. Nothing less than the outcome of the war itself may depend upon our success."

I confess that when Holmes expressed himself in these stark terms I was brought up short, my trembling hand forgotten for the moment. We had been so long chasing this cursed message that I had quite lost sight of what its contents might mean.

"Holmes, what if 158 never arrives? What if Count Bernstorff refuses to forward it? We know he is appalled by the contents. The telegram from hell."

The detective's brow contracted in thought before brightening. "He must forward it, Watson. If there is no acknowledgment of its safe receipt, the Wilhelmstrasse will recall him and the count will find the water in Berlin so warm it will make the spa at Baden-Baden seem like an ice bath." He shook his head, like a cur shaking off rain, as if to reassure himself of his reasoning. "He may procrastinate. No doubt he has, hoping for some development that may delay or divert the necessity of obeying orders, but in the end, he will do as instructed. And we must be prepared for that eventuality. Have you another cigarette? I seem to be out."

I gave him one and waited while he lit it, trying to look casually about me as I struggled to understand the realities that confronted us. "Holmes, assuming the telegram does arrive and assuming we succeed in having it photographed, why trouble to return the original?"

He shook out his match. "A reasonable question, Watson. But whether or not the message has been decoded, its disappearance, if discovered, may set off alarums and excursions we cannot imagine.

I think it preferable to slip it back inside the embassy as soon as possible and hope Ambassador von Eckardt proves none the wiser."

"That seems a lot to hope for."

"I know."

I made a mental note to carry my revolver with me from now on.

**11 January 1917.** Things have moved much faster than expected. My tremor had mercifully subsided, at which time a messenger arrived with a sealed note for Lionel Undershaft at the Hotel Geneve: "*Pardon the late notice,*" was scrawled on stiff paper with the American eagle embossed on the embassy letterhead, "*but you are both urged to attend a banquet this evening at your hotel in honor of the United Fruit delegation. Do come—you will find it worth your while. F.*"

"What possible reason could Ambassador Fletcher have for extending such an invitation?" I wondered as I attempted to smooth the wrinkles from my dinner dress. "United Fruit, whatever it is, can be nothing to us."

"Only one reason, I am sure," my companion returned, likewise attempting to make himself presentable. "Otherwise he would not have proffered it." Holmes tried to keep the excitement out of his voice but I had no difficulty discerning it.

The supper in question was bountiful beyond reason, the more so when I considered the countless examples of want I had seen in other parts of the city. The company was entirely masculine, numbering the Swedish and German ambassadors among the local diplomatic corps, seated like so many piano keys in serried ranks of black and white, amid glittering chandeliers and gleaming cutlery at an endless white tablecloth. Mestizo servants, attired in eighteenth-century livery and powdered periwigs, hovered behind each diner, ready to replenish our flutes with more champagne—or possibly overhear our talk.

Many fulsome toasts of Veuve Clicquot were proposed by hosts and guests in an assortment of languages that included neither French nor English. Representatives of neither country were in evidence (though American was spoken by representatives of the United Fruit and General Electric companies).

Photographers with flash powders commemorated the event. Some of the more artful took pictures of the brilliant assembly as we were reflected overhead in a clear glass skylight that stretched the length of the table.

There was some confusion at the commencement of the meal requiring the rearrangement of place cards, resulting finally in our being seated to the right of Ambassador Fletcher.

"Sorry for the kerfuffle," the American said in a low voice as we drew up our chairs, "but it was important that we speak." I had never before beheld a man with features so commonplace as those of Henry Fletcher. There was nothing in his pale blue eyes (behind a pince-nez), his undistinguished nose, forgettable mouth, run-of-the-mill mustache, or mournful expression that was in any way memorable. Had I been under oath and asked to describe the man, I should have been at a loss. His bland features were topped with white hair cut close to his head, all the white-ness blurring into a totality of white. He seemed a man designed to be overlooked, though I would shortly learn this was not the case. It is a mistake to judge a book by its cover.

"It might surprise you to learn," murmured Holmes at my elbow, "that the gentleman you clearly consider unworthy of your attention was another of Theodore Roosevelt's Rough Riders in Cuba and also spent a good deal of time in China, as the tattoo above his right wrist indicates. The design and color of that pink-and-blue fish is unique to the tattoo artists of Peiping."*

"And how do you know him for a Rough Rider?"

"That was easily deduced from several photographs of San Juan Hill when I visited his office. He is understandably proud of his association with the former president."

*Henry Fletcher, US ambassador to Mexico*

---

*     Holmes previously remarked on this tattoo in *The Adventure of the Red-Headed League*.

The detective turned to the ambassador. "I take it telegram 158 has arrived," Holmes said in a low voice as he spooned caviar onto a water cracker.

"It has." The ambassador briefly covered his mouth with a starched napkin. "It was submitted to me among others from Count Bernstorff for distribution by Consul Cronholm. I was, as per the usual rigmarole, obliged to pass it back to him for delivery to Ambassador von Eckardt." Here Fletcher cast a sidelong glance at the red-faced ambassador, seated across the table, three guests to our left. As we followed his look, the Kaiser's man—my first sight of the enemy—emitted a bark of laughter followed by a harsh "*Jawohl!*"

*Von Eckardt, German ambassador to Mexico*

Holmes, who had been in the act of squeezing a lemon wedge onto his glistening caviar, casually reached for his champagne instead. "I was under the impression that you were bound not to let us interfere with the president's instructions regarding German correspondence."

"I have not interfered in any way," Fletcher said, smiling and clearly pleased with himself. "I placed 158 back into Consul Cronholm's hands with the rest of Ambassador von Eckardt's correspondence, but I received no instructions that forbade my notifying you of its arrival."

Indeed, appearances can be deceiving. The ambassador, notwithstanding his undistinguished exterior, had displayed ingenuity and initiative for which I would not have given him credit.

Satisfied that the German who sported the requisite saber slice across one ruddy cheek was chatting animatedly with United Fruit, Holmes helped himself to the caviar. I found myself wondering how those vons ever found enough duels to satisfy their essential facial mutilations, or had some resorted to doing it to themselves, an exaggerated form of a shaving cut?

"Can you make out what he is saying?" I muttered.

"The gentleman is partially turned away and my German is somewhat rusty," the detective said, "but it amounts to a hearty insistence that Germany will soon be victorious." Holmes now turned to face Fletcher with an earnest expression. "I—and all those Dr. Watson and I presently represent—cannot begin to thank you, Mr. Ambassador."

"What will you do?" Fletcher asked.

"What I was sent to do," the detective replied. The American was about to say more but Holmes forestalled any questions with an upraised palm. "In view of your news, we must now take our leave, as we have much to prepare."

"Holmes," I protested, "if we leave now it will be most conspicuous."

"In which case it may be desirable to become more so. Might I trouble you for the salt, doctor?"

Without giving his request any thought, I handed it to him and he sprinkled his caviar with it. I wondered at this as caviar is redolent of salt to begin with.

Holmes took a bite and smiled with a gourmand's appreciation before his expression underwent a terrific transformation. He stood abruptly, twisting his head and knocking over his chair in the process. Clawing at his collar, he tore open his cravat and clutched his throat, gasping for breath, his normally pale features suffused a dusky red. As banqueters and servants reacted with astonishment, I managed to catch him as he collapsed.

"Will you make our apologies to United Fruit?"

Confusion reigned for several moments as hotel staff were summoned and Holmes—or Lionel Undershaft, as his passport proclaimed him—now lifeless, was borne from the room on a stretcher. His recovery outside, it is scarcely necessary to add, was miraculous. Time had not diminished the detective's histrionic gifts.

**19 January 1917.** It was slightly after two in the afternoon when black smoke was first detected emanating from a second-story window of the German legation. In short order, the word "Fire!" was yelled by several voices, mainly, as I could make out, in German, but I did detect several, "*Fuego!*"s as well. Toward the rear of the building the sound of shattering glass told of another window smashed.

The inevitable passersby halted to witness the hullabaloo as embassy personnel streamed from the smoke-filled place, many still with napkins around their necks, caught amid their midday meal.

Before they could be seen, the clanging of bells was heard as teams of horses erupted from the fortresslike firehouse on Calle Revillagigedo, dragging four wagonloads of men, hoses, water pumps, and long, unwieldy ladders to the burning site. Hot on their heels, several dozen police followed, boots slapping the pavement like a round of sustained applause. Without waiting for the fire wagons to stop, the combatants leapt to the street, shouting instructions to colleagues and onlookers as they charged the conflagration.

I waited in an agony of suspense, as close as I could get to the embassy, for a police cordon was now thrown up. Could the detective's bold gambit succeed? After what seemed an eternity, the smoke began to disperse through open or broken windows and voices within sounded less clamorous. Soon enough the firefighters themselves trooped out, coiling their hoses, having easily subdued the flames.

"Where there's smoke there's not always fire," commented a bystander.

"Lot of fuss over nothing," a familiar English voice remarked as a tall fireman brushed past me on his way back to his wagon.

I thrust the precious yellow page Holmes had passed me into my breast pocket and sauntered off to Avenida Reforma, where my arrival was expected.

A flight of narrow stairs led me up to the photographic studio of Alfonso Esquivel; where a HABLA INGLÉS sign was displayed in the window on the street below. On the door was presently affixed another sign which read CERRADO, ensuring we would not be disturbed.

Señor Esquivel, less than five feet in height, greeted me in voluble Spanish. English was not in fact spoken in his establishment.

After tactfully admiring wedding and christening photographs that adorned every wall of the señor's studio, I watched as the photographer affixed the crumpled paper Holmes had given me onto a large easel, carefully smoothing the four corners taut as if he were stretching a Renaissance masterpiece.

Now that I finally had the leisure to examine it, 158's appearance proved a disappointment. I don't know what I was expecting, but when all was said and done, it appeared an ordinary telegram, any number of which are sent daily around the world. ARRIVED SAFE AND SOUND. STOP. NEVILLE. HAPPY BIRTHDAY COUSIN MARMADUKE. STOP. SEND MONEY AT ONCE C/O POSTE RESTANTE. STOP. ALL IS FORGIVEN STOP. UNCLE CLOVIS DEAD. STOP.

And so on. Even telegrams in code were not uncommon. Businesses employed them all the time.

With exasperating deliberation the little man wrestled with his oversized Korona portrait camera, which threatened, as he staggered beneath its weight (his legs tangled among those of its tripod), to topple them both to the floor. I would have found his efforts comic had I not been so intent on accomplishing my part of the task. The photographer finally managed to swivel the device to face the easel, endlessly lengthening then shortening the legs of the tripod in an apparent effort to level the image. Still not satisfied, he began twisting the lens of the old-fashioned contraption to adjust the focal plane. It occurred to me matters would be simplified if he moved the easel rather than the camera, but I hesitated to interfere; he was, after all, the photographer and I had no wish to distract or, worse, annoy him.

Pointing to the flattened paper, Señor Esquivel raised an inquiry that required no translation.

"Never mind what it is," I answered with some asperity. "Just take a clear picture of it."

I endured more maddening preliminaries before I understood the photographer was procrastinating. Holmes had given him a down payment but he was awaiting the second tranche before taking an actual photograph. He would doubtless insist on the last third of his commission before developing and giving us the finished pictures.

Where was the detective?

With nothing better to do than consult my watch and revisit pictures of smiling wedding couples while awaiting his appearance (What was taking so long? Had something gone wrong?), I stared once more at the telegram. It was hard to imagine that this yellow rectangle had already disrupted so many lives, let alone consider the possibility that millions more might depend on what it said.

Some of the page was perfectly legible. At the top the words WESTERN UNION TELEGRAM were there for all to read in a plain, large font. Underneath was handwritten the number *158*. Below that, in print once more, the words GERMAN LEGATION MEXICO CITY. To the right, in smaller typeface, I could make out VIA GALVESTON and the date. At the bottom it said simply BERNSTORFF and beneath that, *Charge German Embassy*, without the benefit of an accent above the *e* in *Charge*. To the left of BERNSTORFF was a faint watermark stamp with the sole word INSPECTED, indicating receipt of the telegram by the Mexico City office of Western Union. In between the top and bottom of the message I counted seventeen lines of numbers, grouped in five-digit clusters with spaces in between. What could these groups of numbers mean? And would we ever learn?

With a sinking heart I became aware that my tremor had returned.

Where was Sherlock Holmes?

As if in answer, we heard rapid footfalls on the stairs and shortly Holmes appeared, out of breath, no longer in the uniform of a Mexican fireman.

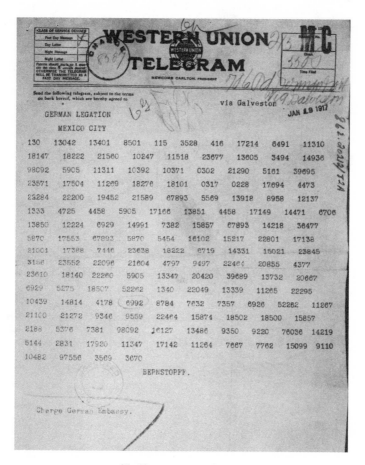

*The Zimmermann telegram*

"*Siento mucho haberte hecho esperar, señor,*" he began, pressing another fistful of dollars into the photographer's hand. Placated, the little man pocketed the money without comment and immediately began photographing the telegram.

"What took you so long?" I demanded. "I was beginning to worry."

The detective shook his head with amusement. "Someone once recommended a general to Napoleon. He insisted the man was an excellent general. 'I know he's excellent,' Napoleon replied, 'but is he lucky?'"

We were back to that mysterious commodity once more. The detective's words popped into my mind as if he had uttered them yesterday.

*"What is luck, really, save a name we give to something that cannot be defined?"*

"And were we lucky?" My tone was querulous by this point.

"By the skin of our teeth, Watson, by the skin of our teeth. What a comedy of errors, but in the end it played in our favor."

"Can you speak more plainly?" Behind us, Señor Esquivel swapped photographic plates in his camera.

"I will try. It began with bad luck, an unforeseen confusion between what is considered the first floor in the Western hemisphere and what such a term designates in Europe."

"I'm not sure I—"

"Señora Vasca told me the safe where the telegrams are kept was on the first floor. I took her to mean what we in England would call floor number one, that is, one flight up from the ground floor. But in Mexico, as in the United States, number one is the ground floor itself, or what they call the foyer or lobby. When I searched upstairs, dragging my fire hose, there was no safe, let alone had it been left ajar."

"Dear God."

"I stood in a frozen panic, Watson. The fire Señora Vasca had helpfully set in a supply closet dustbin would soon be located and extinguished. I was obliged to start another small blaze—a grease fire in the *cocina*—in order to prolong the necessary chaos until I realized my mistake and leaped down a flight to reach my goal, nearly snapping an ankle in the process. Of course, the moment the fire was detected, Ambassador von Eckardt's first instinct, as I knew it must be, would be to slam shut the door of the safe in the room next to his office."*

"But if you were on the wrong floor—"

"So I was. By rights without question I should have been too late. But, as it happens, there was good luck: the ambassador was delayed by a wardrobe malfunction."

"A wardrobe—"

"Ambassador von Eckardt was, you will recall, entertaining a certain Señora Gonzáles at the time, and was obliged to dress before he could move. The señora, shrieking, was in similar straits and the ambassador was obliged to be of assistance. By the time they were decent, the firemen had arrived and one of them whisked von Eckardt to safety, ignoring his protests as he yelled his head off. I can no longer perform such hijinks at my age," the detective concluded, still out of breath. But his ruddy complexion as he watched Señor Esquivel photographing the precious telegram told me my friend had enjoyed every minute.

"And Señora Gonzáles?"

As if the woman's life were an afterthought, it took him a moment to remember. "Oh, hefted to safety by another fireman, to be sure. There was hardly any real danger, you know."

As the now amiable Esquivel uncovered the lens, the detective joined me in contemplating the telegram Count Bernstorff had reluctantly forwarded to his Mexican counterpart. We scrutinized that enigmatic paper as if it bore the cryptic smile of the Mona Lisa.

---

\* Sometimes the old ways are best. Years earlier, Holmes employed more or less this same ruse to procure a precious photograph in *A Scandal in Bohemia*.

"One assumes Ambassador von Eckardt has the key that enables him to make sense of all these numbers," I said. "That being the case, it wouldn't take that long to decode."

"If he has not done so already, to be sure. But once decoded, the German plaintext must be translated into Spanish."

"Spanish?"

"Think, my dear fellow. The German embassy in Mexico City is a diplomatic backwater, not worth ranking above a legation. What could be here worth a German killing or dying for? Nothing that would affect the outcome in Europe, I wager. Ergo, this telegram is intended for a Mexican. Once decoded and rendered into Spanish, it will be von Eckardt's task to deliver it."

"How could a telegram from Germany intended for a Mexican affect the war?"

"Which Mexican, Watson? Pancho Villa? Emiliano Zapata? Obregón? It might make all the difference."

"None of this makes any sense to me."

The detective shrugged. "Formerly we had too much, presently there is not enough data. We have not the benefit of being natives in the know."

I tried not to look at my hand and hoped the detective would not notice. "Well, we know the telegram was sent by Foreign Minister Zimmermann."

"Who is desperate to release his U-boats . . ."

"None of which are near Mexico."

"True. But the late Roger Casement insists there is a plan to prevent America's entering the war, when Germany's U-boats are ordered into action."

I remembered Holmes in my surgery, quoting the doomed man—

*"Twelve weeks of unrestricted U-boat warfare in the North Atlantic, sinking any and all shipping, is all it will take to starve England into surrender."*

Señor Esquivel, still murmuring in his own tongue, was now taking the exposed photographic plates into his darkroom. I turned to face Holmes.

"What are we to do with the telegram, once Señor Esquivel has given us our copies?"

The detective drew me further from the darkroom.

"We must be discreet, my dear fellow."

"Why? We are not conversing in Spanish."

"But can we be sure the man does not understand English? The sign in his window claims he does."

This possibility had not occurred to me. We descended out of earshot to the darkened stairway below the atelier.

"First, as we have discussed," Holmes began, "the original must be plausibly returned to the embassy—"

"I take it Señora Vasca will be amenable to helping you accomplish this?"

"As long as she is persuaded that doing so will somehow advance the class struggle."

"And then?"

"And then we will revisit the offices of Western Union and wire the contents of our copy, number by number, to M in Whitehall."

"Of course."

"Being careful not to employ the person or fist of your charming Señorita Rondón. As I recall, you described the woman as having a good brain for remembering numbers. It would not help should she recognize these and raise any sort of alarm."

"A sensible precaution, I'd've thought."

"Very good, Watson. As Señorita Rondón begins her shift at four, we must send our message home beforehand."

"And M will be able to break the cipher?"

"That's the idea," the detective said dryly. "Though as it happens, Whitehall is doubtless at work on it already."

"I beg your pardon?" I could not have heard him correctly.

"Do you not further recall M telling us that night in Whitehall that His Majesty's government is routinely intercepting American cable traffic from London to Washington? If number 158 from Berlin was bundled through London for the German embassy in Washington on State Department cables, it is likely Admiral Hall had it in his clutches before Count Bernstorff."

"But Holmes—"

He held up a hand. "The count, as we also know, dithered with his conscience before sending number 158 on to Mexico City, but if I'm correct, Blinker Hall was puzzling over these numbers before Count Bernstorff even made up his mind to obey orders."

"You knew this? All this time?"

"I hate to rub it in, old man, but so did you. We were both in M's office."

I could not believe my ears. Or my memory, but the spymaster's words now flooded back—

*"We routinely intercept telegraphic communications between the American ambassador in London and his superiors in Washington. The Americans use a letter code that is absurdly easy to crack."*

I had in truth forgotten, but now I remembered the rest—

*"Spying on our allies?"*

*"They're not our allies yet."*

I was unable to prevent my jaw dropping open. "M has had the telegram all this time? Then why was it necessary for us to go to all this trouble?" I urged with some heat. "Sebastian Undershaft! Opium. All this playacting? Me getting shot again! For us to—"

The detective laid a soothing hand on my shoulder. "Exactly, Watson. Why was it necessary? That is the question."

"Which presumably can only be answered when its contents are learned."

Holmes removed his hand, clearly about to speak—and then, just as clearly, he changed his mind, clapping a hand to his forehead in surprise.

"Holmes?"

"Great Scott." Nostrils flaring, he lifted his beaklike nose like a hound who has taken the scent.

"Holmes, you look like Saul of Tarsus, struck blind on the road to Damascus. Have you connected the dots?"

He struggled some moments longer to contain his excitement, opening and closing his mouth several times as though gasping for air, before answering.

"And the dashes, Watson. And the dashes!"

"Then—"

He heaved a large sigh of satisfaction. "It will keep, my boy."

"Holmes—"

"Let us say merely that it all comes back to you, Watson."

"To me?"

"Yes, you. As I have remarked before, you are not in yourself luminous, doctor, but you are an excellent conductor of light. But let me assure of one thing: telegram 158 is not intended for any of the Mexicans we have named."

Further efforts on my part to draw him out were to no avail, but it was evident from the gleam in his eye that something had excited him mightily. Something he decided not to communicate at present.

"First things first" was his only comment as he held a match to a yellow cardboard square.

"What are you doing now?" I asked.

"You will recall that some years ago I had occasion to decline a knighthood," the detective remarked, observing the flame catch.

"Yes. I thought it a mistake at the time and said so."

"I cannot agree with you, Watson. I am what I have always been, a consulting detective. To ally myself with any faction would compromise not only my objectivity but likewise my independence. Besides, I cannot imagine any party so foolhardy as to welcome into its ranks so meddlesome a fellow as myself, and would be deeply suspicious of any who did."

"And therefore . . . ?"

"I am setting fire to my Communist Party membership card."

**20 January 1917**. It has been a long night and I am horribly
stiff from sleeping fitfully on the stairs below Señor Esquivel's
darkroom. The necessity was a precaution decided upon by Holmes
and myself to ensure that our nascent photographs were not taken
to market elsewhere by their photographer. The tremor in my hand
has yet to cease. It hasn't worsened that I can tell, but it remains
a subject of morbid fascination and I must resist the impulse to
stare at it.

As much from boredom and the need to stretch my injured leg
as to check on the safety and legibility of the facsimile, I limped
up the stairs and rapped on the darkroom door. When there was at
first no answer, my heart began to knock at my ribs. Had the small
photographer somehow contrived to give me the slip? Was there
a window in the darkroom? Had Holmes remembered to check?
Had Señor Esquivel managed to abscond with the pictures—or
worse, the plates?—and was he even now shopping them to the
highest bidder? I knocked more peremptorily (perhaps if I did it

sharply enough, I could rid my hand of the shakes) and the door was opened by an equally sleepy Esquivel.

Divining my purpose, he muttered what I took to be a Spanish oath and admitted me. In the dim light, crowded among sinks and noxious developer fumes, I squinted at soggy images of wedding couples and baptismal babes. Dripping in their midst were two photographs of telegram 158, secured with clothes pegs to a wire strung across the small room. The numbers were legible in both copies, though as inscrutable as when I first laid eyes on them.

The photographer's volubility had deserted him at this hour and he resumed an awkward position in the room's only chair, allowing me to study the numerals to my bewildered heart's content.

What was this message? And what idea had struck Sherlock Holmes so forcibly? Did he in fact know the personage for whom it was intended?

And what was meant by his cryptic remark about my contribution to his flash of understanding? Not luminous but a conductor of light? The detective had in fact referred to me in this way on more than one occasion, but I no more understood what he meant by it now than I did previously.

Holmes, in the meantime, retained possession of the telegram. Squeezing the juice of a lemon carefully around the edges, he succeeded in charring the page with the judicious application of a match flame. Later, Señora Vasca, pleased by the prospect of once more outwitting her supercilious employer and championing the cause of the workers (with an additional contribution to the fledgling party's coffers), would "discover" the paper on the floor near Ambassador von Eckardt's safe and show it to him, singed and perhaps damp from the fire hoses, but otherwise undamaged, wondering innocently if it was important. The ambassador would heave a sigh of relief and assume the page had luckily escaped the blaze. Perhaps he would even reward the charwoman for her diligence.

"But I doubt it," said Sherlock Holmes, "and so I will do it for him."

By noon, our photographs were dry. As arranged, I took both copies as well as the plates from the silent Señor Esquivel in exchange for the last payment of his fee. Blinking with fatigue, I stepped into the chilly sunlight and returned to the Hotel Geneve, where I kicked off my shoes and, still clothed, fell asleep at once. After what seemed five minutes, I was awakened by a sharp knocking and stumbled to my door to find the detective standing impatiently on the other side of it.

"Watson, come, dispatch! If we are late, we risk encountering Señorita Rondón at the telegraph office."

"What time is it?"

"After three."

Gaping stupidly, I ran a hand through my hair. "I must have passed—"

"Later, Watson, put on your shoes! Where's the facsimile?"

Fumbling, I produced one of the two copies and handed it to him. Using my razor, the detective deftly sliced off the top and bottom portions of the page, eliminating the words Western Union and Galveston and the numerals 158, leaving only the center of the message with its mysterious sequenced numbers and the sole name Bernstorff toward the bottom.

"Keep the other copy in a safe place," he instructed me.

In this sorry condition, unwashed and unshaven, my newly mended leg aching with the effort to keep pace with the detective, we fairly trotted to the telegraph office.

By the time we arrived at the North American desk, there were less than thirty minutes before Señorita Rondón was due to begin her shift. Against the possibility of being recognized upon her arrival, I busied myself at a kiosk with telegram forms while Holmes did his business with a slender, sandy-haired youth with a reddish beard. Around us resounded the staccato clacking of telegraphers' fists but I was close enough to overhear their exchange.

"I wish to send these numbers exactly as they appear to Ambassador Spring Rice at the British embassy in Washington, DC," Holmes explained, "with supplemental instructions to forward it to Sir William Melville at the Foreign Office in Whitehall."

"London, England," the young man confirmed.

"Ah, you speak English," the detective said, with relief in his voice.

"It is required, señor."

The man's speech lacked the least trace of a Spanish accent. "You are . . . ?"

The telegrapher smiled. "Australian, señor."

"You are far from home."

"We both appear to be," the man behind the counter said, evidently amused.

Holmes might have wondered at an Australian at the North American desk in the Western Union office in Mexico City, but he had not the time. "It is vital these numbers be transmitted precisely."

There was a pause as the paper was examined.

"I understand. Please wait. I will calculate the fee." The voice and manner were pleasant but unhurried.

"The sooner the better."

"Yes, yes." Amid the clacking of telegraph keys, I could make out the ratcheting of an adding machine and the voice of the young

man as he mumbled. I caught such phrases as "seventeen lines . . ."
"one hundred and seventy words . . ."

"Numbers," corrected Holmes. "With the name Bernstorff at
the end."

"Yes, yes, señor." The voice was amiability itself. "But we calculate
the spaces between the numerals as if they were words . . ." There was
more ratcheting, followed by the pronouncement: "Forty-seven hundred pesos. Plus, the forwarding instructions . . . would come to . . ."

"Eighteen hundred and thirty-eight pesos," the detective totaled
the sum for him. "I am making out a check on the Banco Nacional
for that amount." So saying he took a pen from an adjacent inkwell
and scribbled the number, appending a signature, though under
which name I was unable to see.

"Excellent, Señor Undershaft."

Pretending to scan the vacant telegram forms stacked below me,
I could hear but not see the conversation. It has been demonstrated
that when one sense is deprived, others take up the slack. In my still-
confused state, there was something familiar about the telegrapher's
voice, which assumed a prominence it might not have otherwise
occupied had I been distracted by the sight of the speaker.

But I was distracted by something else as well. As I scribbled
gibberish on one form after another, discarding each into the rubbish as though unhappy with my wording, I was pleased to note
the tremor in my hand disappeared. From the corner of my eye, I
saw the detective hand over the check. Seconds later, I heard the
emphatic stamp of the telegrapher's endorsement.

I was puzzling over the man's teasingly familiar voice when
a more urgent thought intruded. By my oversleeping, we were
cutting matters close. What if Señorita Rondón took it into her
head to turn up early? Should I have remained out of sight at the

Hotel Geneve? Would it not be prudent for me to leave at once and wait elsewhere? But would I not now risk encountering her on my way out? In our haste, Holmes and I had not had discussed these possibilities.

"I will transmit immediately," the bearded Australian informed the detective. "Buenos—"

"If you've no objection," Holmes interrupted, "I will wait to obtain confirmation the message was received."

As the queue behind the detective was not a lengthy one, the telegrapher smiled. "As you wish, Señor Undershaft." He donned a pair of Bakelite headphones and disappeared behind the counter from whence we were presently rewarded with the sounds of a confident fist.

Leaning on the counter, Holmes turned and regarded me with an expressionless countenance as we listened to the rapid-fire tapping. As I anticipated, the process was not a short one. Even with the Australian's nimble fist there were a great many numerals and, as Holmes specified, they had to be transmitted exactly as they appeared on the original, every space properly replicated.

I consulted my watch. It was three-forty-six.

The tapping continued. Amid the roomful of competing casta-nets, I could make out the nearby starts, stops, dots, and dashes of our own telegrapher. They were meaningless to me but presumably recognizable in Tampico, Galveston, Washington, and, with luck, ultimately, London.

Three-fifty-eight. The vigorous clattering behind the counter continued. Señorita Rondón might on occasion be early but for a certainty she would never be late. As I stared blindly at the pile of telegram forms I had defaced, I found myself confused by a feeling I could not name. Something was hovering at the edges of my mind but I could not think what it was. In my dotage, was

I starting to become like my friend? Unable to connect the dots?

"Here is confirmation from Tampico." The sandy-haired youth was smiling and putting on an alpaca coat that he had retrieved from a nearby stand. "It is the end of my shift, Señor Undershaft."

"*Muchas gracias.*" Holmes slipped a wad of pesos across the counter.

"*De nada, señor.*"

I turned away just in time to avoid being seen by Señorita Rondón hurrying to her station as our telegrapher disappeared from his.

ʅ

6:30 P.M. In Holmes's room at the Hotel Geneve, the detective and I were seated in opposing armchairs.

"What happened after Tampico?" I wondered. "Did the message reach Galveston?"

The detective shrugged. Had it been forwarded from Tampico? Did Galveston pass it on to Washington and thence to London? Was M now in possession of those enigmatic numerals? In theory, as with all telegraphic communications, the answer was in the affirmative. But until confirmation tomorrow we could not be sure.

"Did you check that all the numbers were identical?" I asked for the third time.

Languidly, the detective produced his copy of Señor Esquivel's photograph. "I did. And our telegrapher was equally if not more punctilious."

"And the plates?"

"No one will ever find them."

Another silence. We both experienced a feeling of anticlimax.

"Do you feel peckish, Watson?"

"I can't say I do, Holmes."

We regarded one another warily. I was spent as if I had been in the Royal Marsden these past months, cutting and suturing round the clock. But the only surgery I've attended was my own. I have been from pillar to post, crossing oceans and (unsuccessfully) avoiding bullets.

"So we've sent the wretched thing off to London," I said, sulkily. "Now what do they expect of us?"

Holmes busied himself packing his old briar. I found his silence maddening.

"You need a new pipe," I remarked with some irritation. "How long have you kept that thing?"

"Too long," he admitted, not looking up. "I expect we're to make our way home somehow."

"How are we to do that? And what have we accomplished? After all this?"

Holmes struck a match on the pewter ashtray embedded in one arm of his chair and lit his charred pipe, puffing contentedly as the bowl glowed red. The procedure took longer than necessary, which I gathered meant he was unsure. This served only to aggravate my testy humor. In that moment I did not remember the previous June after Juliet's death and the decline of my surgical career. I did not remember how I had been at morose loose ends when the detective with cracked ribs and a black eye had knocked at my door. I did not recollect how the summons to Whitehall had brought me back to life. All I could experience at present was a sense of depletion and futility. Had our forwarding the telegram from hell to M been successful, and would it mean anything if it were? Were those numbers worth all our travel, travail, hurts, and deaths?

Holmes was in the act of shaking out his match when we heard a cough outside the door. Silently he blew out the light, set down his pipe, and lay a finger on his lips.

Thinking, as he did, that we had been attacked more than once, I quietly retrieved my revolver from my overcoat pocket with the five bullets Von Bork had mockingly left me, but my hand shook as I held it. I passed the weapon to Holmes, who stole close to the door and cocked the hammer.

After another interval in which no sound was heard save our own shallow breathing, a sibilant rustle drew our attention to a familiar yellow envelope sliding across the doorsill.

We waited, motionless. After another cough, padded footsteps on the other side of the door withdrew. Eyeing me briefly, Holmes uncocked the pistol and I let out a breath.

"What have we here?" he bent down and plucked up the envelope. "Addressed to Sebastian Undershaft . . ." Absorbed by the new arrival, he returned my revolver, holding it negligently by the barrel. It was of no further interest to him.

I slid the bulky item back into my coat pocket and watched as the detective held the envelope up to the light and tried to peer through it.

"Holmes, for heaven's sake. It's a telegram."

Eyeing me a second time, he tore open the envelope and scanned the message.

"Well?"

"YANKEES THREE PIRATES TWO. STOP. CINCINNATI SEVEN CUBS FOUR. STOP." Bemused, the detective sank into his chair and continued to read aloud: "BROOKLYN DODGERS TEN DETROIT TIGERS THREE. STOP. . . ." his voice trailed off. "I've no idea what to make of this. BOSTON BRAVES ZERO—"

"Those are baseball scores." I drew close and peered over his shoulder.

"Baseball?"

"Rounders. America's answer to cricket. But they're all wrong."

Frowning, he twisted to look up at me. "Wrong? How do you mean?"

"I mean these scores are nonsense. The baseball season doesn't start until April and it's only January. Holmes, you were in America for two years!"

"Watson, you never cease to amaze." He renewed his scrutiny of the telegram. "Hullo, here's more at the bottom. IF THESE OUTCOMES DO NOT SATISFY TAKE A MATCH TO THEM. STOP."

"A match? Let me see."

He handed up the telegram for my inspection, remarking, "Curious locution. Why not say simply, 'Burn after reading'? Wait!" With an oath he rose abruptly and repossessed the page, holding it up to the light. "Ah. Let us see."

Striking a second match, he waved the flame behind the text as close as he dared to the paper.

"Mirabile dictu, Watson!"

"Don't burn it, man!"

He cast a patronizing look in my direction, as much as to say he'd done this sort of thing a thousand times, and together we watched as hidden brown cursive slowly emerged like a spirit photograph between the lines of pasted teletype:

*Your mission accomplished. Night train to V.C. leaves at 8. Tickets held at Window 5. Await instructions in V.C. M.*

"M." Holmes could scarcely keep the satisfaction from his voice. "A worthy successor to Mycroft, if I say so myself."

"V.C. What is V.C.?" The only V.C. I could think of was the Victoria Cross.

"Veracruz, dear boy." He was tugging his valise from under the wardrobe. "The port on the Gulf of Mexico that leads to the open Atlantic. The implication being that a ship of some sort waits to carry us home."

"Holmes, stop a bit. This makes no sense."

But he was already tossing his clothes into the bag without troubling to fold them. "It's almost seven. Hurry, Watson, there's no time to lose!"

"Holmes, you must listen to reason. How can a message written in invisible ink in London appear in a telegram issued in Mexico City? The message may originate in England, but the paper comes from the local offices of Western Union."

He stopped and looked at me, smiling broadly. "Is it possible you do not understand? Our instructions were sent by M in a separate telegram—doubtless in his own code—directing that his real message be transcribed by hand in lemon juice by his agent in Mexico."

"And who might that be?"

"Eliminate the impossible—" he began.

"And whatever remains, however improbable, must be the truth," I completed his maxim, having heard it a thousand times. "That would make it—"

"Someone who works for Western Union. It was he who supplied the baseball folderol amid which to insert the writing. And observe, there is no watermark on this telegram with the stamp that reads *Inspected*, which would be the case if this message had been genuinely received instead of generated here on Western Union's Mexico City premises."

I stared at the paper with growing excitement. "Nor are the words 'via Galveston' and 'Tampico' anywhere to be seen!"

"Excellent, Watson. Really, you are coming along. Now where does that leave us, do you think?"

It took several moments for me to grasp his meaning. "The young Australian?"

"Who else?" His expression was practically a smirk. "It would not astonish me to learn it was that same hand sliding the telegram under our door just now."

"The Australian?" I could only repeat.

"The last time he was Welsh! And female. With a stiletto instead of a telegraph key."

There was a roaring in my ears and I was obliged to grasp the back of the nearest chair for support before I finally managed, "You mean—'Reilly'?"

He laughed, fairly chortling with satisfaction. "And Irish, as well, I'd forgot. Our self-anointed 'guardian angel.' I admit it was difficult to recognize Violet Carstairs with short, reddish hair and a beard."

In a flash the spy's words came back to me. The accent wasn't Australian but the husky voice had indeed been familiar: *"The police will turn me over to the BOI, who will contact M, and I will be shunted elsewhere on another neutral vessel. Somewhere I will be of further use."*

"'Further use' proved to be Mexico City." Holmes remembered the same words.

"It was he, following us from the time we arrived!"

"Watson, there is no time to lose!" With a third match, he set fire to Reilly's message.

**21 January 1917**. After midnight. The discovery in the Western Union office that my tremor disappears when I write has had the curious effect of impelling me to keep scribbling, as though the exercise might constitute a therapy that could result in a cure, or, at the least, a remission. At all events, it prevents my becoming fixated on my symptom and wondering what else it portends. My hand remains steady so long as I wield my pen, though writing here, I was initially dismayed to see that my hand still shakes recounting the day's events—until I realized it was the erratic motion of the train rather than my penmanship. Holmes is asleep in the upper berth, insisting, as he has since I was shot, that I occupy the lower on these occasions. The blue night-light here will not disturb him and its dim illumination is sufficient for my purposes.

In truth, we are lucky to be here at all. Our headlong flight from the Hotel Geneve more closely resembled the getaway of desperate criminals than the leave-taking of sober travelers. We barely made it to Avenida de los Insurgentes and the Estación

Colonia by a quarter to eight. At this hour the ticket windows were closing their shutters, but number five remained open with only one prospective passenger before us. The gentleman, his face swathed in a scarf against the night chill, took an unconscionable time completing his transaction. He, too, was evidently taking the eight o'clock train for Veracruz, for he scurried toward it as we reached the barred ticket window.

"Sebastian and Lionel Undershaft," the detective repeated our names slowly.

After another exasperating wait, during which we eyed one another, damp with anxiety, an envelope containing our tickets was silently pushed toward us on the wooden tongue beneath the brass grating.

"*Muchas gracias!*" I shouted the only Spanish I knew as we made for the train, whose whistle now shrieked in anticipation.

When we finally tumbled into our *camarín*, we were so relieved that the shortcomings of the cramped space made little impression at first. The upper berth had already been lowered for the night. The car boasts no WC. Should either of us require it, my lower berth lifts to reveal a commode, open at the bottom to deposit all contents onto the railbed. Later we became aware that our folding sink had a leak and our broad window was cracked.

"It's a mere eleven hours," Holmes declared, hoisting our bags onto the rack. "We will be in Veracruz in time for breakfast."

"And what will we find there besides *huevos rancheros*?" I said, tugging off my shoes. My Spanish was more or less furnished by restaurant glossaries.

"Whatever it is M has provided," the detective returned, climbing the ladder to his aerie and struggling with his long legs to confine himself there. As our journey was not of long duration, we slept in our clothes. I used my overcoat (so cumbersome in steamy Washington but so helpful in chilly Mexico) as a blanket. "But we can at least hope for a peaceful night's sleep. I would think it impractical for the forces of Villa or Zapata to attack us by night."

"You are confident."

He made no answer. Holmes could sleep anywhere, but for me there was no question of rest. My mind was awhirl with anxieties and misgivings. Had M really been so prescient and effective (ten thousand miles distant!) as to pave the way for our escape on such short notice? Or had Holmes's interpretation of the invisible writing on the nonsensical telegram been some form of wishful thinking? The detective had been wrong in the past. Was he, at long last, succumbing to the effects of age? The fact that there even was an eight o'clock train for Veracruz I must count an encouraging sign. At least the detective had correctly interpreted *V.C.*! But for the rest, I remain uncertain. Was it really possible that our Australian telegrapher was formerly a Welsh female singing coach who laid low Herr Bechmesser with a stiletto ("mother's little helper") after the false watch salesman attempted to dispatch Holmes with a potassium cyanide saltshaker aboard the *Norlina*? (I stare at my last sentence with something akin to disbelief.) And who, when leaving us in Boston under arrest, gave us an Irish name? Had he in fact been our invisible shadow from the time we had first set foot in Mexico? Come to think of it, had he been with us even before that, on the Águila Azteca, crossing the Rio Grande? Fighting Pancho Villa's muchachos? In what guise on that occasion? An American cavalryman? Possibilities proliferated in my teeming brain.

In all the time I had accompanied Holmes, had there ever been a case—I've come to regard this as a case—with as many twists and curves as this one? Had we ever been met with so many surprises and shocks along our way? They resembled nothing so corkscrewed as our rail route through the Sierra Madre mountains.

*What did that infernal telegram say?*

We were scheduled to stop at Puebla, but by that time the train's rocking motion had lulled me to a restless sleep. Somewhere my mind insisted our troubles were not yet over.

**23 January 1917**. O my prophetic soul. I have missed a day's entry, a thing which rarely happens, but the events of the last twenty-four hours have been so terrible I had neither the leisure nor the ability to set them down.

We were awoken by a sharp knocking on the door of our *camarín*. In my haste I had forgot to wind my watch, so it was impossible to know the time. All I can say with certainty is that it was still night as Holmes slid off the bed in his stocking feet and approached the door.

"Yes?"

The knocking was repeated, more gently. By this time, I had sat up and slid into my overcoat, exchanging looks with Holmes.

"Señor Undershaft?" We knew that voice.

Holmes slid open the door to reveal a stranger, his face half hidden in the dim light. It was some moments before I recognized our Australian telegrapher. He had shaved his beard and the transformation was remarkable.

"Reilly?"

"Good morning, gentlemen." We were greeted by that same husky voice, though the Australian accent had now been exchanged for Oxbridge. The slender agent stepped into our pigeonhole and slid the door shut behind him. "I'm sorry to have roused you so early but it is important that I inform you of next steps."

"Please sit," Holmes said. "We owe you a great deal."

"It's part of the job," Reilly responded, but I could not fail to detect a note of satisfaction in his tone. Holmes was not the only individual in this cubicle with a share of vanity. With nowhere else to sit, Reilly hunched into the lower berth, his feet grazing the floor.

"We never saw you following us in Mexico City," I added, hoping to add my thanks to Holmes's.

He frowned at this. "You are mistaken. I never followed you."

The detective and I exchanged looks. In truth we had seen no one. Were we being, as Doktor Freud might put it, paranoid?

"What awaits us in Veracruz?" I asked, rubbing sleep from my eyes.

Reilly was pleased to get on with business. "Passage home in a form I suspect you could not have dreamed. When the train reaches Veracruz, a carriage waits to carry you both to *muelle cuatro.*"

"*Muelle cua*—?"

"Pier four. *Muelle cuatro.* The port is large and extremely busy at all hours and so it is vital you remember the address so as to avoid any possible confusion."

"*Muelle cuatro.*"

"Very good."

"And at *muelle cuatro*?" It was Holmes who posed the next question.

"A launch is waiting to carry you to the HMS *Caroline*, a light armored cruiser of five thousand tons. Weather permitting, she will bring you to Portsmouth in eighteen days."

I could scarcely believe my ears. "Do you mean to say His Majesty's government has sent an entire warship across the Atlantic to fetch us home? Can we be worth such expense and risk?"

Reilly smiled. "First Sea Lord Admiral Jellicoe is evidently of that opinion, though it is my understanding the decision was taken at the insistence of Admiral Hall. In anticipation of this rendezvous, the *Caroline* was sent some days ago from Barbados. As Mexico holds neutral status, she must anchor outside the harbor."

There was only the rattle of the train as we absorbed these tidings.

"Eighteen days seems a long time," Holmes said, breaking the silence. "Is there no way the ship can make more steam on her return voyage?"

"Speed is not the issue. The *Caroline* can do upward of thirty knots, but is obliged follow a zigzag course to lessen the risk of encountering German submarines. This lengthens the voyage considerably."

"Have the U-boats been loosed then?" My stomach tightened.

"Not in packs to prey on neutral merchant shipping as yet, but warships of the Royal Navy constitute a legal and tempting target. The skipper who sinks one is typically awarded the Iron Cross."

"And where will you be?" I asked. Dawn light was creeping into our broken window.

"I must return to Ciudad de México,, as my work there is not complete."

"We shall refrain from asking you what that is," Holmes said. "But you take with you not only our gratitude but also His Majesty's and the people of England."

The man who was now Reilly rose and shook our hands. "Gentleman, I can truly say it has been a pleasure."

He slid open the door, uttered a cry of surprise, and fell back into our arms, a large knife buried to the hilt in his stomach.

Following close behind and sliding the door shut in one swift motion as he entered was the tall individual who had bought his ticket before us at window five the night before. He held us at bay, a revolver grasped in his right hand, but even before he unwound the scarf that muffled his face with his left, Holmes knew his identity.

"Von Bork."

The villain smiled. "Did I not promise?" said he in a low voice. "Did I not swear to get level with you if it was the last thing I did?"

As I had first suspected, it was Von Bork who had been following us.

"This man is dying," I said, extracting, as gently as I could, the wide blade and unsuccessfully attempting to stanch the flow of blood gushing over my hand.

"*Gut*" was the satisfied reply.

"Do you really imagine you will get away with this?" Sherlock Holmes asked in the disinterested tone of one who wondered if it will rain on Tuesday.

This provoked a gruff laugh. "But I already have, Herr Holmes. By the time this train stops there will be three bodies in this compartment and I will be on my way."

"All for nothing," the detective declared. "The war is lost."

Under my hand, Reilly's heart had stopped. For him the war was indeed lost.

"*Jawohl*, but who has lost it?" Von Bork was clearly enjoying his triumph and toying with his victims.

"Germany, to be sure," Holmes answered promptly.

Von Bork's grin was now visible in the gathering light.

"*Der Unsinn.* Drivel! The U-boats will be turned loose and the great Sherlock Holmes will have met his end in Veracruz, of all places. Nothing so grand as a waterfall! What a pity you will not witness the demoralizing effect your death will have on the population of your irritating little island."

With my hand still pointlessly pressing on the unfortunate Reilly's chest, I recalled a previous occasion when England had supposed Holmes dead, to say nothing of more recent dismay when news of his demise in America had been received.[*]

"If you shoot, your gunfire will be heard." Holmes was playing for time.

The malefactor understood as much and barked a laugh. "Not over the noise of this rattling old train, I think. I will now trouble you for the copy of Foreign Minister Zimmermann's telegram, number 158."

Holmes hesitated. "I do not have it."

"Gideon Altamont, you try my patience." Von Bork cocked the hammer of his revolver, as I had recently seen Holmes do. The slightest untoward motion of train or man and the weapon would discharge.

Holmes heaved a sigh. "Dr. Watson has the copy. In his coat."

"Give it here. And none of your tricks, Herr *Arzt*. This time I will aim higher than your leg."

---

[*]   Watson refers to reaction in England when Holmes was presumed to have gone over the Reichenbach Falls in Switzerland in the embrace of his nemesis, Professor Moriarty.

"Very well."

"Right hand pocket, Watson," the detective reminded me.

Wiping my hand, slick with the dead man's blood, on my trousers, I reached into my coat, fumbled for the trigger, and fired my revolver through the pocket several times.

The German's eyes bulged in wonderment, as if he had received unexpected news, and he dropped the gun, clutching his stomach, as Reilly had done. His weapon discharged when it struck the floor, the bullet harmlessly shattering our window.

I kept firing until all five bullets were gone and the murderer lay dead beside his victim, his lips curled in a rictus that snarled his bared teeth. And Von Bork was correct: the gunshots could not be heard above the din of the train. I was not aware I was still squeezing the trigger even after there were no more rounds until Holmes laid a hand on my arm, bringing me to my senses. Had he not done so, God knows how much longer I would have continued clicking the empty chambers.

There was no need to speak. Working as one, we rifled the pockets of both dead men, searching for any clues as to their identities that might aid the police, and removing them. With no time to take inventory of what we found, we dropped the items through the commode onto the tracks below.

Holmes then placed my revolver into Reilly's hand, clamping the slender, womanly fingers on the grip and hooking the right forefinger around the trigger. Both the unfortunate man's hands were crimson from contact with his fatal knife wound.

To any new arrivals, it would appear these unidentified two had killed each other, the result of an old grievance or sudden quarrel.

Soon we would arrive at the station at Veracruz. Holmes surveyed the scene we had staged. "I don't believe our fingerprints

SHERLOCK HOLMES AND THE TELEGRAM FROM HELL        231

will be of use to the Mexican police, who certainly have none of ours on file," he remarked. "Where *is* your copy of the telegram?"

"In my shoe," I said, pointing to where I had left both beside the lower berth.

"You're sure?"

I checked, bloodying the folded photograph in the process.

"Good. Leave it in your shoe, Watson."

"Holmes, what about Von Bork's gun? Toss it through the window?"

"I shall dispose of it at sea where it can do no further damage. I am to blame," he muttered. "Had I not been intent on obtaining our tickets last night in time for the train, I might have recognized Reilly's killer then and there."

There was no reply to make to this so I made none.

ꙮ

7:00 A.M. An old fiacre was waiting for us at the station. The driver stood unsteadily in the box, holding up a sign with the name *Undershaft* scrawled in chalk on a small blackboard. Without waiting upon formalities, we sprang into the picturesque carriage with our bags.

*"Muelle cuatro, por favor."*

*"Si, señor,"* the driver, prepared for this request, cracked his whip and we set off amid the already crowded streets, heading toward the water.

I was still huddled in my overcoat, my finger restlessly poking through the bloodstained hole in my right pocket, inside and out blackened and crisped with powder burns.

"The coat must go, as well," said Holmes, reading my mind, as he often did. I knew that *as well* referred to my trusty service revolver, now left behind forever in Mexico. I reproached myself for briefly devoting more regret to the loss of my weapon than to the death of the heroic young man who had repeatedly saved our lives.

**25, 26, 27, etc., January 1917.** I believe that after all we have
endured, I am suffering the effects of shock. As directed, the
*Caroline* followed a zigzag course east across the Gulf of Mexico.
Though the gulf seas proved tranquil, the armored cruiser was
not. Warships are not built for comfort, and this one was traveling
at top speed and turning sharply at irregular intervals. The rapid
course changes and remorseless throbbing of her engines laid me
up almost at once. Added to this, Captain Crooke directed us to
remain in our quarters and out of contact with the crew. Our meals
were served privately.

*Armored cruiser HMS* Caroline

"I'm sorry, gentlemen, but my orders are to keep you sequestered, though you may have access to fresh air on the gun deck when my officers are at mess. And before you ask, we may receive but are not permitted to send any messages and must retain radio silence throughout."

I could not be certain, but I was unable to discount the impression that the captain regarded this assignment—ferrying two civilians across the Atlantic—as a squandering of scanty resources and a chore unworthy of a vessel that had recently distinguished herself under his command in the most significant naval engagement of the war. The *Caroline*, as we learned, had taken part in the action at Jutland and survived to tell the tale.*

"Can you at least bring us up to date on the war?" Holmes asked. "We have not had recent access to the news."

"There is scarcely any point" was the reply. "Nothing has changed, no ground has been gained or lost on either side. Casualties mount for both. Unless you count the revolution in Russia," the captain threw in as an afterthought.

"The what?" I had thought by now that nothing could surprise me.

"A spontaneous uprising, as I understand, apparently the result of wartime losses and famine. The people are howling for the tsar's abdication."

"I don't suppose that makes much difference," said Holmes.

Captain Crooke regarded the detective with astonishment. "It might make a great difference, Mr. Holmes. Should the tsar

---

* The Battle of Jutland, May 1916. The *Caroline*, under Crooke's command, played a vital role and remained in service until 2011, making her the longest commissioned vessel in the Royal Navy, with the exception of Nelson's HMS *Victory*. The word radio, incidentally, was a new term.

abdicate and the Bolsheviks assume power, they promise to pull Russia out of what they insist is a capitalist war.

"Should that happen, we will have lost a key element of our coalition, and German troops presently pinned on the Eastern front will be freed to add their numbers to the Western lines, where Britain and France will be obliged to fight on alone."

There was little to say in response to these tidings although I could not help recalling Holmes recently attending meetings of Mexico's fledgling Communist Party. As he described those proceedings, a Bolshevik revolution struck me as the height of improbability. Now I was less certain. I could not imagine anything like a similar uprising at home, but the world was so changed from the world I had always known, how could I be sure of anything? Whatever unspoken hopes we'd held that matters at the front had somehow changed in recent days, that a breakthrough had been attained, that the German line had finally collapsed, we both had known better. But was it really possible that after all these years, all these men, and all their commanders, nothing had been achieved?

"Thank you, captain."

Our quarters, like all the ship, reeked of rancid grease, coal dust, and machine oil. The *Caroline* carried two six-inch guns, eight four-inch guns, an anti-aircraft gun, as well as two twenty-one-inch torpedo tubes. These were fired without warning for gunnery practice, the recoils like gigantic hiccups, flinging us off our feet or into the nearest bulkheads.

While I lay curled in my berth, Holmes managed to use his topside privileges to dispose of my coat and Von Bork's pistol into the waves where they would never be found.

We received a single wireless communication sent in plain text from London and delivered personally by the captain. It consisted of one word: PROGRESS. STOP. M.

"What does that mean?" I demanded. "Is progress a noun or a verb? Are *we* to progress? How? Or are *they* making progress?"

"A noun, I suspect," said Holmes.

"Does it mean they suspect or know for a fact there is progress?" I demanded. The message bore an infuriating resemblance to the rest of the war news, cloaked in ambiguity and euphemisms. How many times over these last years had I read about "the big push"?

"Really, Watson, you must eat something."

"Later."

Somewhere among all these illnesses and reflections is the growing conviction that everything we have done has been for nothing. The stalemate continues. The United States clings to its neutrality and without its might hope fades that England can ultimately survive the German onslaught. Though we did not discuss M's one-word message further, we found it unsettling. If Holmes was correct, M and Admiral Hall had telegram 158 in their possession before von Eckardt ever received it. And if, in all this time, they were still unable to read it . . .

Somewhere amid my discomfort, I finally spared a thought for the hapless Reilly, that chameleon who slipped glibly in and out of a dozen identities while fruitlessly, I suspected, in search of his own. Was he Irish as the name he gave us implied? Or was that merely another nom de guerre? Did he even have a true identity? He would receive a posthumous decoration and his family, if they could be located (did they exist?), granted some sort of stipend, but was there, in reality, any form of compensation for what the remarkable man had done? As we learned from Mrs. Longworth, who took to drinking sherry, spies do not prosper.

Holmes, too, appears less than himself. He does not suffer mal de mer as I do, or at any rate it doesn't turn his complexion chartreuse, but he is subdued. He rarely leaves my side and tends me like the most devoted nurse, helping me to some fresh air on the gun deck when it is permitted.

The crew, when we encounter them, give us sullen looks. They appear to share Captain Crooke's disdain for this costly and distracting errand, and I worry it is justified. We are asking ourselves what the telegram from hell was really all about and would it, in the final analysis, have made any difference at all to the war had M and Admiral Hall been able to decipher it.

For myself, matters only worsened as we left the gulf through the Straits of Florida, skimming the north coast of Cuba and threading the Bahamas. In the rolling swells of the North Atlantic in the dead of winter, I was sure I was going to die. The five-thousand-ton *Caroline* was tossed about as unceremoniously as a cork, her bow rising at an impossible angle, pointing at murderous slate thunderheads, only to plunge as if down a vertiginous ski slope. At times I was certain the ship would founder. That, too, now seemed desirable. Was this what poor Jonah experienced in the whale's belly? I began to long for an encounter with one of the Kaiser's dreaded submarines to put me out of my misery, but the Imperial German Navy refused to oblige. Even with a steady hand, it is virtually impossible to write and I have lost all track of time. I am not even sure at this point how many days have passed. I cannot tell whether it is day or night, for our quarters boast no such reassuring luxury as a porthole, depriving us of both an orientating view of the horizon or any outside air. The incessant palsy of our engines and our abrupt course alterations puts me in mind of a bean rattling inside a gourd, added to which the repulsive odors make it impossible to keep any food in my stomach.

More than my physical torments, I believe my entire system is rebelling against the totality of this experience, beginning with the war itself, which had already exacted a toll before Holmes ever knocked at my door. What I have seen and endured in the last seven months has quite overwhelmed my capacities. Formerly I imagined myself to be a sturdy, reliable sort of fellow, my injuries notwithstanding, someone to have by one's side in fraught circumstances. I believe Holmes would not have disputed this characterization. But I am no longer sure. I no longer feel I am the man I was.

"There is, however, one important change in your favor," the detective pointed out when I enumerated my ailments.

"I find that most unlikely."

"Look at your hand, my dear fellow. Since you fired the shots that killed Von Bork, your tremor has entirely vanished."

I held my hand before my face, startled to realize this was so. Yet fascinated as I was by this development, uncharitable thoughts now proceeded to cross my mind in which I found myself wondering just what it was over the years that found me accompanying, observing, and chronicling the adventures and cases dealt with by Sherlock Holmes. In my misery I did not recall Holmes as I had often described him, the best and wisest man I had ever known. Instead I marveled that even when years apart had intervened, I somehow always returned to his side for more. Was Holmes my drug? Was I no less addicted than he had been to cocaine? But he had—with the help of the now world famous Doktor Freud—broken free of his enslavement. Could I—should I—not do the same? Could I never resist his siren cry of "Watson, the game's afoot!" and join the new halloo, even when, as it turned out, it put my life in peril, when I was past the age when such folly could be excused by impetuosity and the intemperance of youth? With a sinking heart, I realized the time when such choices were possible was long past. It was too late.

**10 February 1917**. "Von Bork is dead." Thus Holmes began our report to Admiral Hall and M in the latter's office after midnight in Whitehall. Both men had aged in the interval since our meeting the previous June. The admiral's gray hair was now snowy white and the pouches beneath M's eyes were dark from sleepless nights.

I was scarcely in better shape, having had virtually no rest from the time we boarded the *Caroline*. The armored cruiser had maintained radio silence across the storm-plagued Atlantic, breaking it only at the end of our voyage, after we had nipped into the safety of the Solent. Once within that barrier, Captain Crooke alerted Whitehall, and by the time we put in at Portsmouth, M had arranged transport for the detective and myself in the form of a private train. Given the country's wartime privations, this was yet further evidence as to the urgency of our errand.

But my own difficulties were not at an end. One disagreeable consequence of setting foot on terra firma after so long on surging seas was an attack of vertigo. As a doctor I was able to diagnose my condition, which some (who have not experienced the malady) have humorously termed *mal de terre*, but I can attest there is nothing amusing about it. As result of so much tossing about, my brain in its casing required time to settle, which in the hurly-burly of still more travel, it was not receiving. Holmes was obliged to prop me upright as we walked and I lurched like a drunken sailor tottering onto the train, clutching every handhold in sight. Tilting walls looked like floors and vice versa. Shaken still more on the ride up to town, I could not dispel the sensation I was about to slide off my seat.

"Look at the horizon, Watson. That should help," Holmes advised.

Through the dirty window, as we threaded the lacework of tracks into Victoria, London appeared more threadbare and forlorn than ever. In ways too numerous and subtle for me to identify in my condition, the war continued to lay waste to England.

"Von Bork is dead." Holmes's voice brought me back to the present.

"Oh?" M responded, his tone typically neutral, as one who has just been informed the post is delayed.

In the low light, his office looked much the same, though the large desk was piled higher with papers than I'd remembered. The windows shattered by reverberations from the bomb that struck St. Paul's on our previous visit had been replaced, but otherwise the chamber and its furnishings remained unchanged. Like the war itself, I realized. It took a concentrated effort on my part to view the room upright.

Holmes recounted in succinct and I thought rather colorless detail what had befallen us since sailing from Southampton. Aside from occasional telegrams sent from the United States regarding the health of "Aunt Abigail" and communications via Spring Rice in Washington from M pressing us for results, we had not been in contact with Whitehall or indeed anyone in England until forwarding the contents of telegram 158 from Mexico City on 20 January.

The two tired men heard the detective out in attentive silence. Occasionally, M held up a hand to halt his narrative while he made a note. As I listened, I had to marvel at what I heard, the flat recital of our narrow scrapes and the singular individuals whose paths had crossed ours. It was a wonder we were alive, a thought I had not fully permitted myself till now.

"Yes. We killed him," Holmes concluded.

In another era, the detective might have sugarcoated his language, but four years of unremitting slaughter, all we had undergone in the past months, and his feelings about his remorseless adversary had freed him of euphemisms. Even in my dilapidated state I appreciated his use of *we*. It had indeed been teamwork when Holmes had slyly reminded me where I'd stashed my service revolver during our final encounter with that German fiend.

"Well done." This from Admiral Hall, who on this occasion had drawn his chair into the light where he could be seen.

"Unfortunately," Holmes continued, "Von Bork managed to kill Reilly before we could prevent him."

There was silence.

"Who?" said M.

"Reilly," I replied automatically. "Your agent, sent to safeguard us aboard the *Norlina* and again in Mexico City."

M's brows contracted. "I know no one of that name," he said. "Admiral?"

"Doesn't ring a bell."

My dizziness must have affected my hearing. "Reilly," I repeated. I was seized by a sudden comprehension. "Oh! You knew her as Violet Carstairs. The Welsh singing coach? Were you unaware he was male?"

It was impossible to miss the brief exchange of looks that followed between M and Admiral Hall.

"Violet Carstairs." M repeated the name as I had Reilly's. "I'm sorry, the name means nothing to me. Admiral?" he again addressed the white-haired officer.

"Doesn't ring a bell," the man answered like an automaton.

In a shattering instant I grasped the sordid truth and gaped at these two beauties.

"You swine."

"I beg your pardon?" M's tone was innocence tinged with frost.

Holmes laid a restraining hand on my arm, but I shook it off, bile rising in my throat and color to my cheeks. If I'd harbored any doubts heretofore about how this business worked, I shed them now as I struggled to my feet.

"Do you remember what you said to me on the Embankment, Holmes? That day we walked after our breakfast at Craithie's?"

"Watson, this isn't the—"

"You said, 'In war, morality becomes a luxury few can afford.' And then you speculated that if we grew desperate enough we might well be capable of similar barbarism. Well, it turns out we are!" I was shouting now, clutching the back of the chair to keep from toppling. "Poor Reilly, whoever he was, won't be receiving any posthumous decorations, will he? Nor will his family, if they exist, be granted a stipend for their son's sacrifice. You disown him. Why? Because he was expendable or because his ambiguous gender proves an embarrassment easier to dispense with now he is gone? Here!" I somehow managed to tear off my shoe, draw forth the crumpled photograph of telegram 158, and shake it in their general direction as I slid to the floor. "This is what all the fuss is about, what the man gave his life for. What a pity we don't know what it says. Why this man had to die for it! That's his blood, by the by! And why you are now prepared to deny he ever existed!"

Ignoring my outburst and my location, M took the page from my outstretched hand, smoothing it beneath the lamp on his desk, where he commenced examining it.

Sherlock Holmes silently came to the rescue and helped lift me back to my seat. "An attack of vertigo," he explained. "It will pass."

"Doctor," Admiral Hall interposed, oozing contrition. "You have performed Herculean feats. You are overtaxed and overtired. We all are. May I see that?" he asked M, who silently handed him the paper.

I would like to have answered but I was obliged to clutch my chair in hopes I would not tip over.

The admiral held the photograph of the telegram to the light and squinted at those maddening numbers. Evidently unsatisfied, he spread the paper over his knee and bent over it.

With an effort, I recovered my shoe and slipped it on.

"Can you stay, doctor?" M asked mildly. "Or perhaps another time might suit you—"

"I'm perfectly able to follow this conversation," I insisted, for I had no intention of missing anything that happened in this room.

"Very well," the spymaster said, after an indecisive pause in which I knew he contemplated rationales for dispensing with my irksome presence. He decided in the end not to antagonize Holmes, who had made his own position clear. "Admiral Hall, will you bring us up to date on telegram 158?"

The admiral looked up from the page and cleared his throat as if attempting to clear a good deal more. "Thanks to you, we know the message was written in German using the ultrasecret code 13040. We have managed to decipher some portions of the telegram, but not the whole, as yet. . . . Of course, after rendering it in German, it must be translated into English."

"Code 13040 remains vexatious," M chorused, "though it is gratifying to learn you are making progress . . ."

*Progress.* There it was again, that maddening word.

"But if you already had 158 in your possession, why was it necessary for us to wire its contents back to you from Mexico City?" I demanded, still thinking of Reilly.

"To check your numbers against ours, for one thing," said M. "We had to be certain we were talking about exactly the same numerals. I'm happy to say we were." The man offered what I took to be a smile, which further infuriated me.

"And for another?"

"It was essential the telegram be obtained from the Western hemisphere, essential that the American interception of the message originate in Mexico, not London."

"'American interception'? But the Americans had nothing to do with it!" I protested with heat. "It was entirely Holmes who—"

"Oh, but they did, Watson," the detective reminded me. "You will recall it was Ambassador Fletcher, who, at the banquet at the Hotel Geneve in honor of United Fruit, first alerted us to the arrival of 158. He didn't actually hand us the telegram, which, to be sure, would have contravened the president's policy, but he certainly can be said to have put us onto it."

"None of which brings us any closer to knowing what it says," M remarked dourly.

It was then that Sherlock Holmes uttered the most astounding sentence of his life:

"Oh, if it is of any use, I can tell you what the telegram says."

"Nonsense," the spymaster blurted impatiently. "13040 is their most secret code, as you informed us via Spring Rice. You cannot possibly have broken it. To do that—"

"One moment." Admiral Hall rose to his feet, towering over Holmes in his chair. "Have I heard you correctly? What are you saying, Mr. Holmes?"

"You cannot have misheard me," the detective replied, looking up calmly.

Again, I saw the exchange of looks between M and Admiral Hall. These two were connected by an umbilical cord, for the latter gave an imperceptible nod.

"Do you mean to say you have decoded the text of 158?" M took the crumpled paper from the admiral and brandished it close to Holmes. "How can that be? Our cryptographers have been working on the problem for weeks."

"Since you first intercepted its transmission, eavesdropping over American wires," I reminded them.

Neither man chose to dispute this, but both hovered before the detective in his chair as if between them they held a stag at bay.

"I have not decoded it, I have deduced it," Holmes stated, not the least intimidated by his challengers.

"What does it say?" Admiral Hall demanded, at the same time M asked, "How?"

"Or rather," the admiral clarified, "what do you think it says?"

As I had seen him do on previous occasions, Sherlock Holmes collected himself like a steeplechaser before a jump. He sprang to his feet, surprising both men into stepping backward. None of us could have anticipated the vertiginous heights the detective was about to leap.

"It is indeed a tangled skein," he began, "and may require some patience to undo the knots. Last June in this office, you referred to the 'trifling' affair of Pancho Villa invading the United States in Columbus, New Mexico, forcing President Wilson to dispatch troops there."

"Yes, I recall our conversation," said M.

Holmes began to pace, thrusting his hands into his pockets. "That is doubtless what gave them the idea."

"Holmes, you are speaking in riddles. Gave who what idea?"

The detective stopped and faced them, his back to the large map, bristling with steel pins and tiny flags, behind M's desk. "Foreign Minister Zimmerman. I suspect Pancho Villa's escapade inspired him."

"Pancho Villa?" Admiral Hall interrupted. "Why do you keep mentioning him? Where does he come into this?"

"Villa's raid on New Mexico last year set Zimmermann thinking," Holmes said, assuming a professorial attitude. He spoke with none of the hesitation and diffidence that had occasioned such difficulties in America. Here, in intimate surroundings, he felt himself on solid ground. "Put yourself in the foreign minister's place. If the German objective was to prevent America from entering the war, how better than to keep the Americans occupied defending their own southern frontier? Do what Pancho Villa did—only on a larger scale."

"Preposterous." But even as M spoke, I could see the realization dawning in his face and in the admiral's.

"Connect the dots," said Sherlock Holmes.

"You are saying—?" M had resumed staring at the bloodstained photograph of telegram 158, as if the numbers would now reveal their meaning.

"I am saying it is certain the message you hold in your hands from Foreign Minister Zimmermann is intended for Mexican President Venustiano Carranza. It proposes that Mexico invade the United States."

Electric silence, like the stillness before a lightning strike, now filled the room as we contemplated the terrifying implications of telegram 158.

A brisk knock on the door punctured the stillness.

"Not now!" shouted M before lowering his voice. "Do go on, Holmes."

Still on the ascent, the detective lived for moments like this. He had experienced many and relished them all, but never before such an audience as these two men, who between them held the fate of so many and so much in their hands. But to give him credit, present circumstances outweighed his love of the protracted revelation. He spoke slowly so as to be clear, rather than to dramatize, a tutor rather than an actor.

"General Pershing has had little success in catching up with, let alone capturing, Pancho Villa, as Watson and I learned firsthand, and President Wilson has been obliged to expend both resources and energy to ensure that the southern border of the United States does not experience another incursion."

"I begin to understand," M said.

"But let us suppose it wasn't Pancho Villa and his small band of marauders," Holmes went on as though the latter had not spoken. "Suppose it was an entire army. What then?"

"Then it would require an entire army to repulse them," Admiral Hall said, following the trail of dots. "And America doesn't have enough of an army at present to fight two wars, one at home and another on the Western Front."

"Not nearly enough," murmured M. "She would have to choose."

"Watson, you will recall Colonel Owen's reference to America's paltry military resources," Holmes reminded me.

"Yes, with no wars to occupy them, young men have flocked instead to football. 'War without rules,'" as I remembered Owen's description of the game.

Holmes turned again to M. "And you will recall your man in New York, Herr Feldenstein, telling us that one of Von Bork's Hydra heads, Emil Gasche, keeps blowing up munitions factories to add to America's unreadiness."

As this exchange was lost on him, the admiral went on as though it had not taken place. "And given the choice of defending herself or joining an overseas engagement, it isn't hard to imagine which fight the Americans and their president would choose," he reasoned.

"QED," said Sherlock Holmes. "With no American army in Europe to tip the scales, Germany is free to wage unlimited submarine warfare and England is shortly starved into surrender, as Roger Casement prophesied."

M brought the telegram closer to his face, as if that would help decipher its contents. "You say you have not decoded these numbers."

"I am not a cryptographer, but as *e* is the most common letter in both the English and German alphabets, I assume your team has begun there."

This was followed by another silence, more ruminative than electric this time, broken finally by M, who had resumed tugging at his mustache.

"But if, as you concede, you are not a cryptographer, then how can your conclusions—your 'deductions'—be confirmed? Why, for example, would Mexico ever contemplate attacking her huge northern neighbor? America's armed forces may be insufficient to fight two wars, but she could doubtless overcome whatever Mexico has to throw at her."

Before the detective could answer, a commotion was heard outside the thick door to M's office. The two men paid no heed to word of the latest calamity, their attention entirely focused on Sherlock Holmes.

"For a very simple reason." Holmes continued to unknot the tangled skein. "President Carranza was offered a mouth-watering carrot by the cunning Zimmermann. It is doubtless contained somewhere in this telegram, probably toward the end."

"And that carrot would be?" I found myself asking.

"Watson, it was you who led me to it! You will recall I harbored the conviction you had told me something of immense importance during our journey across Texas, but for the longest time I could not recall what you said that had so intrigued me."

"I recall you made some remark to that effect but confess it slipped my mind."

The detective smiled. "As it did mine. But the night we found ourselves in conversation on the stairs below Señor Esquivel's dark-room, I remembered what it was, though I declined to enlighten you at the time. As we crossed Texas, I had remarked on all the Spanish names. *Corpus Cristi. Laredo. Agua Dulce. El Paso* and the rest. All these, you pointed out, had once been belonged to Mexico."

The detective strode to the map. "For Mexico, a successful invasion across the Rio Grande—were it to take place—stands to recover Texas, New Mexico, Arizona, and California, the vast territory lost to the United States in the Mexican–American War of 1848, a conflict of which I was woefully ignorant. Here is the tasty carrot Foreign Minister Zimmermann offered President Carranza!" He swept a hand over a huge portion of the American Southwest on the map. "As I remarked, you may not be luminous but you are most definitely a conductor of light, my dear fellow."

As Holmes spoke, M began gnawing his mustache as I had seen him do when we first met. "Admiral?" The spymaster faced his naval counterpart.

"What we've gleaned of 158 so far is not inconsistent with Mr. Holmes's deductions." It seemed a grudging admission.

All connected, the dots now constituted a clear image. It was the finest hour of Sherlock Holmes. Never, in our long association, had I seen his powers rise to the dizzying heights they now reached.

"No wonder Count Bernstorff called it the telegram from hell," I reflected.

"No wonder," echoed the detective. "If the Zimmermann plan succeeds, Germany will emerge victorious and the world will be changed beyond recognition."

This declaration was followed by a third silence, broken once more by M. "I believe I will have a brandy and soda," he said. "Would any of you gentlemen care to partake?"

He approached a sideboard beneath the map and proceeded to prepare the beverage, squirting soda into his glass.

Admiral Hall raised two fingers indicating he would accept what was on offer.

Holmes and I declined. In the stillness that accompanied this alchemy, Holmes resumed his seat next to mine. "What I've yet to understand," he said, fishing out his pipe and tobacco pouch, "is why it was necessary for us to go all the way to Mexico, Watson here getting shot in the process, if you had the telegram in your possession the entire time."

"I believe you have acknowledged elsewhere that politics is not your métier," Admiral Hall responded, "so allow me a disquisition on realpolitik." He took a sip of the drink handed him by M. "Setting aside the awkward fact that we have been spying on our American allies—"

"Potential allies," M reminded him.

"Potential allies," the admiral agreed, shrugging and taking another sip. "Let us assume for the moment, that you"—addressing Holmes—"have correctly summarized the contents of 158. The fact remains that if it is Great Britain that reveals the existence of the telegram and its treacherous proposal, it will be vociferously denounced as a hoax by America's large German American community. Desperate to prevent America's entry into the war on the Allied side, they will insist the telegram is a clumsy British ruse intended to trick America into joining the conflict."

"A plausible argument, one must admit," M conceded. "And President Wilson will cling to that rationale and remain neutral." He punctuated the quiet by squirting another jet of soda into his glass.

"But surely," I felt bound to point out, "when Germany begins sinking American ships, the president will be forced to change his policy."

"By that time, it might be too late," said the admiral. "At present, all we've intercepted is a series of numbers. We may claim those numbers say what Mr. Holmes says they do, but until now, we have neither completely cracked code 13040, nor until now did we possess an actual telegram, one that shows what this photograph does." He held up the crumpled picture of 158 I had hidden in my shoe. "That it was sent 'via Galveston and Tampico,' that it contains the watermark 'Inspected,' confirms its receipt in Mexico City and so on. What was essential," he concluded, "was a copy of the physical telegram with all these attendant identifications."

"Including a man's blood," I was impelled to add.

"It doesn't hurt." This was the closest they ever came to acknowledging Reilly. The war had coarsened them.

"The question now is whether President Carranza has received the telegram," the admiral mused, swirling the liquid in his glass.

"There can be no doubt," Holmes assured him. "From the German perspective, speed is of the essence. The telegram has been decoded, translated into Spanish, and hand-delivered to Mexico's president."

"Which leaves only the question of whether Carranza will act on the telegram's proposal—and how quickly." M was thoughtfully tapping the paper on his forefinger. "Should that happen, all is lost."

"Oh," said Sherlock Holmes, puffing serenely on his pipe, "I think you need have no worries on that score. From what Dr. Watson and I experienced, Mexico is in a state of near anarchy. Gunfire is intermittently heard throughout the city, with President Carranza himself closely guarded against the possibility of his own death."

"Given yesterday's events, you may be right," M said.

"Yesterday's events?"

"An attempt on Carranza's life. As we are given to understand, the president was unharmed, but the attempt supports your analysis of Mexican instability."*

If this confirmation satisfied the detective, he gave no evidence of it. "As I suggested, Mexico is in no condition to mobilize for an offensive against the United States while its army is divided among warlords,

---

\* Carranza was in fact ultimately murdered in 1920.

each seeking supremacy. Vis-à-vis the United States, Pancho Villa a year ago was the best they could manage. He may have inspired Zimmermann's telegram, ingenious as it is, but there's no way such an invasion could come to pass or represent a true threat if it did."

"But what if you are mistaken about Mexico's capacities?" It was incumbent upon M to explore every possibility. "What if the prospect of regaining so much territory serves to unite those warlords?"

Had Holmes considered this possibility? If not, he was forced to confront it now.

"If I'm mistaken, the United States will find itself under attack. In consequence of having to fight a war on her own doorstep with the scanty military resources currently at her disposal, she could never come to the aid of the Allies in Europe and the war there would be lost. England and Europe as we know it would cease to exist. German would become the lingua franca."

Following this blunt analysis, Admiral Hall finished the last of his drink at a gulp.

"Let us consider what choices remain to us," M now resumed his dispassionate tone. "You have told us what will happen if you are wrong, Holmes. But should you be right, what then? Let us assume, without knowledge to the contrary, that Mexico does not possess the wherewithal to attack the United States. Does that render 158 moot?"

"A pertinent line of inquiry," said Holmes. "In a strategic sense, perhaps it does. There would be no war on America's southern border. But . . ." he trailed off, a faint smile tugging at the corners of his mouth.

"But what?" M prompted with a trace of impatience.

The smile broadened. "But should the American public learn there *was* such a perfidious scheme as the Zimmermann plan—the mere knowledge of its existence, that the proposal was sent using American cabling facilities despite a German promise not to use those facilities to transmit 'anything inimical to American interests' . . ." This sentence was likewise left unfinished.

I twisted myself into my chair as I was again in danger of sliding out of it. "You believe President Wilson will find himself forced to abandon his neutrality?"

"I think it not unlikely. But first," the detective turned to Admiral Hall, "the rest of the telegram must be decoded. The task should be easier now that you know the gist."

"It should," the admiral agreed.

"And then?" M inquired.

Holmes paused to relight his pipe, which had gone out. "Of course these next steps would have been more Mycroft's line of country than mine, but after Zimmermann's message has been rendered in plaintext, would it not seem natural for the Foreign Office to share the telegram with the American ambassador?"

"Ambassador Page," M supplied. A smile now began to creep across his features as well. "The ambassador will of course convey the message to Washington, explaining how it was obtained by *an American in Mexico City.* The blood on the message is a most convincing touch," he added.

Did I imagine he had the decency to look ashamed when he caught my eye?

"The Americans will doubtless clamor for the identity of the agent in question," Admiral Hall interposed, attempting to forecast the next series of chess moves.

M hesitated before deciding. "We will refer to the agent in Mexico simply as . . . H"—here he inclined his massive head in

Holmes's direction—"and insist that to reveal more would be to compromise his utility as well as his safety."

"Whether or not the telegram represents a genuine threat is entirely beside the point," Holmes pointed out. "The press inevitably will learn of this dastardly plan, even if they have to be led to the trough by unseen hands." It was now the detective's turn to acknowledge M with a head tilt. "Once there, they will drink greedily and spew large headlines."

Along with pipe smoke, an aura of satisfaction was creeping into the atmosphere as Admiral Hall now seized on the narrative.

"Public outrage will follow and, if things, for once, go according to plan, President Wilson will have no choice but to declare war on Germany."

"And if he does that," M concluded, "this damnable war will finally end." He turned to face the detective. "And Sherlock Holmes will have helped to win it."

[WATSON'S WRITING ILLEGIBLE HERE, LIKELY

THE RESULT OF HIS VERTIGO. —NM]

It was dawn by the time I reached Pimlico. My latchkey had long since migrated to the recesses of my luggage and the cabbie was obliged to wait while I rummaged in search of it, opening my bag on the curb and reaching blindly among laundry and shaving tackle until I located the small but essential item and was able to let myself in. The house was large, empty, and silent, furniture covered in dust sheets, a musty smell in the air, though the place had in fact been recently tenanted.

I paid the driver, who set down my bag before leaving. I sat in my accustomed chair and stared into space as I heard the front door slam behind me. With that door slam, the succession of events, the travel, the hairsbreadth escapes, the deaths, in a word, the noise of the past nine months all ceased. It had all come to this, an elderly widower alone in his sitting room, staring into space.

What was I meant to do now?

**12 November 1918**. The war ended yesterday and I am taking up my pen for the first time in almost two years. My health has been in tatters since I last wrote, but the sights I saw yesterday impel me to set down my reflections, if only to fill in some blanks for posterity. Yesterday, after four years of unremitting slaughter, at the eleventh hour of the eleventh day of the eleventh month, the guns at last fell silent—but the silence that followed was anything but quiet. With the German surrender, London has exploded with scenes of joy unparalleled in my lifetime, and, I suspect, in the lives any who have survived the carnage. The streets are jammed with strangers of every class and character embracing, dancing on automobiles and rooftops. Among the heaving mass, kisses are exchanged indiscriminately along with tears of grief and relief. Legless and armless men were to be seen twirling awkwardly in their wheeled chairs. The Mall and Buckingham Palace are impassable, thronged with cheering crowds, men and women delirious with happiness.

Where have all these people come from? Before the armistice was announced (for it is in fact an armistice and not, as most prefer to think of it, a German surrender), London had taken on aspects of a ghost city, but now, like animals revealing themselves after a torrential downpour, those who survived the tempest have emerged from their burrows to bask in the light of a new day. I had no idea so many were left alive, though in truth one does not see many unmaimed young men. That generation is gone, and along with many others, including M and Ambassador Spring Rice, neither of whom lived to witness the Allied triumph. In America, a new scourge, the Spanish influenza, has decimated additional millions and even now making its way overseas.

The house in Pimlico had been maintained in good order by the family to whom it was let, a doctor and his wife. The doctor has since acquired a practice in Fulham and purchased a house closer to his consulting rooms on Cortayne Road.

Numbed after Juliet's death I had made no change, but the place now feels too big for me and the stairs are becoming something of a chore. More depressing, Maria has gone to live with her sister and I was obliged to hire a new girl. Maudie is very capable but offers no rapport. Comely enough, she performs her chores with humorless efficiency but does not live in, which is perhaps as well. Sooner or later I must find smaller digs. But where? Still in town? Or do I follow Holmes's example and rusticate?

In the aftermath of the Zimmermann telegram's decryption, events did not entirely unfold as anyone in M's office that night anticipated. True, Admiral Hall's team, whoever they were and however they did it, aided by Sherlock Holmes's summary of its contents, eventually managed to crack the German code and read the diabolical telegram.*

True, the Foreign Office did turn the telegram and its deciphered message over to Walter Page, the American ambassador, who, as anticipated, immediately passed it across the Atlantic to the White House, explaining it had been obtained via the American embassy in Mexico City, thanks to a daring agent whose identity he could not reveal, but whose code designation was H. It has thus not been necessary to disclose Great Britain's original interception of the message, much less the role of Sherlock Holmes in laying hands on the actual telegram or in helping decipher it.

Surprisingly, in March 1917 (at roughly the same time Tsar Nicholas II abdicated the throne of the Romanovs), Foreign Minister Zimmermann, confronted with evidence of telegram 158, admitted to having sent it! Historians, I suspect, may wonder at this, but as I see it, the man had little choice; the evidence was irrefutable as to his culpability, forcing him into an attitude of truculent defiance, insisting from the German vantage point that all's fair in war. In retrospect, the telegram was seen as a desperate gambit by a desperate nation, unlikely of success from the start. But, like England, Germany was running out of everything, including strategies that, however improbable (or reprehensible), might lead to victory. As Holmes had observed that morning after breakfast at Craithie's, in wartime morality becomes a dispensable luxury.

The dissemination of the telegram did not result in an immediate American declaration of war, though it did succeed in provoking

---

* Like millions more, Watson lived in ignorance of Room 40, Admiral Hall's top secret cipher center. The existence of the room, its occupants, and its purpose were not declassified or revealed for over another half century.

popular outrage that drowned out the voices of isolationism and served to silence protestations in the German American community. Still, the impossibly stubborn Wilson chose merely to sever relations with Germany, digging in his neutral heels to the knees. He was, however, fighting his own losing battle.

Germany, now in extremis and beyond rationality, pounded the final nail into their own coffin. They did not choose to wait for an answer to their telegram from President Carranza. Doubtless anticipating his inability to oblige Germany by invading the United States in the near term, the U-boats were at long last released from their moorings with orders to conduct unrestricted warfare in the North Atlantic.

What followed was inevitable. When the Kaiser's U-boats began torpedoing American ships, the president was at last compelled to give way and the United States finally declared war on Germany.

In Wilson's new formulation, the conflict was reconceived as "the war to end wars," "a war to save democracy," and many American lives now joined the roll call of English, French, Russian, and Italian dead in pursuit of that lofty aim. Whether that aim is achieved remains to be seen, but there can be no doubt that the arrival of the American Expeditionary Force, led by the self-same General John "Black Jack" Pershing (formerly charged with the apprehension of Pancho Villa!), served to turn the tide and win the day, as England hoped and Germany feared it would.*

Any account of the past twenty months would inevitably constitute a dreary recitation of my own ailments, the regimens, the

---

* Pershing, landing on French soil, movingly proclaimed, "*Lafayette, le voici,*" which boils down to, "Lafayette, we are here." In other words, America's debt to France for helping win our revolution will now be repaid.

nostrums, and, on one occasion, the surgery necessary to render me ambulatory and prolong my life. Suffice it to say my health has not been so questionable since I returned from Afghanistan almost forty years ago. At that time I was young enough to mount a vigorous recovery; now the process has become more prolonged and the outcome less certain. I cannot help wondering what England's recovery will look like. Will it mirror my own erratic rehabilitation?

One of the therapies recommended for my unfortunate leg has been exercise, but issues of vertigo and an intermittent tremor have rendered me a semi-invalid. Only of late and following the triumph of the Allies have I felt sufficiently emboldened to walk in open air and look at the world once more.

It is and will be, I know, a very different world than any that has come before it.

A different sort of dizziness will inevitably overtake me as I try to navigate it.

London on this Tuesday was bathed in sunshine that partly diluted the city's hungover appearance. Newspapers lay in gutters with headlines in type, font, and size never before seen. "Confetti" in mounds and other detritus littered every street, and exhausted revelers were still to be seen sprawled asleep on benches or lawns. It wasn't revelry alone that had felled them; it was the previous four years.

I had been reading the *Times* at breakfast when it struck me as odd that I had not heard from Sherlock Holmes at this time of jubilation. The more I read details of the cessation of hostilities, the more perplexed I became by his silence, for I knew better than anyone the pivotal role the detective played that had contributed to the Allied victory. But for his genius (and courage), it is questionable whether America would have ever entered the war, or at the very least, entered it as soon as she eventually did, which is to say in time to avert catastrophe.

I now remembered as well, and with a sense of shame, the graceless thoughts I had indulged regarding my relations with Holmes as I languished in my berth aboard HMS *Caroline*. It was no use pretending I had not had them, or to attribute their ugly tenor to my indisposition. In the tranquil aftermath of all that occurred, it is once more clear to me that Sherlock Holmes remains the best and wisest of men and that my long association—painful as portions of it may have been—remains among the most rewarding chapters of my eventful life.

At the same time, I am forced to acknowledge that for all the time I have spent in his company, Holmes remains—and probably always will remain—unknowable. I can list innumerable details of his form and character, his strengths and weaknesses—indeed I have spent a lifetime doing so—without being able to reach a comprehensive understanding of this singular individual. I can tell you what the man has for breakfast, lunch, and supper. I know his musical tastes, what tobacco he prefers and where he keeps it, but, like an onion, Sherlock Holmes comprises endless layers. When all's said and done, his genius remains elusive.

Perhaps it's best that way.

But as I write these words, another thought occurs to me: Could Holmes not say of me what I say of him, that I, too, am ultimately unknowable? Granted, he knows my habits (tea with honey and lemon) and personality (plodding), as I know his, but no matter how much time people spend together—even under the most varied circumstances—is there a point past which each will remain forever a mystery to the other? I enjoyed an intuitive sympathy with both my late wives (one perhaps more than the other),* but beyond that, how well did we truly know one another?

Is it thus with all people? Are we all enigmas?

But where was Holmes? What was he doing? And why, on this of all days, have I not heard from him? In my head I imagined him back in Sussex among his bees, but following the instincts of my heart I knew him to be elsewhere and rang his Baker Street exchange.

The telephone rang several times before it was an answered in a flat voice. "Yes?"

"Holmes, it's Watson. So you are in town. I felt sure of it."

There was some hesitation on the other end of the line before he answered, "Yes," in the same listless tone, increasing my unease. Something was unmistakably amiss, but I was at a loss as to what it might be or how to learn what it was.

"Have you seen the paper?" I began. "The Kaiser is desperately calling for a peace conference on behalf of his people, now faced with famine. There are rumors that a conference of sorts will shortly commence in Paris."

"Oh, yes?"

"It is said the President himself plans to attend."

"Indeed."

"They say he's calling for some sort of world government."

There was no reply to this so I pressed on. "There's to be a thanksgiving service today at St. Paul's and the royal family is due to attend, but I don't suppose we've a prayer of getting in."

"No."

---

\*    Which??

These monosyllabic replies served to alarm me further. "Holmes, I am coming to Baker Street, straightway."

"Watson, you—" but I rang off before I could hear him object.

And so I had been coaxed from my bolt-hole into the late afternoon sunshine, pocketing my copy of the *Times* and making my way through rubbish, swirling around my ankles like Texas tumbleweed, to the Pimlico Underground as I set out for Baker Street.

Baker Street had changed. There was a new tube station conveniently situated not far from 221,* and though the large street was cluttered with rubbish from yesterday's bacchanal, I could see new shops and enterprises were everywhere springing up, like mushrooms after a rain.

"Dr. Watson?"

The woman who opened the door was not yet forty. Her dress was hemmed to her calves and her hair trimmed short in the new ubiquitous fashion I found difficult to admire.

"Mrs. Turner?"

"Mr. Holmes is expecting you." Her smile was warm but somehow impersonal. "Is anything wrong?"

We were standing in the entryway at the bottom of the seventeen steps that led to 221B. I decided tact rather than confidences might be wisest at the moment.

"Not at all. I was just remembering . . ."

"Ah, well, he said to go right up." She lowered her voice. "I am glad you are here, doctor. I fear he is unwell. He has not been taking his meals, nor does he go out for air."

---

\*   Today, outside that tube station, stands an enormous statue of Sherlock Holmes. There are many reasons it might be there, but surely his wartime service is one of them.

Her words, confirming my fears, immobilized me. Those familiar stairs seemed suddenly insurmountable, not from any physical impairment (I could still manage the flights at Pimlico), but because the sight of them after so long brought back a flood of memories—and because I worried what I might find at their head.

Mrs. Turner, now the landlady (she had taken over the leasehold from Mrs. Hudson, who chose to remain with Holmes in Sussex), retreated to her rooms while I returned to my examination of the steps. The worn carpet had been replaced with a severe dark wool nap, but the polished brass stair rods that secured it were the same and the wall to my right still displayed the cameos as I remembered. Details I'd forgotten made me smile at the sight and smell of them. Somewhere I heard an infant squalling. There was a family in the building. Life was going on. Perhaps it had never left off.

With every step I remembered more. How many clients, how many curious cases and mysteries had trod these same steps. A nervous client with some outré—

"Watson! I can always recognize your distinctive tread on the stair."

Holmes stood aside and admitted me to my old lodgings. He wore his impossibly threadbare, mouse-colored robe over his shirt and trousers, but his tieless collar was unfastened and he had not shaved, unusual manifestations in one who was habitually tidy as a cat in such matters. His features had not changed so very much from our time together in Mexico. His hair perhaps was thinner and a shade whiter, but his broad forehead, hawklike nose, and determined mouth appeared much the same. Yet he appeared haggard, as if portions of his physiognomy had been tugged downward by gravity.

For a panicked moment I wondered if he had resumed an old habit. Reading my mind, he pushed the fraying sleeves of his dressing gown and shot forth his bare arms for my inspection. "Not to worry, old man."

I could think of no reply but "Holmes, that robe has fallen to pieces."

"I know. I have a new one in Sussex from Marks and Spencer, but I keep this one here. You have taken the Underground, I perceive."

"And just how is it that you perceive?" I asked, relieved to be falling into our familiar rhythms of exchange.

"From the ticket protruding from the cuff of your new, and if I may say so, most becoming overcoat."

Holmes may not have changed, but 221B, on the other hand, bore scant resemblance to the place it had been during the old times when we'd occupied it jointly. How could it?

The deal table that formerly held the detective's chemical apparatus was long gone. Instead of the post, cavalierly affixed to the mantelpiece with a jackknife, a rolltop desk in which correspondence was pigeonholed had long dominated the sitting room, along with a telephone and a tin of Balkan Sobranie in place of its former eccentric repository (a Persian slipper, as I recollect). And, of all things, an ungainly typewriter.

One curious reminder of our old days together endured: against the far wall, so faint they were hardly visible in this light, I could make out the letters *V R* outlined in bullet pocks. Driven to distraction by the absence of cases worthy of his attention, the detective occasionally fought off fits of boredom by indulging in indoor target practice. On that occasion (to the consternation of Mrs. Hudson), he succeeded in outlining the old queen's initials in bullet holes.

For reasons best known to himself, Holmes had never had the wall replastered or papered over.

In place of curtains, the windows that gave onto Baker Street now boasted large Venetian blinds, half-mast at this hour to repulse the November sun. The effect was to throw much of the room into shadow. In these conditions and at this hour, it was time to click on the lights, but the detective had not done so, further evidence to my mind that something irregular was going on.

But by far the most conspicuous change was the most recent: an assortment of thick volumes lay strewn about the room, various places held with strips of torn paper inserted between the leaves. These tomes were so unlike the detective's typical reading matter that I stooped to examine what proved to be a volume of Gibbon's *Decline and Fall of the Roman Empire*.

"This looks to be quite a change from ancient English charters and the origin of the Chaldeans," I observed, nudging one of the large books aside with the toe of my shoe to make a path for me to reach my chair. Over the years I had seen Holmes research many abstruse subjects for reasons I could never entirely understand. "Shall I turn on the lights?"

"Later, perhaps."

"Holmes, what is going on? I insist you tell me."

Before answering, he adjusted the position of the book I had moved, restoring it to its place amid the cluster on the floor.

"Watson, you once remarked with justice that my knowledge of politics was 'feeble,'" he began. "As you know, events of the past decade have compelled me to educate myself. I may remain naive, but it can no longer be said that I am ignorant."

"I never said any such thing."

"Others have and you have implied as much. Therefore, in my
dotage I have begun reading history, even as in his old age Count
Tolstoy taught himself ancient Greek."

"I know nothing of Count Tolstoy or his Greek," I responded,
examining the volume of Gibbon a second time, "but what has
prompted this fetish? Shouldn't you at this moment be rejoicing at
the greatest triumph of your career? Though the world may never
learn it, you may claim to having helped ensure the Allied victory
everyone is celebrating—the dawn of a new day and a brave new
world."

Not raising his eyes to mine, he began packing a pipe. "I very
much fear it is the same world." Before I could protest, he went
on. "You will recall how appalled you were when you learned I
was ignorant of the Mexican–American War. But"—and here he
paused to light his pipe and spoke between rapid puffs—"I have
since been forced to conclude such ignorance is no longer excus-
able." He sighed. "It *does* make a difference."

His state of mind as much as his opinion alarmed me. I divested
myself of my new coat and drew up a chair opposite, reaching for
the tin of Balkan Sobranie. "May I?"

"Of course."

"So." It was now my turn to fill a pipe. I went about the business
slowly, trying to collect my thoughts. "You have decided that your
ignorance of history warrants your present lack of enthusiasm for
the part you played in it? I fail to follow your reasoning. Having
helped secure the victory, do you now believe you are not entitled
to be pleased by it? You may not be able to take credit for your role,
but that is hardly novel in your experience. Yet I daresay when the
dust has settled you will be summoned to Windsor and—"

"Presented with another bit of ribbon to add to the collection in my drawer."

"I was going to suggest a knighthood might be a more fitting acknowledgment for your extraordinary services—"

"Following in the footsteps of Roger Casement? I think not. We have trod this ground before. Besides, it was you, not I, who was actually shot, my dear fellow, to say nothing of Reilly, killed. And what form did Reilly's acknowledgment take, I'm forced to wonder?" he added in the same listless voice, so unlike his crisp, self-assured utterances.

But however delivered, this rejoinder served to spike my guns. He heaved a sigh that was far too heavy for my liking. "Watson, the dust is never going to settle. What do you know of the Congress of Vienna?" He gestured with his pipe stem to another book.

"Something to do with Napoleon?" I hazarded, puzzled by his change of subject. "I seem to recall learning about it in school."

"Very good, Watson. The Congress of Vienna was a group effort to fasten Europe back together following Napoleon's final defeat at Waterloo. In 1815, the victors and the vanquished convened in that city to redraw the map of Europe."

"And what conclusion have you reached?"

"An elementary one. That theirs was not a permanent solution," he responded, still without looking at me. "Lord Castlereagh, who led the effort, wound up cutting his own throat. And a century later, here we are again. Don't you see, Watson? No matter what service I may have performed, no matter the outcome of any forthcoming peace conference, a hundred years from now—perhaps less!—we will all be at each other's throats once more. League of Nations or not, the human race will never cease being human."

"But we progress—" I fumbled, but he cut me off with a bitter laugh, holding up a hand like a policeman.

"Progress! There is no such thing, Watson. All progress is illusory."

I now understood—the blinds had not been lowered to block the sun. Sherlock Holmes's eyes glistened in the looming dark, water tremulously quivering in them like a dam about to overflow or give way altogether.

"If that is the case," I could only say, "what are we to do? Cut our throats like Castlereagh?" I regretted the words as soon as they left my mouth for in his present state I had no wish to put ideas in his head. It occurred to me to point out that the results of the Congress of Vienna had endured for over a century, but I knew this was not the case. He would point out that the hundred years following the congress had been as full of war and destruction as any before it. "What about your words the night you knocked on my door? You said we must do what we can to save civilization."

"Of late I am less sure that civilization can be saved—or that it is worth saving," he replied.

It is hard to argue with someone who is smarter than you are. Fumbling for another topic, I drew forth my copy of the *Times* and commenced flipping pages in search of something, anything, that might jar his mind from its present location and away from the fate of the unfortunate Castlereagh. I had always admired rather than envied Holmes's genius, but I sometimes wished he had less brainpower and I a bit more. Mind racing, I was struggling to make out headlines in the gloom, when I stumbled on my last hope.

"I say," I fairly shouted, "there's a concert tonight at Wigmore Hall!" He made no reply. "Holmes, did you hear what I said?

Eight o'clock! They're playing . . ." I was unsure how to pronounce it. "Lisht?"

There was a pause.

"Liszt," he then corrected me.

"Yes! 'Three Hungarian Rhapsodies.'"

"Humph" was his noncommittal response after a silence.

"And Rachmaninoff . . ." I added as my last hope. This was the best I could do. I could hear my own labored breathing. Long seconds ticked by in the silence that followed, but then he surprised me.

"What Rachmaninoff?"

It was hard to see the small print in this dim light. "It, uh, looks like . . . twelve études? A Frenchman is playing."

". . . Cortot?"

"Yes, that's the one. Alfred Cortot."

He grunted with reluctant approval. "The Liszt is superficial . . . they all begin in a mosque and end in a tavern."

"Ah, yes, but the Rachmaninoff—" I gibbered. I had no notion what I was talking about, but I understood my object was to engage that mind whose confines he presently could not escape—"*I must have my musical injection*," he had said to me that night in Pimlico. "*It is the one habit I cannot break.*"

"Rachmaninoff. Not profound, but beautiful," he conceded. "And, perhaps, a trifle archaic by now. One could probably omit some of the repeats and the pieces would be none the worse for it."

"Probably better," I concurred wholeheartedly. I heard him chuckle. He knew what I was doing. "Do you suppose we could get in?" I asked in the most casual tone I could manage.

This was followed by another indecisive silence, and then, "It's early enough. We might be on time to begin the queue . . ."

I dared not speak for fear of breaking the spell.

"What have I done with my tie?" He was throwing off the tattered dressing gown and absently searching for it. Was he genuinely excited about the prospect of a concert or merely humoring me by proposing to go? At this point, I didn't care.

"Is that it, hanging from the desk?"

"Invaluable, Watson." Holding the tie in his hand, he straightened up and offered me a melancholy smile. "Shall we do what we can to save civilization? I should hate to miss the Rachmaninoff."

# AFTERWORD

Like its predecessors, my sixth Holmes novel adheres—more or less—to the "accepted" chronology of Holmes's adventures as recorded by Watson and ordered by W. S. Baring-Gould in his *Annotated Sherlock Holmes* (Clarkson Potter, 1967), and revised in Leslie S. Klinger's *The New Annotated Sherlock Holmes* (Norton, 2005–06). I have no wish to reinvent the wheel, merely to add a few spokes. Readers of the Holmes World War I story, *His Last Bow*, set in August of 1914, learn that Holmes has spent the previous two years undercover in America, as the Irish American sympathizer Gideon Altamont, after which he finally succeeds in busting Von Bork's German spy sabotage ring and predicts the war's victorious outcome—after much travail. I took off from there.

Though this novel was written without harming or using AI in its composition, many of the events it recounts are so off-the-wall the reader could be forgiven for asking: How much of this stuff is true?

The answer, as it happens, is most of it. I've occasionally simplified things and mushed a few dates and railroad routes, but the
gist is fact.

German Foreign Minister Zimmermann *did* send a coded telegram via Count Bernstorff in Washington to German Ambassador
von Eckardt in Mexico City. The telegram (photocopied in this book)
*was* intercepted by British intelligence (M and Admiral "Blinker"
Hall). A crack team lead by naval captain Guy Gaunt in top secret
Room 40 succeeded in breaking the German code in which the
infamous telegram was sent and passed it on to the Americans. It
*did* propel America's ultimate decision to declare war on Germany.
(Incidentally, there was a whole other part to the Zimmermann plan
involving Japan, but that turned out to be one too many balls for me
to catch so I left it out.)

The British agent who laid hands on telegram 158 in Mexico
City really went by the code name H. Too good to pass up.

The piquant exchange between Holmes and Watson on board
the *Norlina* actually occurred not so many years later on the Twentieth Century Limited, between George Gershwin (lower berth,
"genius") and Oscar Levant (forced to occupy the upper, "talent").

Dwight D. Eisenhower and Douglas MacArthur *were* in the
West Point backfield playing against the Carlyle Indians in 1912.
Super athlete Jim Thorpe played for Carlyle. Army lost big time.

Within two years of his encounter with Holmes, J. Edgar
Hoover was running the ultimately renamed Federal Bureau of
Investigation, a post he tenaciously held, along with its considerable
power, for thirty-seven years until his death in 1972. Everybody
was afraid of him.

Alice Roosevelt *was* married to Nicholas Longworth, who *did*
become Speaker of the House. Alice liked to startle callers with

a snake around her neck. I may have elongated the snake and changed its make. Its actual name was Esther Spinach. (Don't ask.) Alice died in 1980, still in Washington. I think I invented her affair with Count Bernstorff, but Alice got around.

Pancho Villa *did* conduct a raid on US soil, which probably inspired Zimmermann's Hail Mary pass to keep America out of the war.

World War I and its appalling casualties really happened.

I slightly altered the route of the Golden State Limited train in the American Southwest to get H & W where they were going a bit faster.

There was a concert Tuesday, November 12, 1918, at Wigmore Hall, in which Liszt and Rachmaninoff were performed.

And so on. You get the idea.

In fact, the Zimmermann telegram was not Germany's only Byzantine scheme to win the war; one other surely had the effect of prolonging, if not ending it: knowing of Communist opposition to Russia's participation—and losses—in what the Communists deemed a capitalist conflict, Germany arranged to extract Vladimir Lenin, the Bolshevik leader, from his Swiss exile, and return him to Moscow. As they anticipated (and as Captain Crooke dreaded and Señora Vasca hoped), Lenin withdrew Russia from its alliance with France and England once he was in power. With Russia out of the war, Germany was able to free up fifty-two battalions in the east and deposit them on the Western Front, thus enabling the mutual massacre to continue.

If the United States had not piled on, Germany might have won.

The fates of some other characters may also be of interest:

Roger Casement, the Anglo-Irish journalist knighted in 1911 by the British government for exposing the crimes of King Leopold's

Belgian Congo, was hanged by that same government for high treason in 1917, despite pleas for clemency by the US Senate, George Bernard Shaw, and Sir Arthur Conan Doyle. Joseph Conrad, who had known and liked Casement in the Congo, was conspicuously silent. No one knows for sure whether Casement's sensational "black diaries," identifying him as homosexual and which helped sway public opinion—and the jury—against him were forged by British intelligence or not.

Sir William Melville, another Anglo-Irishman, the first M, was the first chief of the initially named Secret Service Bureau, subsequently SIS and MI6. (Mycroft obviously came first but the bureau had not been formed or named until after his death.) Melville died in February 1918, but I've kept him alive a few weeks longer. There are intriguing rumors that Melville—or M, if you prefer—was Houdini's handler when he spied for the US and Great Britain on tour in Europe in the run-up to the war.

Admiral "Blinker" Hall, the man who arrested Roger Casement after a German U-boat dropped him off in Ireland, ran the secret Room 40 decoding center. He died in 1943, in the midst of World War II. Hall made a lot of questionable unilateral decisions regarding telegram 158 without authorization from the British government, but that's another (long) story.

Cecil Spring Rice, British ambassador to the United States and close friend of Theodore Roosevelt, died in in Canada, in February 1918, of Graves' disease, as Watson diagnosed, almost at the same time as his fellow Anglo-Irishman, Sir William Melville, in England. Although according to Philip Hoare's masterful account, *Oscar Wilde's Last Stand*, Spring Rice may have been murdered, "after he uncovered a 'German plot.'" We can easily imagine what that was!

Tsar Nicholas II, with his wife and children, were shot by revolutionaries in the cellar of Ipatiev House (the "House of Special Purpose"), in Yekaterinburg, Russia, on July 17, 1918.

President Venustiano Carranza joined the ranks of murdered Mexican presidents in 1920.

Pancho Villa, whom Pershing could never capture, was gunned down in Parral, Mexico, 1923.

German Foreign Minister Arthur Zimmerman resigned from office in August of 1917, probably in connection with the telegram fiasco. He died in Berlin in 1940.

Emil Gasche, aka Captain Franz Dagobert Johannes von Rintelen, was a member of the German nobility and a veteran field agent in the intelligence wing of the German Imperial Navy who operated covertly in the still-neutral United States, sabotaging American munitions factories and fomenting labor unrest before World War I. He died in London in 1949.

General John "Black Jack" Pershing led the American Expeditionary Force that resulted in the eventual Allied victory, the one and only U.S. general ever to hold the rank General of the Armies. He lived long enough to see a second Allied victory in World War II and died at Walter Reed in 1948. There are many streets and squares named for this remarkable man, whose name (like Lafayette's) now means nothing to those who utter it.

HMS *Caroline* was captained by Captain Crooke (I wish he'd had a less improbable name) and saw action at Jutland. After Nelson's HMS *Victory*, she remained the longest commissioned warship in the Royal Navy.

Reilly is less easy to pin down. He is my mash-up of two real people, the eighteenth-century French trans person and adventurer

Chevalier d'Éon, and the early twentieth-century Russian Jew known as Sidney Reilly, Ace of Spies, about whom Wikipedia says:

> Sidney George Reilly MC, known as the "Ace of Spies," was a Russian-born adventurer and secret agent employed by Scotland Yard's Special Branch and later by the Foreign Section of the British Secret Service Bureau, the precursor to the modern British Secret Intelligence Service.

Holmes and Watson, of course, live on.

# ACKNOWLEDGMENTS

It is self-evident that without the genius of Sir Arthur Conan Doyle, Sherlock Holmes and John H. Watson, M.D., would not exist. And so it might be said of many of us who stumble in Sir Arthur's oversized footsteps. None of us seems able to fill those shoes, let alone walk in them. Still, we try. . . .

With that ginormous debt acknowledged, there's a host of people I need to thank for having helped me to write this book.

There are two books with the same title, *The Zimmermann Telegram*, written over fifty years apart, that were crucial in inspiring and helping put together this story. The first *Zimmermann Telegram* was written by the American historian Barbara W. Tuchman in 1958 and published by Macmillan. The second, written in 2012, is by Thomas Boghardt, senior historian at the US Army Center of Military History in Washington, published by the Naval Institute Press.

Over the years I have acquired quite a library of Holmesian research. There isn't room to cite all the books I consulted, but I think I must acknowledge several of the late Michael Harrison's volumes about Holmes's world and Victorian London, *In the Footsteps of Sherlock Holmes* and *The World of Sherlock Holmes*.

For information regarding American and Mexican railroads of the period, I am indebted to Lynn O'Leary and Jonathan Tiemann; for things (and language) British, to David Robb; for things Mexican and for extraordinary hospitality and guidance, to Alfonso Arau, Lorenzo O'Brien, Carlos Sanchos Gomez, and Alejandro Bermejo, who guided and escorted me through my

Mexico City research. They showed me loads of pertinent locations, including the remarkable telegraph museum (originally the Ciudad de México offices of Western Union), adjacent to the Plaza Tolsá, with its special exhibit devoted to the Zimmermann telegram, plus Porfirio Díaz's nearby jaw-dropping idea of a post office.

For wrangling the photographs in the book, I am indebted to Frederick Courtright and my sister, Deborah Meyer.

Writing a book—for me, at least—involves imposing on the time and good nature of several friends in order to give the manuscript the equivalent of an out-of-town tryout. I am indebted to Frank Spotnitz, Michael Phillips, Alan Gasmer, Barbara Fisher, Matthew Robbins, Richard Rayner, Bob Wallace, Jeremy Paul Kagan, Jim Sjveda, John McNamara, Leslie Klinger, Michael Elias, Michael Scheff, Alan Kay, Paula Namer, and John Collee for patiently reading, and in several cases rereading, the book, and for the many helpful suggestions and corrections they offered. The same may be said for my son-in-law Dan Colanduno and my daughters, Dylan, Madeline, and Roxanne Meyer, who all contributed to the end result.

It goes without saying that if that result falls short, the fault cannot be traced to any of the above helpers but is mine alone. It takes many people to shepherd a book to publication and I must not neglect imperious Otto Penzler, the Don Quixote of The Mysterious Press, and his crew of merry men and women at Warren Street—Charles Perry, Julia O'Connell, Will Luckman, Luisa Smith, Maria Fernandez, Wendy Marquez, and a special hats off to Amy Medeiros, the greatest copyeditor who has ever torn me apart. All bestowed upon me their expertise and their extraordinary patience.

And special thanks to my indefatigable agent, the one and only Charlotte Sheedy.

Finally, my biggest debt remains to be paid to Leslie Fram, chief critic and cheerleader, whose comments and enthusiasm kept me going when I succumbed to attacks of insecurity.